AM I...

By SJ Sherwood

Published by Blue Ned Ltd.
27 Mortimer Street, London, W1T 3BL

First published in the United Kingdom in 2023.

A CIP catalogue record for this book is available from the British Library.

ISBN 978-1-9997929-9-2

For Caesar and Laelia.

Thank you for changing our lives.

Blank Page

I know a snake in the grass when I see one.

There's one sitting opposite me pretending to be my friend.

'Do you know what a "betrayal bond" is, Kieran?'

I shake my head, letting my attention drift back into the session. 'Nope, but it sounds painful.'

Edward Carrington-Smythe Jr II smiles one of those fake smiles that make babies cry.

'Let's rephrase it, shall we?'

'You can rephrase it how you like. I'm not paying for your time.'

Ted—as he likes to be called—smiles again, and I recall how I belly-laughed when I first saw his name engraved on the nameplate on the door of his practice. I have continued my internal snipes each time we meet. It's the only refuse I have against these sessions that I'm terrified will define the rest of my life.

'A "betrayal bond" is often referred to as a "trauma bond". "Betrayal" is a more accurate description of what is psychologically happening. Are you familiar with the second term?'

I have a good idea of what he's looking to prize out of me as I suppress the urge to smartarse my way out of his question—my usual default when my back is against the wall.

Instead, I smile and shrug and shake my head.

'An indication that someone is "trauma bonded" is if they repeatedly enter into volatile relationships and then find it difficult to leave, especially when there are clear abusive interactions. Does this sound familiar?'

I'm deeply tempted to give him the two-finger salute as I leave the room and never return.

But I don't.

Because I can't.

The law is all on his side, not mine. So I do my best to think about his question in an honest way, fighting against my secondary thought that I would have been better off with a woman therapist. Or at least a man who was closer to my age.

'No… and if you're meaning "Stockholm syndrome", then perhaps you should be sat here, and I should be sat there.'

He smiles again.

It drips with fake friendship.

'"Stockholm syndrome" is a good connection. Let's stay with that thought if you don't mind?'

'To be honest, I do mind. No disrespect to your profession, but you're way off. Because unless I missed it, I've never been taken hostage by a terrorist organisation, which means I definitely couldn't have fallen in love with one of my captors, assuming one of them was a woman. And I'd like to point out that I'm not gay or bisexual, not that it would matter to me if I were; it's just not how I'm wired, and seeing as you keep digging into this shit, I thought I'd set it straight. No pun intended.'

I smile and sigh slightly, checking the time and seeing I have twenty-three minutes of this headache left.

'How are you wired, Kieran?

'Brown to live, blue to neutral. It's working fine.'

'Which means what to you?' he says, sounding like an algorithm waiting for a predefined answer.

'That I consider myself a balanced individual with sound rational judgements.'

'So you don't see yourself as someone who overreacts or is led by their emotions?'

'It's what I said, right?'

He smiles and makes a note on his pad, ink smudged on his second finger and thumb.

'I'd like to go back to your comment in the previous session when you said that you think people are "jealous" of you.'

'I don't think I said that?'

He flips back a couple of pages in his notepad.

'You said you encounter a lot of jealousy as one of the youngest CEOs in your chosen profession. People are surprised to find out your true age.'

'Then I wasn't being clear. What I had meant to say is that I'm often judged like I had it easy, like I was handed it on a plate. Excluding some luck, I've worked hard for what I've got, and I do encounter jealousy because of it.'

'So you're competitive?'

It's a repeated line of questioning that stinks of a trap. I've already fallen into the jealousy snare, so I dwell on his strategy, letting my barrister's advice smoulder through me.

'Competition is for losers.'

He frowns, unsure, waiting for me to continue.

'I'm competitive with myself, not others, and I try and focus on what I'm unique at. It's something I got from my dad. It's much better for your mental health, and it's why I'm successful at what I do.'

I can see he doesn't believe me, but I'm not a professional sportsman, and I've learnt that sometimes, the more you compete with those around you, the less you get.

'Did your friends like her?' He says.

'Hell, yeah! They thought she was perfect. I mean, she was, or at the time, I thought she was!'

'You met on social media?'

It's another question I've answered a hundred times.

To him.

To the Police.

To everyone.

Serena and I connected on Tinder and chatted through the App, but it then fell away, like so many of those fleeting conversations. I didn't give it a second thought, moving on to the next match. A fortnight later, I was at a conference in Bath where I was giving the keynote. There she was, sitting in the third aisle, centre row, smiling that sexy, inviting smile. It came at me full wattage, and I felt like I'd been hit by a brick, almost wrong-footing my presentation.

Later, we caught up and chatted at the bar, pretending like the Tinder thing had never happened, enjoying the chance encounter. That night, I tried to find her Tinder profile again, but it had been deleted, or at least I couldn't find it. I couldn't find her on Facebook, which, at the time, I thought was weird, but then again, people delete their accounts all the time. When we did manage to go for dinner a few weeks later, Tinder came up, but she was quick to dismiss it, like it was somehow beneath her, and social media, in general, was something that haphazardly got stuck to the bottom of her shoe.

It was the first of many lies.

Social media was her haven.

A stomping ground she owned.

LavishLondonLashes had five hundred thousand followers at the time and was growing by the day.

Serena was genetically blessed with the thickest and longest lashes I had ever seen, parked under perfectly framed eyebrows, lit by ice-grey eyes. Her Instagram account was her growing business empire. An influencer on the rise who was rapidly monetising as she learnt to work the angles.

A star in the making.

'Would you call your relationship with Serena "on-and-off" at the beginning?'

'We dated a few times, and then she'd disappear and reappear, but it's not my definition of "on-and-off". It wasn't like we argued or fell out. We both had busy lives, so it was... you know... convenient. It worked. It was adult. Casual at the beginning.'

'But it's fair to say that it kept you intrigued?'

I think about his question and its implications for my future.

'She was great fun. Sexy. We were each other's shiny new toy if you know what I mean.'

'Did you date in between?'

'In-between what?'

'Seeing her.'

I chew on his question.

'It wasn't like we'd declared our undying love for each other. We didn't have kids and a mortgage and a dog and credit card debt. But no. I didn't date in-between.'

'Did she?'

'Did she what?'

'Think that the relationship between you was exclusive?'

I let his question dance in the air because my problem with Teddy-Boy is simple. He's in his early sixties, and we are worlds apart in how we view relationships, even if he did once take psychedelics and dance naked at festivals back in the day. So how do I explain fucking on Tinder to a dinosaur without convicting myself in the process?

'I didn't ask her, and she never mentioned it.'

'Is it fair to say that the disappearing and re-appearing intrigued you, even excited you?'

'Can't say I gave it much thought.'

'The high arousals of an intense relationship, especially at the beginning, followed by low-to-non-existent intimacy, can create a sense of danger, even fear. This kind of interaction can make "healthy relationships" boring by comparison. It's an addictive emotional cocktail that can have devastating impacts within a relationship.'

'Ted, we had some ups-and-downs, which you know about, and she could be a livewire. But I want us to be clear. I didn't kill her.'

I hang up from a call with a client, one that I shouldn't have taken, glancing at the time on my laptop.

Fifty-three minutes to finish off and get out of here and over to my next meeting.

Tight.

Doable.

I start to edit the final slide on my deck when the door to my office opens. It's Abbie, our team secretary. I wave her away, but she ignores me, stepping past the threshold of my office as if I had beckoned her in and not out. She's young and trendy and always smiling, as well as stubborn and wholly entitled.

I like her.

She's fun and witty.

She also has a first-class degree from Manchester in economics and should be doing something better with herself than running around after us. I make a mental note to discuss her career and see if she'd be interested in becoming an account director. It has to be better than making tea and taking calls.

'There's a woman at reception to see you. Says she has a four-thirty with you today. It's been in the diary for two months, apparently! *The Leaf-Project*. Something to do with Indonesia.'

I frown: '*Leaf-Project?* Indonesia?'

Abbie shrugs.

I switch screens and bring up my calendar.

'It's not there,' Abbie says. 'I've checked.'

'She's here, now?'

'In reception.'

'You'll have to apologise profusely and rearrange for next week. I need to finish this and get out of here.'

Abbie turns to leave when I call out.

'What did you say her name was?'

'I didn't. But it's Scarlet Jackson from ZBA Environmental Research Institute. They don't come up on Google. Says she met you at the Awareness Conference in Bath.'

'Does she have brunette hair, tallish?'

Abbie smiles, and it's a touch familiar, but I guess I asked for it.

She nods.

I check the time again and sigh, more to myself than Abbie.

'Send her in.'

I glance at my presentation, irritated, more at myself for leaving it so late, but buoyed by the sudden stabs of excitement that attack my emotions.

I shut the lid of my laptop, staring through the glass that divides my office from the open-planned space beyond. I concentrate towards the reception, swelling with pride as Scarlet Jackson, aka Serena Brown, glides around the first desk that separates our main floor space from the reception area.

It's twenty-seven degrees outside, and Serena is wearing a tight-fitting dark-blue dress, more suited for a club than walking the streets in a heatwave. Her hair is in a ponytail, braided to an arrow and glows under the spotlights above. She's wearing white scuffed Nike's. As she
follows Abbie, she swings her hips, legs moving in front of her with the poise and strength of Lipizzaner Stallion. The whole motion is subtle enough not to be obvious but striking enough to glue your attention.

I watch on myopic, sensing a quietness descend through the office as her presence suffocates the natural hubbub.

Our Finance Director, who is sitting in the office next to me, throws me a lucky-bastard smirk as I stand to greet Serena, who glides into my office with a surge of energy that threatens to swallow me and Abbie whole.

'It's true!' Serena says with a cock-sure grin that delicately creases her flawless skin.

'What's true?'

'That you're a CEO with a view of Green Park. I stand humbled. I bow before you.'

'You checking me out?'

'Don't be silly. You wouldn't lie to me; it's not in you.'

Abbie steps out of my office, smirking behind her eyes. I can't decide if Serena's poking fun at me or just playing—but then I never can. She has this knack of catching people off guard, which I both distrust and like in equal measures.

'*The Leaf-Project*! Sneaky!'

'Thinking on my feet.'

'Is this a surprise visit, or are we in this part of town?'

'I have a meeting around the corner, and when I stepped out of the taxi and saw that I was early, I thought, well, I can go for a coffee, or I can come here and check on my gorgeous man.'

She leans in, smelling of lilac and pine, and kisses me on the cheek, wiping the residue of lipstick from the side of my face.

'Oops,' she giggles. 'I wouldn't want to get you into trouble.'

'That's hard, seeing as I'm the boss.'

'Only here, darling,' she says with a wink.

I smile.

'Do you have time for a coffee?' she says, her long eyelashes fluffing in front of me.

'As wonderful as it is to have you here, I do have an important meeting in fifty minutes. I should be finished at six-thirty. Seven, latest. When will you be done? We could get something to eat afterwards if you're free?'

'Would love to, honey, but I've planned dinner with my colleague.'

I half wait for the rest of the sentence, but it doesn't come, and I suddenly view how she's dressed in a different light.

A club.

A night out.

A colleague.

A male.

She steps to my window to admire the view of Green Park, and a jealous rage smashes through me. We've been dating for six weeks, and we both have opposite-sex friends who aren't intimate. The last thing I want to do is come across as the possessive, controlling type, which I'm not and never have been, but she has a way of pushing those buttons within me.

'I'm assuming we're still good for Friday?'

'Are you really that busy that you can't spend ten minutes with me?'

I knew before I opened my mouth she wasn't going to answer my question about Friday.

My jealousy antenna flicked again.

'We've been on this one for nearly eight months and are at the sharp end of the deal. I need to kick you out. I'm sorry.'

'Don't be silly, it's me that's sorry. I should have called. You can at least spare two minutes for the abridged tour of the office as you push me out the door?'

'I can.'

I open my office door and lead the way. Our office space is small, with only forty employees, and the building itself is thin and narrow, having recently undergone a refurbishment before we took the lease. We share the floor with four other start-ups. The open design and frosted sections give a spacious atmosphere despite the odd dimensions from a 1750s original build.

We walk past finance and marketing and then IT.

Serena pops her head into one of our break-out rooms and comments on the space. Our head of account management stops to introduce herself, and I prickle with embarrassment as I get caught between saying a 'good friend' rather than my 'girlfriend'. It makes me question what we represent to each other apart from being sexually compatible in a way that I've never experienced before.

Conscious that the minutes are counting down, I border on frog-marching Serena towards the main elevators.

We chat.

The small talk, a touch strained, like it's a first date. I'm struggling to take my eyes off her dress, which hugs her figure in a way that drives me crazy.

'You look good in a white shirt,' she says. 'You should wear one the next time we climb into bed.'

'Hopefully, that'll be Friday.'

She doesn't comment on our pending date, and I want to kick myself for showing my insecurity.

The lift pings open, and it saves me from myself. I seem to have developed into that person who can't believe his luck at dating the prettiest girl in his group.

'Oh… sorry, do you have a toilet I can use? Sorry, sorry, I know you're pushed.'

'Sure, there's one down here.'

I guide her to my right, and we walk toward the bathrooms. As I approach, I see the office caretaker put a sign outside.

Out of Order.

I huff, irritated.

'We have one in our office. I'll have to get Abbie to see you out if that's okay?'

'Didn't I walk past a disabled toilet on my way in? I'm sure that's closer?'

I have to think for a second, but she's right. There's one on the other side of the corridor, away from our reception area but closer to this point.

'Sorry,' she says, smiling.

It's sexy.

Naughty.

Controlling.

'It's okay. This way.'

We walk on when I get this tightness inside, like she's toying with me. She's walking slower. She doesn't really need the toilet. She wants to start another conversation.

I say my goodbyes and mumble that I'll call her later when she steps in close. The surprise and speed of movement are enough to nudge me backwards. I stumble backwards into the toilet, helped by the kiss she plants on my lips to help me on my way. The lights flicker on, and she locks the door behind her, leaving her lips on my mouth.

Were we seen is all I can think.

It could cost me everything I have worked years to achieve and some.

But it doesn't stop me.

I don't want to.

I'm lost to a new lust I've recently discovered, grateful, somehow, that I'm the beneficiary of this moment and not somebody else.

My Friday night has come early.

I grab for the hem of her dress as my career shoots through my mind.

I blank the thought, rocked by a deeper sense that I'm crossing more than a professional line as my hand slips inside her pants, and a groan drowns my fears.

Chapter 3

I leave Teddy-Boy's Practice and head for the station as my anger gyrates from peaks of rage to lows of self-pity. It's an internal rollercoaster I'm struggling to contain. The more I scratch at this mess, the more confused I become and the more desperate I feel. And despite Teddy's so-called impartial stance, his inquisition into my personal life is more prosecution-led than he's letting on.

It's a situation I'll discuss with my barrister when we next speak.

I walk on, having secretly hoped these sessions would throw some light on how I got sucked into this maelstrom. They haven't, and I'm beginning to doubt that they ever will. I'm growing more convinced that his nit-picking is an underlying jealousy towards who I am and my lifestyle in general. I'm sure he'd tell me I'm suffering from Transference Neurosis or some other Freudian bullshit, but I've seen that green-eyed trait enough times in my short career to recognise it a mile off. Inadvertently, he has taught me my biggest danger is myself. I've become self-obsessed, where I'm the centre of a circular conversation about my predicament and my pending doom.

I need to stop.

To stop fretting about my defensive shows with Teddy, trusting that the old fool is wise enough to see through my fragile ego and give a fair assessment of who I am. He doesn't have to like me. He just has to see the truth. If he can't, or won't, then that's why I have an expensive barrister to do my barking and to tell the world I'm a normal Joe who's drowning in a shit-swamp of someone else's making.

Wrong place.

Wrong time.

I have to keep this at the forefront of my mind, or I'm going to sink to the bottom of the sea like thousands of others before me.

I enter the station, realising I had unintentionally lied to Teddy-Boy.

I don't ever recall asking my inner circle if they liked Serena or not. I assumed they did. What wasn't there to like about her had been my default thinking. She was fun, gregarious, and had a knack for remembering everything you ever said. She had this gift of being present, never distracted by others or her own thoughts, even if you bored her. It was a mesmeric, easy charm. Unique in our distracted world. I would buzz with excitement when we were out together and she turned heads, which inflated mine. I'm not going to apologise for the adrenaline rush I got from her being on my arm.

Our finance director at Eco-Blue drooled over her if we ever went for team drinks and Serena joined. She would playfully flirt with him. He took it well, and he liked her. They got on. My best mate, Daniel King, thought we were a great match, and he wished us luck. Hatti, his wife-to-be, wasn't a Serena fan, but then other women weren't, from what I could tell. They were scared Serena was going to steal their man, but she wasn't like that. She was proud of her sexuality and saw female jealousy as part and parcel of life's negotiations. An unavoidable Tax. From what I could tell, those eyelashes pissed off every woman she ever met.

Teddy-Boy's right about the excitement Serena generated within me. He knows I'm lying to him. At the beginning of my relationship with Serena, I was never sure if we were dating or not, and it kept me on my toes. I was busy with work and life, so it didn't overly matter. I would sometimes stop to think about where she was and what she was up to. She did have this knack of when I thought she'd left my life for good, butterflying back into my sphere with plausible excuses of business deadlines and dramas at work, bamboozling me with attention and compliments.

We'd go out and eat gourmet, guzzle champagne, followed by intense sex. Combined, it nulled my lingering doubts about commitments and our future together. All of which I'm struggling to articulate to Teddy-Boy.

I sense he's secretly scoffing at the casualness of online dating. He thinks I'm a player. I'm not. He doesn't seem to get that people lie about who they are and what they do. Photoshopped pictures dot every page. The whole process is a hit-and-miss lottery of avoiding the desperate and the unbalanced. It's all underpinned by a swathe of unwritten rules that you need to learn the hard way. It sounds cheap when you begin to articulate them, and so what if you sleep with a few people you don't like to get your needs met? And if churn is your game, then dating apps give you that choice.

I don't care about Teddy, but I do care about the jury.

Nobody seems to believe me that I met Serena at the Awareness Conference. It's true, as was her Tinder Profile. The reason I remember her Tinder Profile so vividly is the picture she used. She was dressed in a flimsy summery dress at what I assumed was a pool party in the Med. She was holding a glass of champagne, sunglasses delicately balanced across her head. She had a fresh, honey-coloured tan, a sulky smile and a twinkle in her eye, which suggested so much more, and one I can vouch she delivered on.

Then there were those lashes and eyes.

I remember swiping right and thinking this girl is going to be hit on by everyone whose profile she matches. It even crossed my mind that she was too good for me, and I was embarrassed at my lack of self-respect. It's why when we did match and initially chat, it struck a deep chord.

One I will never forget.

Our first date was at a hotel bar near Piccadilly. I'm never late, but she beat me at my own game. I'd have bet serious money she was going to play the fashionable ten-minute late rule. Instead, there she was, waiting at the long bar with a bottle of champagne on ice and an empty seat beside her. I can still recall that surge of adrenaline at seeing the bar stool, knowing it had my name rubber-stamped across it. I was struck, too, at how different she looked from the conference. Shortly after, she invited me to a Japanese-themed party to celebrate a marketing deal she'd been involved in. Serena showed up as a Geisha, along with a sunblock umbrella.

She looked native Japanese.

But that was Serena.

The perfect chameleon.

And I liked it.

She pushed my boundaries at every opportunity she had, relentlessly.

An ingrained habit, wrapped up in the personality of who she was.

Her smile was a combination of sexy and spiteful.

Her laugh was the same combustible mix.

Her tone danced a delicate balance between rock and silk, the delivery leaving you unsure if you'd been complimented or insulted.

She loved the ambiguity of being Serena, and she loved her *LavishLondonLashes* Instagram profile even more.

Now she's dead, and I'm starting to wonder if it was me who killed her after all.

Chapter 4

Serena nudges me awake.

It's not what I'd call aggressive, but it's not gentle either. It's a behaviour that began immediately when she started to stay over and one which feels ingrained into what makes her tick.

I acknowledge it, as I always do, by turning onto my back and waiting for the ritual to continue.

Eyes closed, she pushes up without kissing me and climbs on top, simultaneously wetting her hand and then herself before pulling her panties to one side.

She glides me in.

It hurts.

Dry skin on dry skin, but the moment passes, and we're soon connected in our mutual warmth.

She's not a selfish lover, not even close, but this is about another part of her personality. Each morning, I'm nothing more than an object to be used and then discarded. I've questioned myself if I should be letting this happen. But I am, and I do, so I must be okay with it, or at least a co-conspirator in her game.

I watch her gaining speed and wonder who she's thinking about or what fantasies are cascading through her mind. I'm confident that I'm not part of them, and I ping with both jealousy and relief in equal measures. There's a certain peace to be had from the lack of emotional commitment. There's no effort required on my part. I don't have to pretend to enjoy it.

We're both off the hook to let our minds go to those dark, exotic places, limited only by our imaginations.

I'm confident Serena is already there and has probably been there in person.

I groan.

It's fake.

My jealously stabbing at me some more. I'm a fool to let those emotions rule, especially as I'm the benefactor of her vivid sexual inventiveness. I've accepted that you can't be as good at this as Serena is unless you've practised the art.

It's a fact I'm maturing into.

I let my negative thoughts evaporate and detached myself even more from the experience. At the end of my bedroom, I have a mirror. I can see the top of her head bob up and down in its reflection. It's strangely more erotic than seeing her flawless body carve away at mine.

I grow bored of my own detachment, deciding it's time to join the party. I groan and relax into being her toy. I allow myself to go to my fantasy of choice, time folding away.

I groan.

It's loud and genuine.

She stops and smiles, then peels herself off.

I'm not convinced she even got to the point she wanted other than to scratch her morning habit.

'Shall we go out for breakfast?' she asks like nothing just happened.

'Sure. Where?'

'It's a gorgeous day. You choose,' she says with her best Fox News smile.

I'm hungover and spent, but I nod okay. I don't know how she does it. It's like there's a nuclear reactor which keeps her burning twenty-four-seven.

I look at my phone for the time, and it's later than I thought, nearly eleven. It must have been past three when we finally collapsed into bed.

I turn back for a quick snuggle, hoping to change her mind, but she's rolled away and is heading for the shower. She pads naked out of my bedroom, and seconds later, I hear the water hit the walls, and it's my unofficial notice to get out of bed.

It's a struggle.

I chastise myself for spoiling my Saturday with cheap champagne and even cheaper prosecco. I head for the kitchen to make a coffee, remembering I don't have milk. Serena's right behind me, dressed and looking like she's just left a spa and detox retreat.

'Come on... let's go. The sun's out, and the sky's blue. This one's on me.'

I find the reserve for a five-minute power session to get myself showered and dressed and out the door, doing my best to leave the zombie version of myself behind. We take the short walk to Kensal Rise and head for *The Tree-House Café*. The decor is a mishmash of anything they could find that they thought was trendy. I find it a touch pretentious, with its school-style chairs and rustic tables, but the food is organic and fresh, and the glass roof spills the room with natural light.

I go for the full English while Serena orders poached eggs and avocado with no sourdough bread. When the food comes, she drizzles her meal with additional avocado oil while I squeeze ketchup on the corner of my plate.

Opposites attract, I think.

My hangover continues to sing through the front of my mind.

We eat and chat.

The conversation is light, and there is nothing to ignite a debate or a simmering hurt. I'm not sure if it's the delayed reactions from the alcohol still in my blood, but I've heard this chat before—the same stories, the same ticker-tape running, like we've exhausted the menu and need to start from the beginning.

I clock it all like a distant echo.

To a degree, she's gushing too much about how compatible we are and how we like the same things—foods, culture, travel, sex. She likes to zoom in on our ages and how it's been worth the wait for both of us. Though I'm older by three years, we're at the magic number—still young enough, but old enough at the same time to know best. I think it's too early in our relationship to talk about the longer term, but like her morning nudge, I go with the ride, enjoying it more than I care to admit.

I ask for the bill and an extra coffee to get me through as Serena starts on another story about work that I heard in full last night. I'm waiting for my moment to suggest we head back for another round between the sheets, followed by a movie and some sleep, when she beats me to it.

'I meant to say, darling, but I have to work today. We have an important event that has been brought forward by a week. I should have worked last night, but you're too sweet and gorgeous to resist. That white shirt tipped me over the edge.' She giggles. 'You don't mind, do you? It looks like you need the time to recover, anyway.'

I let her words drift in the space between us, wrong-footed by my insecurities, my hangover, and the disappointments that chop through me.

'Hey... sure... no problem. I definitely need a couple more hours of sleep. I wanted to get on the bike later, anyway.'

'I knew you wouldn't mind.'

She stands, brushes at the front of her dress, looking more like she's finished an all-nighter and is now heading home to recover.

I wonder if that's what I am?

A port in the dark.

She kisses me long and hard on the lips, then leaves with a wave as I'm hit with another annoyance.

Picking up the tab has become the norm.

On one level, I don't mind. It's only breakfast, and I'm confident I earn more than Serena—a lot more. But those offers to pay never materialise, and there's something off in how she presents it.

She'd be better off saying nothing, and I wish she wouldn't offer.

I stand and squeeze past a row of chairs to pay at the counter, catching my reflection in the mirror on the far wall. My skin is grey, even in this bright sunlight. My eyes puffed. I've been drinking too much since the onset of this relationship. I need to rein it in.

Serena suddenly appears in the reflection behind me.

She's doubled back to the zebra crossing and is heading for the station.

I watch on, intrigued, surprised she's not ordered an Uber.

She's reading messages and replying. I can see she's lost in her digital chat, and I wonder who she's communicating with. I'm struggling with this newfound jealousy, and it's poisoning me in a way I'm unfamiliar with and don't like.

The green man appears in the light, and Serena starts to cross the road. I spot a young dad pushing a toddler in a pram, heading in the opposite direction. The dad is chatting with his son, laughing about something, but I can see a growing distraction at Serena's lack of awareness.

She's heading straight for them.

The dad veers to his left, but Serena changes direction and continues to drift their way.

She's lost in the void of her phone.

Texting and scrolling.

The dad stops and waits in the middle of the crossing, making a point. Then he clears his throat, and it's like I can hear him from where I'm standing. I don't know why, but it strikes me Serena is deliberately ignoring him. It's that same feeling I had when she slowed her walk in my office when I was hurrying to get her to leave.

The dad shouts his presence, but it comes too late, and Serena clips the corner of the pushchair with her shin. The man says something as his son rocks violently in the seat. Serena shouts back, jabbing her finger toward the man's face like it's his fault, her rage pouring from her in a high-octane outburst.

There's a tension and a moment's silence.

I can see the man is caught unaware by the onslaught of temper.

It's his toddler's screams that bring him back to Earth, and he crouches beside the pram to soothe his child.

I expect Serena to apologise, but she doesn't. Instead, she leans forward, examining her leg, making a show of pulling indignantly at her tights. The man stands, and they are dangerously close to each other. I tense, expecting the escalation and hoping in the same thought that it doesn't come because I don't want to get dragged into their fray.

Then he points to his temple, and then at her, and moves on as the lights go green. She says something back but doesn't move, staring him out. Then she checks on her leg, obsessively adjusting her tights, which look undamaged from where I'm stood.

They're only tights, I think.

A car driver gently toots his horn as he points at the green light and for her to move. She throws him a murderous stare, pointing at her leg like it's broken and she needs an air ambulance and full medical team on standby.

Embarrassment prickles at all my senses.

For her.

For the dad.

For the car driver.

I watch on as another driver sounds his horn for Serena to move. Her piercing look and unwillingness to accept responsibility for what's happened is something I'm all too familiar with—even comfortable around.

My mother reacts in the exact same way with my father. It took years for me to see the truth behind its meaning.

Serena was giving everyone the stare of "annihilation". And if that trait lies within you, it eats at your soul and never leaves.

Ever.

Chapter 5

My murder charge meant I scraped bail by a flea's whisker. It was aided by my clean record and my barrister's silver tongue that matched his eye-watering fee. Curfew is a painful twelve hours that I mostly spend sleeping or pacing my flat like a caged bear on the brink of insanity. I deeply resent the constrictions on my life, but my alternative is remand in custody, so I grin and bear it.

I make another tea, more out of boredom than thirst, as a crystal blue sky brightens my room, but not my mood. I would normally embrace the hot weather, but wearing shorts with an electronic tag is an attention grabber I don't have the nerve for, especially since I'll be meeting my dad. The visual upsets him.

Workout bottoms are now my default wear.

I currently have twelve pairs.

Online shopping is my new distraction.

I wait until ten-past before heading out the door. I'm nervous about a technology glitch that could see me behind bars.

Once outside, I quickly march, burning off my pent-up tension. I catch the overground and then the underground to St Pancras. It doesn't take long, and I'm hot, sweaty, and excited as I head toward street level and into the buzzy summer crowd.

In the mid-distance, I spot my dad people-watching as he waits for me to arrive. He must sense my presence, turning to greet me with his fatherly smile. There have been moments between us that I'd rather forget, but I've never stopped admiring who he is and what he's done for me. Every time I see him, it cloaks my own pains in comfort and gives me hope I'll get through this chaos that has become my life.

He's had a hardcore weekly routine of walking, yoga, swimming, and eating only two meals a day for over a decade. It's paid dividends and is a lesson for my own later years, but he's not looking that good of late. He's lost too much weight, and there's a jaundiced hint to his skin that his permanent suntan can no longer hide. I guess at seventy-six, he's teetering on the brink of old age, and I have to accept that my pending trial is affecting him as much as it is me.

'How you doing, son?'

'I'm good.'

We hug as if we haven't seen each other in years, and I can feel the sharpness of his ribs under his loose-fitting shirt, and it gives me another jab of guilt.

After the divorce from my mother, the little he had left, he managed to set up a home in Majorca. He never once moaned about the terms of the settlement and how screwed to the wall he was because of the second-rate barrister he hired and the belief he held that my mother would play fair.

Instead, he knuckled down, kept his mouth shut, and rebuilt his shattered life piece-by-piece, slowly finding himself and his mojo again. His small wine import business has paid enough for him to clear his mortgage on his property in Majorca. He's even scraped enough together to buy a box studio near Heathrow Airport, where he stays a few days each month when he comes to England.

We walk past the Google Building and head to Coal Drop Yard as my dad talks about how this place used to be full of drug-dealers, pimps and street prostitutes—and look at it now. It's a wash of luxury flats, a bespoke mall, all butting into a tech hub and the train gateway into Europe.

Turning into a cobbled area, we head for a small bistro we like, finding seats outside. We sanitise our hands, and sit and order food from a waiter who is wearing a mask. My dad doesn't drink—or not any more—despite his part-time profession, and I can't. I have a blood test in a few hours, all part of my bail conditions and conditions linked to the night of Serena's death.

Our soft drinks arrive, and we chat about Majorca and how it's too hot and too full of Brits, like he's a local and not the ex-pat that he's become. He hints that he's dating, which brings a youthful chuckle to his voice. It eases the pain in his face and reminds me more of the dad I know and the happier days we once enjoyed.

'Any news on the trial date?'

I shake my head. 'My barrister is telling me to expect late October or early November. He still hints at a dismissal, but I doubt it. I'm going to have to go through the motions unless the police miraculously find a new suspect, which isn't going to happen because they would have to actively look for one in the first place. Carter's convinced it's me.'

My words hang in the air, and my dad nods.

'Thanks again for picking up the legal bills. It's not going to wipe you out, is it, as I've been thinking that I should sell my flat? I was never that attached to it, to be honest.'

'You're my son, and I believe in you. I'm okay for the money and, anyway, who else would I spend it on—your mother!'

We laugh. He'd rather commit Hara-Kiri before giving her another penny. Then his eyes flicker and mist with a milky sheen, and the moment turns on us as if we've stepped onto an emotional ledge.

We hold each other's stare, and I rock with guilt, or is it shame? I'm never sure of the difference because they both axe at my heart.

He asks me if I've heard from Ryan.

I shake my head.

After the divorce split our family, my older brother, Ryan, moved out and then decided to emigrate to Australia. Since that move, he has had close to no contact with us. He's spoken to me once since I was charged, and his lack of interest or empathy towards my plight is depressing and makes me thankful he's not on the jury. He'll speak with my dad, but only if my father makes the call and the conversation never extends beyond fifteen minutes.

As for our mother, Ryan doesn't even acknowledge her presence any more.

For him, she's dead.

And maybe she is for all of us—emotionally, anyway.

'You keeping busy?' my dad asks, breaking the moment.

I shrug. 'I'm trying. I get on the bike when I can, but I'm bored out of my mind. I've too much time on my hands. Too much time to feel sorry for myself.'

'You have to make this period work for you. The obstacles are where the opportunities lie. Don't forget that. It's how you're going to survive this.'

We share a smile, but it's weak and lacks conviction from my side. Doubts about my culpability on the night of Serena's death continue to dance in the shadows of my mind.

'You look terrible, son. Is there anything else I can do?'

I shake my head, thinking the same about him or are we both projecting our fears onto each other, locked into our own personal hells?

'I'm scared, and my concentration is shot, but overall I'm okay. I need to get to October or November or whenever it is this trial will be and then put this behind me. That's it. That's my mission right now. Simple but complex.'

He nods, although I can see he doesn't agree.

'Get your mind as straight as you can. That jury is going to be looking at you for two weeks. You're innocent, and you have to carry that within you every single day you step into that court or something else is going to poke through. Something you don't want. You listening to me?'

I nod, unable to hold his stare.

My mind rocks with guilt.

About him.

About Serena.

About my brother.

'I meant to say, I'm seeing Mum tomorrow. Anything you want me to tell her?'

'Yeah, she owes me a couple of million plus interest. I also want my pound of flesh back. I need it at my age.'

I enter the police station, and it triggers all the insecurities I harbour over my case. My fears flush through me in a surge of guilt toward Serena. I struggle to contain them, detached from the moment. I've come to dread these weekly visits that are part of my bail conditions. Even the smell of the building rams home the close call I had at staying out of the worst parts of the system until my trial.

The duty officer recognises me and looks on impassive as he reaches under his desk and buzzes open the door to my right. I enter and am met by another man, young and fat—a civilian who runs the show in this crowded room.

'This is the third time you've been late, Harrison. It's getting logged against your record.'

It's another barbed warning from the pen-pusher who has no real power other than the inflated one ramming through his mind. He's picked on me from day one, and I'm inclined to tell him he should be more concerned with his Cuban heels and the people who are laughing behind his back than worrying about me being a few minutes late because of a broken-down bus.

My barrister has already given me the pep talk about the process and the people who run it. There are those whose sole job it is to bait defendants. I didn't believe him at first, but I now know it is true.

It's like they win a prize—a holiday in Barbados—if they push you over the edge and you end up breaking your bail conditions.

I can see in his eyes that he thinks I'm an entitled rich kid who got drunk and angry and killed his girlfriend because he had nothing better to do.

Well, I didn't, I want to scream, but it's not him I have to convince.

It's the twelve people on a jury and maybe one more.

Me.

I sit, and he makes a show of checking on my electronic tracker. I'm not even sure it's his job, as the tracker is run by the monitoring service. I seriously debate whether to ask him if he wants to polish my shoes while he's down there, but I don't.

My barrister is my new mentor.

What he says, I do.

Instead, I glance through the room at the other curfew bunnies. They all look as guilty as the Devil himself. Some of them stare back with the same suspicious eyes. I'm the guy who walked into a drug den rather than the A-List event I thought I was going to.

They have a point, and it's how I've felt since this all started.

The wrong person.

The wrong room.

The wrong time.

A nurse appears from the door at the far end of the room, and she hands me two small plastic pots and points me in the direction of the toilet. I gulped a litre of water when I was having lunch with my dad, so I'm more than desperate to go. I head for the cubicle as she hands a set of pots to the guy sat next to me. She's wasting her time, and she knows it because he stinks of booze and has the bloodshot eyes of a vampire.

I close the door and start to pee, wondering what the youth's life is like compared to mine. He's institutionalised through and through, and I must look the multi-millionaire to him, to the others, too.

I've never taken drugs and, apart from the odd beer here and there, didn't discover drink in its full glory until I met Serena.

Champagne is our choice of weapon.

I still can't tell why it became central to our relationship other than it did. It was one of many minor shifts I allowed to creep into my life when I should have been more vigilant. Like neglecting my friends, being late for work, my presentations not being as finessed as usual; the list is as endless as the crimes in the room behind me.

Even my fitness regime evaporated, and the extra kilos from those nights of indulgence still push at my belt.

My internal justification was that my single-life had to bump into a serious relationship at some point. What's the point of building a financially secure future and the career you dream about if you can't experience it with the people you love? I used to believe that an experience unshared wasn't an experience, but I'm not so sure any more.

It's all how you view it.

I retake my seat as the *how* and the *why* continue to loop through my mind, as they have done since that fateful night in May. I suddenly recall the trip to San Diego, where Serena joined me. Eco-Blue had won an industry award for our Beach Initiative in Southern Sri Lanka. The idea was brought to me by a fifteen-year-old girl who had been on holiday with her parents and had watched from her hotel room as the young boys from the local village burnt plastic water bottles on open fires. They were paid in Coca-Cola to clean the rubbish from the Surf Camps. The billowing black smoke was destined to shorten their lives. It distressed Jessica enough for her to do something about it. She came to Eco-Blue with a detailed plan to employ the boys to collect the bottles from tourist beach spots and set up a recycling plant. Eco-Blue raised three million, and the Sri Lankan Government matched the investment, granting the all-important licenses and access to set up a recycling facility outside of Galle. It didn't control the village politics, but it was a start.

Apart from the recognition that came my way, it was a joy to work with Jessica. Her enthusiasm and lack of cynicism towards the world and its corrupting influences were beyond refreshing.

She never lost sight of her purpose for the disadvantaged boys.

Eco-Blue gave her the finances, but Jessica supplied the real wealth with her insight and energy.

She still sends me updates on the Project that have become an oasis in my pain-filled days. Apart from my dad, she's the only other person to say she knows I'm not guilty.

Stated with the true conviction of a corruption-free teenager.

Our wannabe dictator comes out barking orders, reminding us all to be on time in a week as we're dismissed except for two. The boy with the vampire eyes is staying as is a young Afro-Caribbean youth who looks shell-shocked at not being allowed to leave, tears welling as he stutters: *'wh... at... me?'*

I'm sure Vampire Eyes is not even aware he's about to replace his small room with his stolen 55-inch wide-screen for an even smaller room with no TV and a heavier metal door.

I'm mocking his life, I know. But it's the only way I can push the image of us not ending up in the same cell as each other. I'm going to be eaten alive if I fall into the system full-time, his revenge on me for my spiteful thoughts imminent and permanent.

I'm not cut out for that life.

It's not who I am.

So how the fuck did a thirty-two-year-old CEO on the make end up on a murder charge?

I look through the room, the light of wisdom
clearing my mind.
I lost my head when I should have kept it.
It's that simple.
That stupid.

Chapter 7

I check the time on my phone, allowing my eyes to flick up to the Art Deco clock near the entrance to the restaurant.

It confirms what I know.

Serena's thirty-four minutes late and counting.

My seething thermometer is beginning to rise, made worse by the fact that I'm a punctual person. It was drilled into me by my dad, and nobody likes to be on the receiving end of someone else's superiority play.

Me included.

It's not the first time this has happened. A practice that's been parachuted into our relationship from nowhere and one I fear is heading to becoming chronic.

The barman with the tattooed hands catches my eye. He's good at his job and understands how to max his tips. I order my second G&T, a double, not that I want the first one, but I need something to dull the gnaw of embarrassment at what I'm sure is going to go down as a blowout. On top of the pending awkwardness of leaving alone, it took me a month to secure a table in what should be a gastronomic pleasure if I ever get to taste the food.

My drink is placed on the coaster in front of me, bubbles breaking the surface of my drink. A waitress approaches with two menus held close to her chest. I half ignore her, expecting her to turn to the groomed couple off to my left, when she smiles in my direction, mistaking the elegant blonde as my girlfriend, announcing our table is ready. I flush with embarrassment, as does the blonde. Her boyfriend laughs nervously, and before any of us can say anything, the maître d' is taking charge, directing the waitress and the couple towards their table. She apologises but, in the same whisper, manages to remind me that the table needs to be vacated by 10:00 pm.

I nod that I understand, but we both sense it's looking more unlikely by the minute that I'll be taking the booking.

I reach for my drink as I check my WhatsApp Messages from Serena. She hasn't messaged since late morning, but I can see she was online less than three minutes ago. I scroll back to see that we had arranged to meet in the Bar at 7:30 pm. I was ten minutes early and had been standing here like the Proverbial Lemon for close to an hour. What's bothering me more is that I've had this uneasy feeling all day that I was going to be stood up.

Why, I don't know, but I do, and my own premonition appears to be coming true.

I ignore my paranoid thoughts and WhatsApp her.

I wait.

No response.

I re-read my message, deciding my tone is bordering on the aggressive. My pissed-off mood filtering through.

The message isn't opened.

I grow impatient and text through my network provider, shifting tone.

The message is delivered but isn't read.

I call, and it rings and rings, flicking to voice mail.

I seethe more as fantasies of Serena having sex with another man crash into my mind from nowhere.

It makes me open my new Instagram Account and check out *LavishLondonLashes*. This morning, she posted a picture of her using a new eyelash brush. I'm no expert, but it looks the same as the type my mother has used her whole life. Serena's bragged how she's now charging six hundred pounds a post, and companies are beginning to line up to pay her fee. When I think how hard most people work for six-hundred pounds, it makes no sense, but it's the world we live in, I guess.

I stir my G&T, splashing the drink across the front of my trousers and on the side of my shoes.

I huff, brushing at the front of my crotch.

I'm doing a shit job of looking relaxed in this dimly lit holding pen for couples and aperitifs.

I knock back my drink and seriously debate ordering a third before common sense takes hold.

Tonight is never going to happen. I have to know when I'm beaten.

I pay and head for the door, where the receptionist gets my coat. She is pretty and chatty, like I'm not on my own. She works hard to make me feel better about the situation, adding that she looks forward to seeing 'us' again to experience *Scars* Restaurant.

I thank her and slip outside to be alone with my embarrassment. The cool evening breeze attacks the alcohol in my blood. It makes my emotions erupt from behind their delicate wall.

I check again to see if any of my messages have been acknowledged.

They haven't.

I spark with a new anger and jab at my recent calls, connecting to her phone. Hearing it ring brings to life her ex-boyfriend within my mind. I've never met him, but he's vivid and real within my imagination. Clarke was apparently an up-and-coming Formula Two racing driver destined for the top. Like the lateness, he's a recent introduction into our relationship, and he's appeared one too many times for my liking. Their relationship was all set for wedding bells and happy-ever-afters until he started to push her around and blacked her eye.

I listened and nodded, never commenting beyond my obvious distaste. But I was deeply offended at the undercurrent warning that came with the unexpected and unrequested story. And like today, there was this element of the story that didn't seem to sit in the groove of truth.

'Hi, Darling. What's up? I thought you were out with the boys tonight?'

Her light tone puts me straight on the back foot.

I clear my throat.

'Where are you?'

'Home, watching a movie with a glass of wine. Our work drinks were cancelled, so I thought I'd take the opportunity to have an early night. It makes a change to get some "me" time. I was about to have a bath, so you caught me just in time. You sound like you're in the street? Going anywhere nice?'

I'm struggling to think what to say, and I can hear my own short-tempered breaths filling my lungs.

'I'm not out with the boys. I'm at *Scars* Restaurant or, more precisely, I'm stood outside *Scars*.'

'Oh… you cheat! I thought that was our treat for next week. How could you go without me!'

The playfulness in her voice stabs at my resolve.

'It was this week, not next. It was tonight.'

Nothing.

I don't even hear her breathe. The vacuum of the silence sucking even more at my confidence.

'Darling, we said next Friday. I distinctly remember the conversation. You were telling me about the pitch to the Microsoft Executive and then how Abbie had been waiting on hold for over an hour but finally secured the booking for the 22nd. I have it in my diary. I'm looking at it as we speak.'

'I said the 15th, today, and we spoke about it yesterday. You told me about your pending Instagram post and the new fee, and we were going to celebrate.'

'No, baby, we didn't. I would have remembered. It's not something I would forget. I also don't discuss my posts pre-posting. I've always been like that. I've been waiting for us to go to *Scars,* and there's no way I would mix up the dates. *You've* given me the wrong date. Definitely, *you* have. This is *your* fault, not mine, so please don't push this onto me and ruin my night.'

'No, I didn't,' I hear myself shout. 'We discussed this yesterday, along with your post and... and you've deliberately stood me up. I even knew you were going to do this.'

Silence.

Followed by a laugh.

'Now you're being ridiculous. Why would I do that?'

'That's my question to you?'

A man walking in the opposite direction stares at me. I ignore him as I pull the phone from my ear and scroll through my WhatsApp messages. I can see we've discussed the restaurant and the food and how much we're both looking forward to going. Even the time, but I don't see the date. She's right that

Abbie made the booking, and I recall Abbie sending me the email confirmation.

Yes, I think.

Abbie.

Email.

I switch to my work emails and find the confirmation of the booking.

Bingo, I say to myself, until I see that I didn't forward it on to Serena.

I'm frothing inside at myself but more at my so-called girlfriend.

I know my personal agency.

We discussed her pending post and the time and date of dinner. It's not the sort of thing I forget, especially as it's against my better judgement to use our team secretary to organise my personal diary. That's not the kind of company I run.

'Serena, I said the 15th. Tonight.'

She's hung up.

I call back.

It goes straight to voice mail, and I manage to hold myself from leaving the message I want to leave, but I don't hold myself from sending a sniping text.

I get an instant reply.

Show me the text with the date?

I scroll through our messages again, my anger sliding from its peak into annoyance, followed by irritation, before dropping into doubt, which becomes edged with shame for shouting and losing my calm.

I was too convinced I was right, and I wanted to make my point.

It's not an excuse, but I've been stressed at work, and we suffered a kick-in-the-teeth from a nineteen-year-old university student who came to us for thirty-five thousand to develop a sea-filter to capture plastics. I um'd-and-ah'd, and meanwhile, he was savvy enough to pitch us off against a rival company who joyfully announced a two-hundred-and-fifty thousand package in development funding. The kid even made the front of The Times and promptly left Southampton University to set up his business. I'm pissed at myself and for the negative press it generated for Eco-Blue.

Maybe I did tell her the 22nd, I think. But whether I did or didn't, there is passive-aggressive behaviour that has crept into our relationship via the back door. Whatever I say, the opposite has started to happen. Or, I don't even get an answer. There's nothing committed. The door always ajar for a side manoeuvre. It is behaviour I saw happen between my parents and ultimately destroyed my dad as he fought endless circular battles he could never win. He spent most of his married life stuck in an emotional rabbit hole.

The thought pulls me to a hard stop.

I either let history repeat itself or I draw this to an end.

The choice is mine.

The power resides within me.

I hail a black cab and collapse on the seat, angry. I'm tired, and I want to rest my mind. But I can't. Instead, I continue to torture myself about how much better Mr Formula Two Racing Driver was in bed compared to myself. I'm not sure what is happening to me and why I can't shake what Serena says from my mind. Her voice and her words somehow get planted deeper within me.

Indelible.

As we approach my street, the traffic begins to get backed up. I pay and jump out, deciding the walk will do me good. I cut through a side street toward my flat. I'm now more disappointed than angry in how the evening has panned out.

The only person to blame is myself.

I should have listened to my own advice.

I should have known better.

I approach the communal door to my block when movement in the darkened alley between my block and the neighbouring flats catches my attention.

I tense.

A man on the next street was mugged outside his house for his watch and car keys only a few days ago.

I suddenly wonder if it's a rat or even a fox until a woman's outline morphs into view.

I blink into the darkness.

It's Serena.

She steps from the full darkness into the greys of the shadows, seductive and slow. It's then I see she's dressed in stilettos, the ones that make it seem like she's perched on her toes. She's wearing sheer stockings and a long trench coat that she slowly pries open to reveal nothing but black underwear.

She beckons me in with the turn of her heel and a thrust of the hips.

I gasp to myself and do as I'm told, lost to my pleasure and surprise and a growing lust I can't control.

I say nothing as her coat is pulled back some more to reveal her lithe, hard body.

She smells of the bath she said she took.

I look her in the eyes and then slip to my knees, burying my face into the heat of her body.

A delicate groan dances on the wind of the night, followed by a distant cough of a male and the trot of a walking dog.

Their noise brings me back to what I'm doing and where and all of its potential consequences should we get caught, or for me, anyway.

I'm about to stand when her hand presses at the back of my head to keep going.

I resist and then willingly yield.

Enjoying myself and her, and somehow understanding that being watched is really giving her the connection she wants.

Chapter 8

I have the same thought every time I enter our family home: *It's my dad who should be standing where I am.*

He should be admiring this view and enjoying his golden-years in a place he worked hard to get and wanted to keep.

He cherished those rare quiet moments in the morning, drinking his coffee and watching the Thames bend below our family home, high on Richmond Hill.

We moved here from Kent when I was six, and my brother was ten. Looking back on it, I didn't want to come, I was crying at leaving my friends, but I soon settled, as did Ryan. It's a safe place to live with good schools and lots of outdoor activities, many of which have stayed part of my life.

Cycling for one.

I turn to face my mother. The quiet snarl never leaves the corners of her mouth. She has newly dyed blonde hair and an orange fake tan. She's convinced it makes her look younger. It doesn't.

I think she looks more jaundiced than my dad.

My second thought is always the same after lamenting for my father: *what the hell am I doing here?*

It's been a diatribe of veiled criticisms since I walked through the door, all under the banner of she's only thinking of me.

I wish she wouldn't.

"*What are you wearing?*" were the first words out of her mouth.

Apparently, grey doesn't suit me. It dilutes my skin tones, and t-shirts make me look common.

"*You're late*", which wasn't true. We changed the time a week ago as I had an appointment with my barrister that he couldn't shift. I arranged to come at midday, and I knocked on her door at 11:50 am. I knocked because I don't have a key to our family home, despite still having a bedroom, but I allegedly said 11:30 am. Therefore, I'd kept her waiting for twenty-minutes.

She knows I'm like my dad when in comes to time-keeping and that I am never late.

Maybe that's the problem?

I'm too like my dad, and she can't stand it.

My brother is too much like her, and she can't stand that either.

"You *never come to see me any more!*" Perhaps I'll give her that one because I definitely don't see her as much as I used to.

Her favourite and go-to didn't take long to get tossed my way.

"*You're so fussy with your food. I never know what to cook even when you DO come over.*"

It's another one of the many fabrications that have miraculously become truisms in the relationship between us. I enjoy my food enormously, but since I was a child, I've never eaten chicken or had a particularly sweet tooth.

On one level, I'm gob-smacked to see she's gone to the trouble to make Caesar salad and homemade trifle.

On another level, I'm not.

It's how she operates. I'm used to it. I wonder if dementia has finally set in. I hear dad's cutting cynicism about her suffering from selective memory, except when she stepped into the divorce courts. There, her recall powers of all the hurts she'd suffered, and the list of what she was entitled to fell from her lips in a chronological order that redefined photographic memory. It was bittersweet for my father. He was glad to be free of her, but considering she's never paid for anything in her life, it was a high price to pay.

She places my bowl in front of me, and the first thing I notice is my salad is devoid of croutons but not hers. It's a stupid thing to get irritated about. I almost laugh. I don't even want the salad or even the croutons, but I bristle inside, having to grab my thoughts and stop myself from spilling a cutting remark.

So I have lettuce and chicken, I think.

'Don't tell me you're not eating chicken again? You told me it was back on the menu?'

Impossible, I think, but it's easier to say.

'How they're treated and the amount of antibiotics pumped into them is unacceptable. I just couldn't continue. I'd rather eat something else. Grass-fed meats work, or the lettuce is perfect. I can be a vegetarian for the afternoon. It's slimming.'

'You're impossible to keep up with, Kieran, do you know that! You should have told me it was off-menu, and I could have looked for some lamb or beef. Not sure on the grass-fed bit as they're all herbivores last time I looked.' She chuckles to herself, cutting into her chicken. 'It's delicious. You don't know what you're missing.'

'Yes, I do,' I say.

'Sorry, I should have mentioned it. I've had a lot on my mind lately.'

'It's so difficult to keep up with your fads and practically impossible to second guess that weak constitution of yours. Anyway, if you *actually* came to see me more often, I wouldn't be in this ridiculous situation with you pretending to be vegan, or whatever it is, and me having to throw perfectly good organic chicken into the rubbish.'

I let it all wash over me or, as much as I can, especially the weak constitution part. Like so many of her assessments of my character, they're simply not true—not even close—and it's taken me years to work through them. If anyone in our family has a weak constitution, it's her. From what I can see, she has a permanent appointment with her GP. Hypochondriac should be her middle name. I take after my dad. I don't get colds, flu, or even food poisoning unless it's A-Grade Salmonella.

I can't recall the last time I went to the doctor.

The thought makes me worry about my father. He looked dreadful yesterday. The worst I've ever seen him.

'You know, it's been nearly seven weeks since you came to see me last.'

'Like I said. I've had a lot on. It's a stressful time for me right now.'

'I'm still your mother, and you should make time for me no matter how stressed you are.'

I nod my agreement again. I do it a lot in her presence, feeling that all too familiar heat of shame or guilt or whatever these emotions are that constantly engulf me. She's right that we used to talk on the phone more frequently, and I would visit every two weeks or so, but over the years, the gaps have become progressively longer, and I secretly sympathise and envy my brother's no-contact. The truth is that I've started to feel guilty about not feeling guilty. Apart from the fact we share DNA, I'm struggling to see what else we have in common. There's no listening or interest from either side in each other's lives, and I seriously wonder if she knows what I do for a living or even cares.

'You know your mistake,' she says, breaking my thoughts. 'You should have stayed with that girl. She was good for you. She wasn't like the usual trash you end up with.'

The comment throws me as it simultaneously stabs at my heart.

Trash is a new one, and she's referring to Serena, whom she met once and didn't like—I think it was mutual, but Serena never commented.

I see the corners of my mother's eyes crease into a smile as she knows she's hit the bullseye.

It takes me a second to realise who and what she's talking about.

She's referring to Rowan, the only other girl I've loved apart from Serena.

'The timing was wrong,' I say with a croak in my voice. 'She wanted to live in Ireland, on a farm, and have babies. It wasn't my path. Anyway, Ireland is too wet. That's why it's green. I prefer a dryer climate.'

'You called her boring, and she wasn't. That's you being mean. Just like your father to make sweeping judgements of people.'

I snap back.

But only in my mind.

It's a lesson I've learnt the hard way, and I'm mostly good at it.

I loved Rowan, and if I remember, my mother called her fat or on the plump side, which wasn't true. She had a thyroid issue for a short time, which meant she gained some weight until it was stabilised, and then she returned to her normal figure. We met while travelling, and she lived in London at the time, training to be a nurse, so our relationship flourished when we both returned. She was fun, smart, hard-working, and slightly crazy in that Irish way. She came from a village south of Cork. Her parents were farmers, and she wanted that life with a hive of babies. It wasn't like I was against it, either. I entertained the idea and looked into the commute and how to make it work. But so much was against us that I reluctantly came to the decision that it was doomed to fail.

My mother's comment now made sense. I did say I thought I'd grow bored of the commute and the small village mentality. I never called Rowan boring because she wasn't. She's gone on to fulfil her dreams of having babies, three so far, and she married a farmer.

Good luck to her, and I wish her the best of life because, in contrast, I'm stuck taking this shit with a murder trial hanging over my head.

Where did it all go wrong is my eternal question.

Maybe I should have taken that one-way ticket to the Emerald Isle after all?

I finish the rest of my wet lettuce and fork the chicken around my plate, the nine-hundred-pound gorilla beating his chest in the far corner of the kitchen.

Kieran Harrison's murder trial—who's going to mention it first?

I've taken the first swipe by telling her I have a lot on my mind. You'd be hard-pushed to miss the electronic tag strapped to my ankle. It's sat outside of my jeans. It was a mission to get them on. I wore them to make a point that hasn't been taken. She's not going to ask, I know it. I can still see the shrug of her shoulders when I first told her I had been finally charged by the Crown Prosecution Service.

'That's life,' she said.

She never asks about my father or Ryan.

My brother is convinced that if one of us dies, she won't attend the funeral. I laughed at him when he said it, but I'm thinking he might be right. I have zero chance of prison visits if, God forbid, I get convicted.

I shudder at the thought.

'Kieran, I'm seeing a pattern here?'

'What's that? Zigzag? Herringbone?'

'Just like your father: childish. How you ever became CEO is beyond me.'

Progress, I think. At least she knows I have, or had, a title.

She continues.

'You never ask me about *me*. What I'm up to or doing. You do know that I'm going to the Galapagos Islands next week for a trip of a lifetime? Do you even care?'

'Next week! Sorry, I thought it was next month. As mentioned, I've a lot on my mind.'

I pause, wondering, hoping that she gets the hint and will ask about me and, how I feel and if she can help.

'Yes, we're flying on Thursday. Annoyingly, they've changed our flight, so now I have to get to the airport at 5:00 am instead of 11:30 am. Such an inconvenience. I'll have to book a room at the airport now.'

'Yes, a terrible inconvenience. Richmond to Heathrow is such a trek. Is Henry going with you?'

'Of course, Henry is going with me. He's my boyfriend.'

'Sure he's strong enough? He doesn't look like he can climb into a cab, never mind a grand tour of the Galapagos Islands.'

'That's not funny, Kieran. It's the sort of comment I'd expect from your father. It's why we divorced. Henry drives a Porsche, you know. He paid cash for it.'

'I thought he was an ex-broker, not a drug dealer.'

'Stop it. He asked me if you wanted to come and he'll pay for your flights. That's extremely generous of him.'

I lift my leg, pointing to my electronic tag.

'My passport has been confiscated.'

She looks at my leg and smiles.

'Well, when that rubbish is all over, and you get your passport back, I'm sure we can fit a trip in somewhere. Spain or the South of France would be nice. It would be good for you to bond with Henry. He seems fond of you, but I do wonder why sometimes.'

Teddy-Boy takes off his gold-rimmed glasses and cleans the lenses with a glass-care spray, which he takes from the chipped table next to his chair. It's a cheap ploy he's used before to slow things down and to leave me stewing. DCI Carter does the same. The more unsettled I become, the more likely my anxiety is going to make me say something I regret.

I've been warned by my barrister, and I'm glad that I have.

I take a deep breath and ease out my tension.

He finishes the mechanical clean and then slips on his frames, squinting as he does.

The finished look is a heady mix of 70's porn star and 80's accountant.

'Did you love Rowan, the Irish girl you mentioned?'

It's an easy answer.

'For a time, yes. It was a good relationship that lasted over six years. Had our circumstances been different, I might well be with her now.'

'Do you regret that?'

I smile to myself.

I'm not entering that rabbit hole with a Jack Russel behind me.

'Not one bit. I see it in the context of its time.'

I sound like my barrister, who's been coaching me, which I'm not sure is allowed in the ethical sense but is definitely appreciated.

I continue. 'She has three kids on last count, and I know she wants four. She married her farmer and lives the rural life. It wasn't for me. For a while, I thought it could be. Anyway, it was a long time ago. Life's moved on.'

'It was still important enough for you to mention it.'

'You asked me about my day with my mother, and I told you she called Rowan boring, which she wasn't. I only mentioned Rowan in the context of my day.'

'Are you two still in contact?'

'She used to send me a birthday and Christmas card, but... since... the incident, I haven't heard from her.'

'How do you feel about that?'

'When things go wrong, some people lean in and some out. It's a pity that this mess has probably brought our friendship to an end, but I understand. Anyway, she was never going to send me cards forever. I'm surprised it's lasted as long as it has.'

'And you returned the sentiment with the cards?'

I nod.

'Did you send her a card when you were dating Serena?'

I prickle inside, urging myself to lie, but I resist the temptation. My barrister's voice about being open or, as much as is feasible, so I don't unwittingly tie myself into a mess echoes in my ear.

'I sent Rowan a Christmas card, yes.'

'Did Serena know that you'd sent it?'

I shake my head.

A nondescript smile cracks across his face.

'How do you think she'd have reacted had she known?'

'It was still early in our relationship. I didn't think it was necessary to mention it.'

I sound defensive, but I hold the stare because I think I'm right, and it's up to me if I want to send a card to someone or not. Ex's included.

But he still makes a note in that fucking notebook before looking back at me.

'Did you love Serena?'

The question unsettles me even more than I am, and I don't know why—some latent guilt over the Christmas card, perhaps?

'Maybe,' I say.

'Describe "Maybe"?'

'I thought that I did, but I'm not sure any more. Perhaps it was more infatuation. You know... Serena was different. There's not many people like her.'

'You knew that you loved Rowan. That tells me you have a benchmark for love within a personal relationship. What's the difference between Serena and Rowan?'

'They were totally different personalities and at different points in my life.'

'So you wouldn't say there's a similarity in type?'

'They were nearly eleven years apart from when we first met, and you're confusing me with your questions. It's like comparing a Ferrari with a four-by-four. Apart from the fact they both have wheels and an engine, there's no comparison.'

'Tell me about your dating history. When did you lose your virginity and how?'

I cough out a laugh.

'Are you serious? Can you ask me that question?'

'I can ask what I like, as you can of me. You don't have to answer. Yes, I'm serious. I'm interested to know more about your relationship history. I take it you've never thought about it before, which, by the way, isn't unusual?'

I stare at him long and hard, wanting to bolt from the room, not because I'm scared of the question, but because I have flashes of it being read out in court and my mother and dad hearing it as it shames me and them in the process.

I'm also struggling to see what the connection is between my current situation and some random teenage fumble I had back in the day.

I fidget with agitation.

'You don't have to answer?' he repeats.

But I do.

My barrister has been clear with me about these sessions. Too many unanswered questions will be spun against me.

'I lost my virginity when I was seventeen. It was late compared to my friends. It was to a girl I knew from sixth-form. We got drunk at a house party and went upstairs, and it happened.'

'Did you date afterwards?'

'No.'

'Do you think that's normal?'

'I was seventeen.'

'Drink seems to have played a big part in your relationships.'

'That's not true,' I snap, regretting my reaction the moment I open my mouth.

'Let me rephrase: Drink played a large part in your relationship with Serena?'

'I experimented with drink in my teenage years and a bit at university, then I didn't touch much apart from the occasional work drinks and beers with some friends. It was never more than two, and I usually made one bottle last for hours. That changed when I met Serena. She had a thing about champagne, and I picked up the habit.'

'How was your dating at university? Anyone serious?'

I shake my head.

'When would you say was your first serious girlfriend?'

'I did Ethical Finance and Economics at Durham. Part of our course was a year working on a water irrigation project. It was run by a US company, and it consisted of three months in Somalia and then nine months in their New York office. I met a girl called Cassey. She was an intern with the US company. I would say that was my first serious relationship.'

'How old were you?'

'Twenty-one.'

'How long did the relationship last?'

'A year... ish. It started and finished with my time on the work placement. When I came home, I finished my degree, went travelling, and met Rowan.'

'Tell me about Cassey?'

'What about her?'

'Her personality, your relationship, where was she from?'

I sigh.

Irritated.

'She came from Long Island old money, which she played down. She was highly strung but great fun?'

'Describe "highly strung"?'

'Why can't I describe "Fun"?'

'Please do.'

I let Cassey float back into my mind. I haven't thought about her for years. She came across as a caged animal let loose. A strict family who kept a too tight-a-rein. She rebelled slowly over time, no doubt finding all sorts of trouble in the years that preceded me. I heard later that she had developed a cocaine problem. She came across as someone with commitment issues, which is partly what attracted her to me. I was always going home after a year, and I still had the world to see, or that's how I felt. I played the English card when we first met. She wasn't a fan of her Long Island set. She said all they did was fuck each other, take drugs, and then bitch about each other behind their backs. She was quick-tempered but never at me. Her sex drive was a pure ten and up there with Serena. I turned down a threesome with her and a female friend she knew from college. To this day, I don't know why I rejected the opportunity. I lost my nerve and bottled it.

I should have done it.

Idiot, I think, but Teddy-Boy is going to get the watered-down version.

'She was full of beans. Wanting to do stuff, kinda restless spirit. She had family money and the confidence that goes with it, so she was easy to be with. Looks wise, she came across as East Coast money, definitely not a cheerleader type if you know what I mean.'

'Sophisticated?'

I smile to myself.

It's not a word I would use for her.

Intelligent, yes.

Sophisticated, no, although I suspect she could be if she had to.

I nod.

'After Cassey, you met Rowan?'

I nod again.

'Then after Rowan?'

'My focus went on work. I was hurt that the relationship with Rowan had broken down. I then got my break at Eco-Blue. I was CEO at twenty-nine. Eco-Blue was everything I had ever dreamt about, career-wise, and I threw myself into it. I was on the path I wanted, playing at the level I wanted. I was comfortable there.'

'Then, after you became CEO, you casually dated until you met Serena?'

His tone shifts.

I can't pinpoint it exactly, but it sounds judgemental, like I'm a player who used his job and title to get laid.

He's tried to take me down this path before.

He's going to have the jury hate me.

'I had long periods when I didn't even look to date. I was completely focused on building Eco-Blue and my career. There was some casual dating in between, but most lasted a few weeks, and it was never anyone from work. I was and am a workaholic. I often do eighty-to-a-hundred-hour weeks. I'm young and ambitious. What's wrong with that?'

'Many one-night stands in that period?'

'None of your business.'

He makes a note.

Why didn't I just say *No*, I think?

Idiot.

'Each time you could have become closer to someone, your career became the dominant factor, and you didn't commit?'

'Pardon?'

'Whether it was serious or a short-term relationship, you were the one who ended the interaction, if I understand you?'

'If you put it like that, then yes. But is leaving New York at the end of a contract ending a relationship?'

'You could have stayed?'

'Not true, I had another year to do at university.'

'You didn't look to continue the relationship with Cassey? Coming home was a convenient out?'

'You're twisting my words. I was twenty?'

'I say again that you've enjoyed many casual relationships and one-night stands? It suited and suits your life?'

'I disagree.'

'Were you about to leave Serena?'

'No, I wasn't about to leave Serena. Our relationship was coming to a natural end. There's a difference.'

'Yet her death left you free to continue your career?'

'Her death has stopped my career.'

He skips through his notes, each page echoing louder and louder through the room.

He stops on a page, and my heart pounds to a new beat.

'I quote,' he says. '"My work was starting to be affected by the constant escalating arguments. I'd had enough, and I'd had enough of Serena."'

'My relationship was affecting my work, and I'd had enough of the petty arguments.'

'That isn't what you said.'

'It's what I meant.'

He smiles and makes a note in his notepad, glancing across at the clock on his wall.

'That's all for today. Thank you.'

Chapter 10

I shake hands with David Goldenberg, my barrister.

He's looking relaxed, having spent the weekend in Marbella. He was celebrating his fortieth birthday, one he described as "sick". It was followed with a schoolboy chuckle that I suppose means he drank too much and relentlessly chased the opposite sex, not that there's much else to do in Marbella from what I can tell.

He lets go of my hand with his bone-crunching grip and enthusiastically guides me to his client chair. He is easily one-twenty kilos of pure muscle and must pump weights religiously from the size of his arms and chest. How he finds the time is beyond me, although I suspect there's a laser focus built into his personality.

I sit in the wooden chair that is badly chipped and at odds with his Stella reputation and hourly rate. I hope the quality of the furniture isn't a foreshadowing of my future life as I take a sip of the hot tea his paralegal handed to me as I stepped into his chambers.

Small talk is a skill that I have lost since I was charged, and my mind wanders as David chats on about his Marbella trip and some Argentinian steakhouse that he reckons is the best in the world. I nod and smile, wondering if I'm paying for his Costa-del-Sol story that bores me senseless. I'm eight years younger than him, and when all this started, I had expected my barrister to be at least fifteen-to-twenty years my senior.

It was my dad who found him.

He made it his mission to source the hungry, rising star of the pack, and David ticked all of my father's criteria.

I'm beginning to see that David's immature displays and street-cred words that sound farcical over his public-schoolboy eloquent tones are a carefully crafted game to deflect your attention and to throw you off guard. When my father divorced, he went cheap on the solicitor, who in turn went even cheaper on the barrister. My mother's counsel was in a different league and tore into my father's settlement proposal like a shoal of piranhas. "Pay cheap, pay twice", my dad later quipped. It was a harsh lesson he wasn't about to let me commit. Prisons are full of naïve individuals who believed in justice rising to the top like cream.

It doesn't.

The world is a complex place, and with a twenty-plus stretch hanging over my head, my dad wasn't prepared to let me take any unnecessary risks with my legal team.

So far, David's delivered on the goods. His first win was to keep me out of remand and away from the animals that grace their walls. You wouldn't know it, but he's a Cambridge graduate with a first in law and was top of his class. I think he's adopted, too. He's originally from Nigeria if the little green-and-white flag that sits on the shelf in his Chambers is anything to go by. Next to it is a picture of him dressed in his graduation robes, towering over two proud-looking and white older parents. There's genuine joy and love that is shared in the picture by all. There's no doubt on my part that I'm looking at his primary caregivers. He had all the right offers to enter the corporate world, where I'm sure he'd have paddled his way to the top with his eyes closed. By his own admission, he decided to go left instead of right. He picked criminal law, something that had apparently fascinated him since he was a child.

That's where we part opinions.

I'm not convinced by his statement.

I like him, and we get on, and he's good, but every time we meet, I'm struck with the same uncertainty.

A paradox of sorts.

There's something about him that's corrupt, something that I can't put my finger on, a Lagos wide-boy at heart, maybe.

It all started when I saw his car. And I'm not even sure how he fits into it, but he drives an Audi R8 Spyder in carbon black-and-red with a personalised number plate, and Marbella is his dream destination. Negroni, his poison of choice.

I'd stake my freedom that his lifestyle isn't funded by representing your average opportunistic criminal via the legal aid system. I'm not saying David shook hands with the Devil, but I'm guessing he's met his mate. Ambition and power and control pour from him in open contempt. He's kept one London drug lord out of the system, whose associates are frenziedly knocking at his Chamber door from what I can see. They're in danger of making my sixteen hundred an hour look more pro-bono by the day.

It also makes me the hypocrite in the room because, apart from my dad picking up the tab, as he has for most of my life, I believe in Justice, and I want my conscience and record clear. I don't think David cares about anything other than winning, and I'm starting to believe my dad isn't interested in the truth, either.

It unsettles me.

It shouldn't, but it does.

The truth is what I crave.

'How's the therapist?' David asks, running his hand across his balding scalp.

'He keeps digging into my sex life. It's demeaning.'

'It's a process. Let it run its course. The most important thing for you is not to react.'

I nod.

He continues. 'On reacting, I had a call from the prosecution.'

I tense.

'The police have interviewed a waitress who apparently saw you hit Serena.'

'She is such a fucking liar!'

David stares at me, hands raised, palms out.

'You know about this girl?'

'I know who she is, yes.'

'And you didn't think to tell me!'

'Because it's a bullshit story, and I wasn't even cautioned by the Police. It's a nothing.'

'A nothing?'

'Yes, a nothing.'

'Tell me about this "nothing"?'

'I never laid a finger on Serena in our whole relationship. For the record, I've never hit any girlfriend, or anyone, for that matter. Violence is not my default response to my problems.'

'Thank you for the clarification. Now what happened at *Line Caught* on the eighteenth of March?'

The name of the restaurant triggers an in-pouring of memories, ones that I've been suppressing as my emotions get tasered by his question.

I drop my head into my hands, knowing how the action must look. That week of the eighteenth had been a mini-heatwave in London and was the precursor for the summer we're having. I'd returned from a conference in Geneva, and it was hotter at home than in the Sahara. Serena had been travelling for work, and we hadn't seen each other for close to ten days. She'd been busy on Instagram, so it oddly felt like we'd been in touch. She had posted a picture that I thought was too raunchy and pinged at my jealousy. I'd booked the restaurant from the airport in Geneva before taking off and went straight there from

Heathrow when I landed, the ache in my guts when you long to see someone driving me forward.

Serena was late, of course, but she looked fabulous when she arrived, that delicate perfume she always wore instantly grabbing my attention. The restaurant was bustling, and the tapas-style menu added to the vibrant hustle as waiters and waitresses scurried between the tables to keep the small plates coming.

For me, it had started as the perfect romantic evening. It was a warm night. The food delicious. The champagne flowed, and I couldn't wait to get home and make up for our ten day sexual abstinence, especially as she was wearing the dress from the post that had made me jealous.

'I ordered the bill, and the waitress was this tall Russian. The kind that doesn't wear any make-up and looks like a ballerina. From nowhere, Serena accused me of checking her out as the waitress walked away to get our bill.'

'Did you?'

'The waitress could have been naked and spreadeagle on our table. It wouldn't have mattered. I was so on the hook for Serena I didn't care for anyone else.'

'When she accused you of flirting with the waitress, what happened next?'

'Correction. She accused me of checking her out, not flirting, which is what pissed me off. Serena looked amazing. She always did. I was in love. I'm not some dirty old man who has to secretly pawn over an eighteen-year-old waitress with my partner sitting opposite. I was passionate for Serena, and when did being passionate become a crime?'

David tenses, and I regret my last sentence as the prosecution is framing their case as a "crime of jealousy". I lost my temper, hitting Serena hard enough with a single punch that she fell backwards. I then systematically smashed her head into the corner of the coffee table as my rage continued. Had I called an ambulance after I had calmed down, she might have lived. Her cause of death, a cerebral haemorrhage.

'Did you lose your temper, Kieran?'

'No, but I did get irritated. Irritated at the injustice of it—like now.'

I let that one hang in the tight space of his chamber before I continue.

'Serena wouldn't let it go. She escalated, starting saying she constantly catches me checking out other women. It was bullshit. None of it was true. Then she got up and stormed out. She made a theatrical fuss about it. Everyone's looking. It was embarrassing, because those kinds of things are, plus it wasn't true. I didn't lose my temper, but I was bloody irritated at the stupidness of it all and the fact my evening had been ruined, especially after the effort I made to get there.'

'The prosecution is saying that you slapped Serena across the face as you stepped outside into the street.'

I take a deep breath and look David in the eye.

'As I keep saying. That's a fucking bullshit story. It didn't happen. Not even close.'

'So what did happen?'

'She ran out. I ran after her. Some waiter-cum-doorman-hero-type thought it was a scam and that we were doing a runner on the bill. He came after me and grabbed me around the neck as I was trying to grab Serena's arm to stop her from running off. He pulled me back, and as I fell, my hand shot up, and I caught Serena under the chin. It hurt my hand, so it must have hurt Serena. Knuckle on lip. The next thing I know, she's on the floor, and her bottom lip is bleeding.'

'The police came?'

'Yeah, but they let it go almost immediately. It was a stupid moment that should have never escalated beyond some minor bickering at the table. Even that shouldn't have happened.'

'How did it finish?'

'I paid the bill and left.'

'What did Serena do?'

'She was gone by the time I settled everything. She went home—or I'm assuming she did.'

'When did you see her again?'

'A week later.'

'And?'

'And, nothing.'

'Humour me. Explain, "And nothing."'

'We didn't really talk about it. It was a bit like it didn't happen, which, saying it now, sounds pathetic, I know. But that's what we did. It was like it never happened. The truth is we met up, drank champagne and fucked.'

'The police?'

'I got a call the next day. They asked me a few questions and told me I might have to come in and give a statement.'

'And you never did?'

'I never heard from them again.'

He stares at me, his mind doing the calculations of how this is going to sound in court.

'Any more so-called "accidents"?' he says, using his fingers to frame speech marks.

I shake my head.

'No... no more accidents.'

The late morning sun pours through the windows of *The Tree Café*. The sun warms the right side of my face. I'm sat in my favourite seat, and there's a hustle around me that's comforting and helps calm my galloping loneliness.

I glance over and attempt to catch the waitress's eye. I ordered a coffee that hasn't arrived, and I'm certain I'm being ignored. My name made the local press, and notoriety—if that's what it is—doesn't sit within my personality, or the waitress's from what I can see.

I turn back and spot Dan, my best friend, stride toward the cafe. He looks over and sees me through the window, giving me a thumbs-up and a fat smile. A few seconds later, he's through the door and immediately legitimises my presence with his positive energy. The waitress, who'd been ignoring me, comes over, smiling, and without bothering to look at the menus, we order full-English breakfasts, with extra toast.

Old habits die hard.

Dan orders tea and I politely remind her that I have a coffee waiting.

'Bro, you're looking good. How's it all going?'

'You're such a fucking liar. I look shit.'

He laughs.

'Now you say it... You need a shave, bro. That rugged, outdoor look doesn't suit you. You're too pretty.'

'I love you, too, mate!'

'You're gonna look back on this period and laugh about it one day.'

'I'm not sure. I want to forget this ever happened. Officially, I'm in panic mode. The court date looks set to be the second week of October. It somehow makes it more real, not that it isn't.'

He nods, and we hold a stare.

I left Serena's the night she was killed and dropped a spare key to my flat with Dan, as he was going to let a tradesman into my property to do some work while I was away in Edinburgh. We were together for about forty minutes and it could prove crucial in my overall defence.

My state of mind and general appearance being paramount.

'Seriously... how's it all going? And no problem if you can't talk about it.'

'There's so much outside of my control that it scares me shitless.'

'That's a good thing, no?'

'How's not having control over your future a good thing?'

'Sometimes you have to trust the professionals. You've got a top barrister. You're innocent. What if trying to control every little detail and fretting about stuff is making it worse?'

I shrug.

I'm not convinced.

I want my future dependent on me, not twelve random people I don't know and never will.

'As part of my bail conditions, I have to see this psychotherapist. What I thought would be a nothing is starting to mess with my head. He's digging into my past, my parents, my sex life. He picks at every choice I've made like getting to this point was pre-destined. I know in my heart he thinks I did it. I fucking hate him and his sessions.'

'You sure you're not reading too much into it?'

I shrug, then force another smile.

He's probably right, I think. I'm coiled too tight right now.

I look back at Dan. We've known each other since Durham University, close to fifteen years. Since that night in May when Serena was killed, he's the only friend, apart from Hatti, his wife-to-be, who's stayed in touch. My vibrant network mysteriously vanished overnight, sucked into a black hole, never to be seen again. I don't even bother to call them any more. The pain is too much for both them and me, and I end up justifying who I am, which I'm sure makes me sound guilty.

I've often wondered if things were reversed, would I be like Dan or one of my absentees?

Our breakfasts arrive, and we tuck in.

Dan switches subjects and chats about Hatti and the preparations for their winter marriage in Stockholm this December. I'm pencilled in to be the best man. I've already said he should give the job to someone else. He won't have it, and I'm deeply proud that he's kept his confidence I'll be a free man with a passport returned and ready to travel come December.

Hatti and I were friends from school, and I know I have her vote. It was me who introduced them. Their baby is due in two months, and he's stoked about being a father. He tells me about the latest scan, and I'm hit with an unexpected slap of jealousy. I can see Dan's life before him. His dreams coming true. Being his own boss and having enough to be a husband and a father is all he's ever wanted. I used to poke fun at his lack of ambition, but he's having the last laugh. There's something deeply unhealthy in my myopic drive to the top, and I wonder what it says about me and if it is why I dated someone like Serena.

'Can I ask you a question?' I say.

'Sure, bro, anything?'

A touch of egg drips onto his 300 Spartan-style beard.

'Do I have anger issues?'

His eyes smile first, followed by the crease in his cheeks, breaking into a laugh.

'You've got to get out of your own head. Seriously, you're going to convict yourself if you're not careful. I mean that. As a mate, I'm telling you that you've got to get off your case and trust the professionals.'

'But I can be snappy... I know that much about myself. I'm not the most self-aware person on the planet.'

'You have an opinion, so what? You're a smart guy who likes to debate. There's a reason why you were a CEO at twenty-nine, and I'm still scratching my balls.'

'So I'm not aggressive.'

'Bro... chill. Look, sometimes your assertiveness can come across as aggressive, but it's who you are, and it's okay. It's not like you scare people. Don't sweat it.'

'Okay... thanks. Another question?'

'You're not going to give me indigestion, are you?'

'Did you like her?'

'Who, Serena?'

'Yeah, Serena.'

Dan breaks our eye contact in a way that suddenly worries me. I wait, watching him fold a piece of bacon between a slice of toast. There's a deliberate slowness to his actions, and it makes my insecurities burn hotter than they already are.

'Bro, I don't get where you are going with this?'

'What's there not to get about it? It's simple. Did you like her, or didn't you?'

He takes a bite of his sandwich, wiping at his beard as he does.

I wait.

He swallows his mouthful and then sips at his tea.

'And...?'

'Honestly... no, I didn't like her. I mean, I did at first. I thought you two were the perfect couple, the celebs within our circle. But it's like you became someone else. Not the Kieran we all love and know. Sorry, bro. You asked.'

'Fuck... I thought you were going to say she was great! Seriously, is that what people thought?'

'How many times did I meet her? Four, five, but that second time you came around for dinner, she put Hatti on edge. Hatti reckoned she was flirting with me, which is the drink talking. But my point is Serena had this strange effect on people, and it wasn't always good. You were smitten. All in, and it changed you, and not for the better.'

'You've got it all wrong.'

'Mate, you were always running after her, like a little boy who was scared he'd get into trouble if you didn't. That time you came for dinner, you guys left early because she wanted to leave. We'd barely finished eating. It was fucking rude, dude. I promised Hatti I wouldn't say anything, but now you're pushing it. It was like Serena had cut em-off.'

'Come on... it wasn't that bad. I liked her. I was showing my interest. What's wrong with that?'

'It's none of my business, but if she said jump, you said how high.'

'Come on… no way!'

'You asked, and now you want me to change my answer because you don't like it?'

We stare at each other for a long moment, and I can see Dan believes in what he's said.

And it hurts because I know there's a semblance of truth in what he's said.

'She was a good-looking girl, I mean smok'in, and I get why you were attracted to her, but as a couple you guys didn't work… it was… you know… unbalanced. And, by the way, that doesn't mean I'm saying you did what they say you did. I wouldn't be here if I thought that. Hatti says trouble walked in her shadow, and it takes a woman to know a woman. You were fuck-drunk, bro, and it played with your mind. I don't judge you for it. But you were.'

I blow out hard, letting his words sink in.

'Is that why you guys stayed away, because Serena flirted with you?'

'Don't twist it, bro. We stayed away because you were never available. You were either working those crazy hours you do or away with her. When were we supposed to meet up?'

'Anything else?'

'About Serena?'

'No… The fucking Pope!'

I can hear his mind churn through the gears.

'If you're asking.'

'I'm asking.'

'Hatti did a marketing degree at Bristol, right?'

I nod.

'Well, she made a comment one day that Serena seemed to know nothing about her industry. I know she posted all those pictures on Instagram, but that's not marketing—she's taking pictures of her eyelashes, and a ten-year-old stuck in her bedroom can do that. Hatti said it was like she'd never worked in an office environment. Some of Serena's stories didn't add up. Did you ever meet any of her work colleagues or go for a drink with them? All her travel, odd, no? It wasn't like she was global head. How long did you know each other—a year?'

'Nine months?'

'In nine months, you didn't meet her family, her work colleagues, or any of her friends?! Even a Neanderthal like me knows that women want their best mate's approval about a serious new man in their life. It's weird, bro.'

I laugh nervously, unsure what to say because he's right.

It's weird.

But it was our truth.

One that I took as normal.

Unless I wasn't the "serious" new man in her life?

Chapter 12

I open my eyes to find myself lying sideways across the hotel bed. My feet dangle over the edge. The top sheet has threaded itself between my thighs and across my shoulders, locking me into a Jiu-Jitsu hold of sorts.

I feel for Serena.

She's not there, and I raise my head, squinting into the semi-dark room, anxious about something, but what, I'm unsure.

'Serena,' I whisper, hearing the flush of the toilet.

I listen to her pad across the bathroom, heavy-footed for someone who moves with a ginger step. She turns the shower on. Then the water breaks its rhythm as she steps in, and I relax, knowing she's safe and only a few metres away.

I slowly tune out, my mind drifting through a raft of thoughts, tumbling to a stop on work. I dwell on our second quarter numbers, the poorest for a while, before reliving the pitch I made for funding on our latest Scottish re-wilding project.

I was awful.

Unprepared.

We've not heard back as of yet, but I'm not expecting good news.

I push the anxiety from the memory away, focusing instead on the slow lap of the sea breaking outside the room. Its gentle beat keeps perfect harmony with the wave of my champagne-induced nausea. A sickness that has become an all too common occurrence in my daily life.

I untangle the sheets from between my legs and sit up. My head feels heavy. My eyes sore.

Food and empty bottles of champagne litter the room like debris from a Wedding. Our clothes are strewn across the chaise-longue and floor.

It's a rock star life, I'm not enjoying.

I bend forward and peer between the curtains. The sky is an inky, star-filled night. The Cornish coast of St Ives drifts off to my right, the coastal town of the same name to my left.

I'm now officially thirty-two, but I feel sixty-plus.

We hired a car for the weekend and, following an eight-hour drive, ramped up the stakes with a hard-core pre-birthday celebration that started in the hotel bar, followed by the local pub, before ending up in our room.

I honestly don't remember ordering the food, but I cringe at the memory of Serena insulting a local in the pub. It started out as friendly banter but soon escalated. From nowhere, she'd challenged him to a five-game, winner-takes-all pool competition, which he declined. She baited him relentlessly, and our weekend was nearly over before it started.

I'm not sure how I got us out of the pub in one piece.

Luck, I think.

The skill I need to develop with her is: *no*.

It's a word I've never struggled with until we met. She has this way of rolling past my defences. I recognise the skill and nuance of her technique because I use the same approach to corral people into funding our projects. And it's weird to watch it performed so adroitly on myself. At first, I found it cute, even erotic, but it got out of hand. Eco-Blue lost out on a round of government grants. It was the same with the student from Southampton University and two other small projects we should have won, one my team pushed hard to get. I know when my game is down, and it's been down for a while. I can't blame Serena directly, but considering the limited time we spend together, the impact of her on my life is disproportionally high.

I've been ignoring the dynamic for too long, secretly hoping it will equalise.

It hasn't, and I'm beginning to think it never will. I've spent years designing my life, creating the career and the freedom I desire. I want to make a difference, and it's why I picked the job I do. It takes time, energy, and focus. A small impact here and another one there can have a massive ripple if it's done right. I've proved that I can do it on a consistent basis as long as I have time to think and focus and be undistracted.

All the things I've let go of late.

I need a pee and pills, then sleep in that order.

I stand as I hear a champagne bottle pop.

I'm dreaming, I think?

Even Serena isn't that crazy.

'Hello Birthday, boy. Surprise. Surprise!' she says, stepping from the bathroom.

The light spills from the room, catching her in its beam.

I swallow, re-checking my focus and then my mind, unsure what to say or think.

It's not the two champagne glasses she's holding that are taking my attention.

Or the black lace and semi-see-though corset and stockings, which hug her body like a second skin.

It's the black strap-on that is dangled in front of her and is pointed at me that has my notice. It's fastened to her hips, like it was meant to be there; forged especially for Serena.

She saunters over.

High-heels denting the carpet, a smile in her eyes that I've never seen before or can't quite describe.

Dangerous and inviting, like she's about to slit my throat.

She hands me a glass of champagne, saying nothing, her head tilted, eyes barely visible behind those *LavishLondonLashes*.

She pushes the glass to my lips, smiling as she does, like what she's wearing isn't there.

Isn't between us.

We sip together.

The bitterness and the fizz numbing my hangover as it accelerates my anticipation.

'Touch it,' she says.

I hesitate.

'It's okay… touch it,' she repeats.

I do.

It's hard, warm, and lubricated.

She moves her free hand between my legs, inviting me with her eyes to drink some more.

'Are you scared?' she whispers.

I nod.

'But you want it, don't you?'

I nod again.

She smiles with more dangerous intent.

'I've been saving this special moment for today. It's my gift to you, baby.'

She pushes me back, and I fall onto the bed, the champagne splashing across my shoulders and neck, the glass bouncing to a stop on the carpeted floor.

Serena straddles me, taking a sip of her champagne, before pouring the rest of the contents into my mouth.

It spills across my cheeks and chin and soaks into the sheets.

She giggles before bending forward.

'Turn round.'

I hesitate some more, but we both know it's only a game I'm playing.

I do as she asks, facing the bed, my breath tight, my nerves tighter.

I can't believe I'm doing this.

But it's Serena.

She has this power over me, over everyone, from what I can tell. She's attuned to something within me that I can't articulate. It's like she understands who I am better than I understand myself. She always did. I knew it from the second I saw her in the audience at the conference. Maybe I even knew it from seeing that picture on her Tinder profile. It's part of her magic and what fascinates me about her. She's allowed me to explore myself in ways that I've never been able to with any one before, even with myself.

'Relax,' she purrs. 'Permission yourself to enjoy it, baby.'

I close my eyes as she eases herself up.

Her hand reaches down.

I hear what I think is the click of her phone, but I've succumbed to the drink and the pleasure and the utter humiliation to care if she has taken a picture or not.

'Happy birthday,' she whispers, violating who I am.

Or is it the real me?

I'm not sure any more.

Chapter 13

It's my penultimate session with Teddy-Boy, and I've slowly become obsessed with the contents of his report. I'm having to fight the urge to rip his notebook from his hands and shove it down his throat.

His tact this morning has been to relentlessly probe for signs of latent aggression and control issues towards our female staff at Eco-Blue.

He's wasting his time.

I'm squeaky-clean when it comes to work and, my personal life for that matter, Serena being the anomaly.

As CEO, I was acutely aware that I set the tone, especially as I was inexperienced in my role. I made a point to invest in individuals, getting to know them, never once mixing business with pleasure. Team bonding was a major ingredient in our success, even if it was a quick round of drinks on a Friday night to celebrate a tough week.

He switches the conversation to leadership and the shift in gear catches me off guard.

Once again, I'm hit with the thought that he's jealous of my ex-position.

He encourages me on and my antenna is working overtime to see where this is going.

I go with the flow and tell him how I'd become hypersensitive to team ethics and how a poisonous personality can blow your team up if you leave it unattended. He asks me if I've ever sacked anyone, and I nod that I have. I ponder the first person I had to let go. She was a woman, older than me, and one of our account managers, who was perfectly charming whenever she was in my company. But the complaints from other staff about her professionalism and abrasive manner rolled in on a continuous basis. When I finally looked into it, it was obvious she had to go. She tried to sue us for unlawful dismissal. It went nowhere, but it took months to conclude and zapped into my time in an intrusive manner.

I tell him about the incident, but I make it sound like it was a man who I let go.

'Do you like your mother, Kieran?'

Silence.

His question doesn't make sense in the context of our current conversation. I flush with guilt at the omission I've just made, my barrister's warning about transparency echoing within my mind.

'I have a question for you first... if that's okay?'

He nods for me to continue.

'What's the difference between guilt and shame?'

He gently frowns, turning his gaze toward the window.

'I would view "guilt" as breaking your own moral code. Let's assume you believe stealing is morally wrong. If you steal an item, then you would feel guilty because you have broken that code. On the other hand, if you're a professional thief, there'd be no guilt, and you could easily have the opposite emotion—say one of elation at having fulfilled your belief system. In this case, "stealing" is an acceptable part of your life. "Shame" is more personal. Your thinking will trend toward you as being "bad" at your core. You interpret those feelings as if something is fundamentally wrong with you as an individual. Generally, "shame" is more powerful and therefore the more painful to process.'

I nod, and he continues.

'As a rule, if you feel guilty, it can be easier to apologise to someone, which can help you deal positively with the emotion. Shame, on the other hand, requires you to forgive yourself before you can process it in a positive way. This is often much harder to do. Does that make sense?' he adds.

I nod that it does.

'Do you suffer guilt or shame towards your mother?'

My stomach tightens, and I shrug indifferently.

'She's my mum, you know. You've only got one, and you're stuck with the one you have. It's not like I can trade her in for a new model if I want to.'

'Is that what you'd like to do? Trade her in for someone else?'

'No, and that's not what I said. She's selfish. Wrapped up in her own dramas. My dad calls her capricious. Working out she was self-centred to the degree that she is was a bit like when I found out Santa Claus wasn't real. I kind of knew for years, but it was still a disappointment when you have to face it finally.'

'You felt let down?'

He's given me one of his closed questions—a yes or no answer. I've fallen into this trap before. *Yes*, opens a world of hell for me. *No*, has him writing in his notebook and then picking at my definition of "no", usually by throwing up something I've said before that contradicts my current answer.

'More, let down?' I mirror back.

A trick I've learnt from my barrister.

'Was Serena like your mother? Were their similarities?'

I wonder if that's Teddy-Boy's way of asking me if I thought Serena was a poisonous personality.

I look at him, my mood shifting sideways.

Aggressive.

Survival courses through me.

I have a poor and deteriorating relationship with my mother, but I'm not going to let his report or the prosecution turn me into some misogynist killer because I didn't get my ice-cream when I was a six-year-old.

'It's not like she beat me with a stick or stubbed cigarettes out on my arms. She's not some fucking Nazi, and neither was Serena.'

'That's physical abuse. There's emotional abuse, and intellectual abuse, too. They can be as devastating, especially if sustained over a period of time, say an entire childhood. Or a child can be smothered, too. One doesn't get any space to grow, which is another, and extremely pernicious, type of abuse.'

'Well, that didn't happen. She wasn't there enough to smother me.'

He nods, and we stare at each other, my annoyance wanting to bark back as I think of my brother, Ryan. He was always telling me our mum was imbalanced—fucking nuts—were his exact words. I would defend her, which I'm doing now.

'If I say I have a troubled relationship with my mother, then I can see how it is going to come back at me all twisted.'

'Is that what you think I'm here for, to twist your words back at you?'

'You asked me if I liked her or not. The answer is yes. She did a lot of good things for me. For one, she made sure I got the education I did, and she was good with routines and making sure we always had something to do. Even if it was so she could go off and do something on her own.'

'How was your relationship with her after your parents became divorced?'

'A bit more strained, I guess. I get on better with my dad.'

'Tell me more about their divorce?'

'I was sixteen when it happened, but it had been coming for years. My brother always said that their relationship flipped, and once it had, their marriage was over..'

Teddy-Boy frowns, unsure. I continue.

'Sunday Lunch, Christmas, Easter, Birthdays, organising holidays, all started to fall to my dad. He'd always bought our cards for celebrations as our mother could never be bothered, but she started to do less and less of the traditional family things. Then, my dad had to take over the cooking on top of everything else. If he was too busy at work and my mum had to cook, it would come out of a tin and be on toast, which drove him mad. My dad forgot Christmas one year.' Teddy-Boy frowns. 'I know. He was working away, and time got the better of him, and my mother didn't step up. We had no tree, no turkey, no presents. It was weird, and they argued for two days non-stop over it.'

'Did that upset you?'

'I was angry at my mum, but my brother took it worse.'

'What did he do?'

'He liked to throw stuff when he's upset. This time, he managed to get the whole of his bedroom contents, including the bed, out of the window. He then barricaded himself into his room by jamming a broom under the handle. Like in the movies.'

'How did your mother react when Ryan protested?

'It depends.'

'Depends on what?'

'He can be pretty stubborn, my brother.'

'She'd punished him.'

'Of course, she did. It was in her nature. She punishes everyone.'

'How?'

'She'd hit him.'

'Did she hit you?'

'Sometimes, but Ryan got it most of the time. He was always first in line.'

'What did your father do?'

'It never happened when he was there.'

'Did anyone tell him.'

'Yeah... me.'

'What did he do?'

'He always said the same thing. "That he'd deal with it".'

'And did he?'

'If he did, he never did it in front of us, so I don't know. He's a man of his word, so I guess he did.'

'You've never asked him about it, retrospectively?'

'No.'

'How did you feel when you saw your brother being hit by your mother?'

His question bangs into me, hard and straight. I'd never thought about it before. I was scared, worried it was coming my way; fascinated, too, because Ryan would never cry, never show that it bothered him, continuing to frustrate her into a towering rage. He's now a policeman in the Australian Police Force, and he joked once the injustice of some

of those beatings made him want to be a copper.
Secretly, I feel sorry for anyone who is arrested by him,
because he's riddled with a vindictive streak that I
think he was born with and one my mother
unintentionally helped him refine.

'I'd freeze, mostly, and wait for it to pass.'

'And that's it?'

'Yes, that's it.'

Which is true, except one time when it
wasn't. A time that's been haunting me since Serena's
death. My mother had taken a toy from Ryan for no
apparent reason other than spite. He was furious,
flipping into an immediate tantrum. He started
throwing things around the lounge and goading my
mother in the way he knew how. She rushed to grab
him as he threatened to smash the television.

I stepped in between them and, without
thinking, pushed her away to protect my brother.

Hard.

Fast.

Full of malicious intent.

The shock and surprise that it was me making
a stance caught everyone off guard. Her more so.

She tumbled backwards, tripping on herself.

It should have been one of those moments
that passed into our family history as another
argumentative day and nothing more.

But she fell and cracked the back of her head
on the corner of our coffee table, knocking herself

unconscious, blood gushing from a deep cut from behind her ear.

Ryan and I stood there.

Looking at her, wondering what to do, thinking that she was playing it up, even joking with us, until the carpet started to stain with blood.

Then my brother said.

"You've killed her. Shall we run away and blame someone else?"

"Yes", I remember saying. *"Let's go hide in the park. Let's blame someone else. Who?"*

'Is there anything else to add before we finish for today?' Teddy-Boy asks.

'No... nothing to add,' I say.

Chapter 14

I head into Pret-A-Manger and find a table in the far corner of the room. I'm short of breath and have an ache down the right side of my arm.

I take a deep breath and count out to a slow eight.

I repeat, regaining control of my fraught emotions.

Teddy-Boy is becoming the nemesis of my life.

The day I shoved my mother into our coffee table has lurked in the recesses of my mind and has threatened to escape its chains and air its venom ever since I was charged.

Its moment has come, and I'm not surprised Teddy-Boy was responsible for busting its bubble.

On that day, my brother genuinely thought I'd killed her, and he had wanted us to run away and pretend like the house had been broken into and an intruder had killed her. I was nine at the time. I'm not sure how or why, but I managed to pull myself together as my brother was busy getting our coats. I called an ambulance despite him attempting to pull me out of the house and his constant shouts that I had killed her and that we should leave before it was too late.

The medics arrived within eight minutes and saved her life.

The head trauma had sent her into shock, and she had started to breathe intermittently, becoming weaker with each new breath. She had been close to a heart attack by all accounts. The accident fractured her skull. It took two days to stabilise her, and she spent a further three days in ICU. A month to fully recover.

The whole experience has always been a difficult emotion for me to hold because I was both hero and villain in equal measures. Over time, I have learnt to let it go, seeing the incident in its entirety and the circumstances around it.

My mother has a different view.

Occasionally, It still finds space in our conversations, and I can't believe it hasn't reared its head since my formal charge. I'm sure she's waiting for the right moment, and it's partly why I've been hesitant to visit her even more than I already do.

My barrister doesn't know about the event, either. My dad hasn't mentioned it, too. It's the nine-hundred-pound gorilla in the room. I don't need a psychoanalyst to tell me about shame or guilt to know what just happened to me emotionally.

The barista cleaning the tables near me asks me if I'm all right.

Sensing my own vacantness and mild relief that this episode happened in private, I nod that I am, mumbling that I haven't eaten for twenty-four hours, which is mostly true.

I see her eyes smile, and within a minute, she returns with a cheese sandwich and a bottle of water, telling me it's on the house. I thank her, tugging at the corner packaging of the sandwich. I take a large bite, letting the weight of the food calm me some more, realising Teddy-Boy never did ask if I thought Serena was a poisonous personality. I'm not sure what I would have answered. I didn't see it when we dated, but she was the main instigator of trouble within our relationship. She was fused with random sparks of negative energy that I had attributed to her personality and could mostly ignore. Some people are born antagonists. It's a force that drives them forward to success. It's a trait I often see in other CEOs I meet. I have a little of the same bite. It's us against the world, and Serena's ambition to build her own brand was an attractive quality.

Her drive excited me both emotionally and sexually.

Now she's gone.

Dead.

Something I still don't believe, like a form of denial.

She was a woman I loved, or I thought that I did, as I start the uncomfortable analysis of comparing my mother with Serena. It's something I've been doing since Teddy-Boy was shoehorned into my life. I haven't told him of my game, but if I peek in from the edges, there are dynamics that... maybe... I need to consider more.

The chronic irritability, for one.

The selective memory, for two.

The ability to destroy something good and healthy, the big fat number three.

I breathe out hard, rubbing at my temples, my concentration shot for the day.

I close my eyes, allowing my breath to settle and my mind to soften and drift.

And drift…

'*Ryan!*' I shout.

'*Ryan*!'

Then I recall he's on a sleepover, and I'm never allowed sleepovers because I'm too little and too young.

It's not fair.

It's my mother's rule, and what she says is law.

I put my ear to the bedroom door and continue to listen to the shouting that has woken me. I don't like it. It's scary. I want my brother. I want Ryan. He knows what to do when this happens. He joins me in my bed, and we hide under the duvet.

Mum yells that ugly word, and my stomach cramps.

I lift up my hand and pull on the door handle.

I don't know why I do it, but I do.

It clicks open, and the light from downstairs V-shapes across the far wall, bouncing to a stop on my bedroom floor.

I creep out, taking the line of the shadow, the shouts from my mum and dad getting louder with each new step.

A floorboard creaks under my foot.

I stop, scared of the noise I made as much as the ones coming from our kitchen.

My stomach is somehow heavier than me.

'You're never fucking, home!'

I've heard that word before. It's always my mum who uses it. Never my dad. She says it when she's angry at him. At Ryan, once, too. Ryan made me say it in my bedroom afterwards, and we laughed. I don't want to laugh now. I want to cry. I don't, because I'm scared it will make a sound.

I stop at the top of the stairs and sit on the first bend.

'Are you fucking her,' my mum says.

That word again.

'You're insane, you know that. You can manipulate thin-air.'

'Don't you call me insane! You're never fucking here. The facts are plain to see. I'm stuck at home with two boys, and all you do is go to work and pretend you're a fucking saint. Be a man and stop crying over your obligations!'

'I know more about commitments then you ever will.'

'Commitments... you can't even spell it. You're never here!'

'I'm close to signing the deal that will make me the sole supplier for San Jose's Wines into the UK and get us out of the debt. A debt that you mostly created, don't give a fuck about, and think will vanish on its own.'

'Is that the magical deal you've been working with Deborah—Ms I'm-so-prim-and-proper. Let me tell you about Ms Prim-and-Proper. She's a fucking whore, if ever I've seen one.'

'She's married with two children and lives in Portugal.'

'And you're married with two children and live in England, but that doesn't stop you getting on a plane at every opportunity you can.'

'You're fucking nuts. How do you think I pay for this place?'

'I know you spend more time in Portugal than you do here—FACT!'

'You see what you want to see.'

A glass smashes on the floor, making me jump, the tears in my eyes rolling down my face.

I turn to go back to bed, but I can't.

I'm scared for my dad.

For my mum.

For myself.

For Ryan.

'Are you fucking her?'

'Dad! Dad!' I shout.

I run down the stairs and open the door to the kitchen.

My mother swings round.

She's not seen me.

She's holding the frying-pan that lives on the stove. It dented the floor once when dad dropped it. Mum shouted at him for being clumsy. She usually shouts at me, or Ryan, for being clumsy, so it was funny when it was dad's turn to be the clumsy one.

But this isn't funny.

The frying-pan comes out of the dark and strikes him on the shoulder, skidding up and slamming into the side of his face.

Thud.

'DAD!'

His legs buckle, and he falls to the floor.

'DAD!'

Mum screams that word and Deborah and that word and Deborah, lifting the frying-pan high above her head. Dad rolls to his side and then springs to his feet as the frying-pan slams into the floor.

The noise of another tile cracking fills the room.

I cry.

I want Ryan.

I see dad grab the pan from her before he trips her to the floor. Their arms interlock. They scream at each other. Then, Dad sits across her chest and pins her arms above her head.

He does the same with me and Ryan.

He's not laughing this time.

He's screaming that word, and some others I don't know, but I do know one of them.

Crazy

You crazy bitch.

I don't like it.

She's not crazy.

She's my mum.

Then I step back into the shadows and head for my room, scared somehow that this is all my fault.

Chapter 15

After the initial shock of being charged, followed by the numerous calls to my defence by my inner circle, I was cast adrift. My so-called friends evaporated within a month. I should have seen it coming, but I didn't, and this outcast status underpins my panic attacks.

This morning's episode was spiked by my barrister calling me as I got out of bed to tell me I had to give a police statement about the incident at *Line Caught*—the restaurant where the Russian waitress apparently saw me strike Serena.

It's more white-noise and BS, but I still had to work hard to calm myself off the edge, something I'm having to do now as I finish my coffee and head out of the café for my eleven-thirty with DCI Simon Carter. He's head of the Homicide Unit for North West London, or the Major Investigating Team as it's known, MIT for short.

I joked with him once if the acronym had anything to do with the famous Massachusetts Institute of Technology in the US. It fell on deaf ears, and I reckon my quip has to go down as one of the worst-timed jokes in history. It has set the tone for what was always going to be a challenging relationship.

I sign in and am immediately led to an interview room toward the back of the station.

The rooms all smell the same: a delicate balance of stale urine and fresh paint.

The wall camera in the far corner blinks its red "on" light, letting me know I'm not really alone.

I sit and wait, letting my eyes take in the room. The walls are flaking, and the plaster is riddled with small dents. There's no window in case escape was on my mind, not that I have a passport or any particular place to run to if I'm being honest.

Today is a formality, I tell myself.

A stroll along the beach and not a foreshadowing of my future. I don't even have to do it. I could refuse and leave, but that would be a mistake. It would work against me, plus my barrister has briefed me to within an inch of my life. All I have to do is stick to the script, and all will be fine.

Or that's the hope.

I wait.

Yawn.

Tap my fingers on the table in mild irritation.

I'm sure DCI Carter is busy, but even if he wasn't, this was coming. It's his superior play. It's his way of psychologically wearing me down in the hope I make a school-boy error and save the government hundreds of thousands of pounds in taxpayer's money by tripping over my own tongue and heading straight to jail.

The door opens, and DCI Simon Carter steps in, breaking my thoughts.

'Apologies for the wait, Kieran.'

I say nothing, sitting more upright, keeping a pleasant smile on my face. He could have kept me waiting for ten hours, and I would have had the same reaction.

He pulls out the chair opposite and sits, opening his laptop in front of him.

The screen lights his face in a blue glow.

'You understand why your presence has been requested today and that our session is being recorded?'

'I'm here to give a statement for an alleged incident that happened on the eighteenth of March at the *Line Caught* Restaurant in Soho, London, and I acknowledge that this is being recorded.'

His eyes smile at my barrister-quoted sentence.

'Thank you for confirming.'

I smile back, thinking: *'fuck you, too'*.

Carter presents himself in an open, inviting way, like it's rude not to engage with him, something Teddy-Boy could learn from. It took me weeks to see through the deliberate construct of this alpha detective. My barrister had heard of him and warned me not to mess him around, not that it was ever my intention to do so, and perhaps says more about my barrister's general clientele than it does me.

My conclusion of Carter is simple: he's a man of opposites.

He's overweight with soft, puffy wrists who can arm-wrestle the Hulk. He walks at the pace of a

Buddha, but he's Olympic quick over fifty-metres. His jovial approach is why I cracked my MIT joke, but he's a man who hasn't had a belly-laugh in his entire life. And you'd never guess that he's a veteran of eighteen-years who's investigated some of the worst homicides committed in the UK with an astonishing conviction rate.

He's known for getting his man or woman.

And he's on my case with a simple conclusion.

I'm guilty, and he's going to put me away for life.

My barrister heard that he personally pushed his contacts within the Crown Prosecution Service to make sure I was charged when the case was in the balance.

I want to hate him.

That would be the easy route for me to take. I could have someone to blame and wallow in its comfort until the day of my trial arrives.

I don't.

It's the opposite.

I admire his determination because I recognise that same drive within myself. I just wish he'd use his gritty focus to find Serena's killer instead of closing the book on me. I've even made the mistake of begging him to do it, and it's had the opposite effect from what I can see.

Carter goes through the motions. Ones I'm familiar with, and it takes me a few minutes to see the error that isn't mine.

When the police arrived at *Line Caught*, I thought they'd seen the ridiculousness of the situation and had left shortly to deal with more serious matters. I'm wrong. There'd been an incident report, and Serena had given a full statement the following day, as had the waitress. The statement from Serena proclaimed that I'd punched her in the face and then shoved her to the ground, spitting at her as she fell.

Serena never mentioned any of this to me.

On one level, I'm flabbergasted at what I'm hearing. On another, I'm not. There's the Serena I knew when she was alive, and then there's another version I'm getting to know now she's dead. I'm not sure either of the versions I have is close to the person who crossed my life for the better part of nine months.

The police officer in charge of the incident at *Line Caught* didn't contact me to follow up. No one is sure why, and it's looking like an admin error that could work in my favour—right now, I need all the favours I can get.

'To be clear,' I say. 'I didn't strike or spit at her. She slipped in the heat of the moment, prompted by the over-zealous actions of the waiter, who thought we were doing a runner from paying the bill. She was wearing stilettos, and the pavements in Soho aren't the best. It was an accident created in the heat of the moment.'

He says nothing, smiling with a sense of relief as he hits the full-stop button with an added thump.

He then reads back my statement with the bored voice of someone who's done this thousands of times.

I change nothing.

'I'll get two copies. You can sign, keep one for your records, then you're free to go.'

'I was always free to go.'

'Correct, you were always free to go.'

I smile back, and he continues.

'I do have a question regarding your original Statement.'

'Any additional questions around the original case should be conducted with my counsel present.'

'It's more a confirmation than a question. But it's okay if you don't want to answer, although you will be saving everyone a lot of time by being co-operative.'

I think about what he says.

'As long as it's only a confirmation.'

'You only ever had one spare key to your flat, which you gave to Dan?'

'Correct.'

'Serena never gave you a key, and she didn't have a key to your place?'

'That's correct,' I say.

'Thank you for confirming.'

He smiles and leaves with his laptop under his arm.

I'm left alone again, stewing on his question, or technically, three questions, the stench of urine returning. I try hard not to look at the camera, ignoring the blinking red-light, wishing I'd bought a take-away drink to have something to do with my hands. I pretend to be at ease as I rage inside at the injustice of my life descending into this chaos of limitless problems.

When I was first arrested, Carter skilfully asked if I wanted to admit to voluntary manslaughter. Plead a loss of self-control. If I saved an expensive trial, the sentence could be reduced by a third. The rest would be split between prison time and community service. I'd need a bit of luck and a lenient judge, but I'd be looking at no more than five-years behind bars if it went my way.

My barrister told me I was smart to keep my mouth shut as the manslaughter charge would have turned into the murder charge with an admission of guilt behind it.

I look up at the camera and wonder if Carter is watching from another room.

He must be, I think.

His detective instinct is yelling at him that I'm lying about the key.

I almost want to tell him he's both right and wrong.

I didn't go in because she wouldn't let me in.

I didn't go in because I lost her spare key.

A key nobody knows I had.

Including Serena.

Chapter 16

I sip a cold beer, feet perched high on the bannister of my balcony. A hot London night echoes below me with all its urban sounds. The days and weeks of curfew that have slipped into months are taking their toll. I pine for the company of the city I inhabit. The bars, restaurants, and evenings out are all off-limits.

I stare at my electronic tag.

My fetter of silicone.

Apart from the constant reminder of its implications for my future, it's now sore to wear. Being home alone with nothing to do, I've put on weight. Drinking beer isn't exactly helping nor are the biscuits, chocolates, crisps, and anything else I can find to dull the boredom. I will have to call the monitoring agency in the morning and have them adjust the strap. It's going to be a bureaucratic ball-ache to sort. Not that I have much else to do with my time.

I wish and want to take my dad's advice and use this time more constructively. There's active time versus dead time, and I've fallen into the negative side of the camp. I haven't read a book, watched a film, or completed a project, small or large, in months. Meaningful concentration and conversation are close to impossible. Unless I'm eating, sleeping, or numbed from beer, I can't escape the wild chattering of my mind.

Like DCI Carter's question about Serena's key.

It sparks within me.

I take another numbing sip.

Thinking.

Dwelling on the consequences if my guilty secret was ever laid bare.

It would have me convicted on the spot.

Of that, I have no doubt.

I stole her key when I left on that last night. It was sat in the glass bowl by her front-door, inviting me on. It was an impetuous moment, and I don't have a concrete answer to why I did it.

I left her place angry and pissed off. I went to Dan's to drop off my flat key so that he could let the electrician in the following morning. We chatted about Serena, and he made me feel better about my decision to call time on what was being a toxic relationship. I had another drink with him, which was stupid. I left, and I don't know why, but I stopped for one more in the pub opposite, catching a replay of an American Football match with the Dallas Cowboys.

Another stupid move.

I could blame the alcohol for going back, but that would be too easy.

It was my conscious choice.

I wanted to finish the argument about sharing keys. One that had become the window into our future relationship.

So yeah, I went back with a few drinks in my blood.

I caught the tube and then jogged from the station, driven by my twisting impatience and need for answers. Even now, I can still feel the hollowness in the pit of my stomach at suddenly not having her key when I reached the communal door. Angrily, I rang the intercom system, childishly leaving my finger on the button. I waited below her window for her face to appear, shouting her name. She looked at me, grinning, but didn't come down. I found out later she was on the phone. The police have never been able to trace who she called. It was to a pay-as-you-go. A burner they call it. The SIM was purchased in Manchester over a year before, paid in cash. The calls were received in the Camden area of London. It was a number she'd called over eighty times in the last month of our relationship.

Eighty times, I think.

Carter questioned me hard about our leisure activities. He was convinced she was calling her drug dealer.

He wouldn't entertain the idea it could have been another man. Another sexual relationship in her life. It's how I ended up begging him to search beyond me and, in doing so, driving his conviction of the night's events even more.

I don't think drugs were Serena's thing. She was too into her body and her life.

I don't do drugs. I never have.

What's strange about that night is I don't remember much after leaving for the second time, other than a recall of the gnawing sense of loss over our deteriorating relationship and the amount of blood that was across my arms and jacket, like someone's throat had been slit.

The police are convinced I was drunk and am using it as an excuse to hide behind. I'm not and I don't know why my memory is blank for that crucial period.

I'm sure my barrister even doubts my story but he's professional enough to play the game, my willingness to pay his hourly rate no doubt helping his conscience.

I finish my beer and head for the bathroom and then my bed. I climb between the sheets and stare at the ceiling, wondering if I'll ever get an untroubled night's sleep again.

Ryan floats into my mind, as he often does. I hope he's well and I wish we spoke more. Over the years, I've intermittently mourned our lost relationship, but never as much as I have these past months. It was our mother who destroyed the bond between us. It seeped into our lives over the course of us growing up and then reached a point of no return. I often think about that Sunday when Ryan had come home late from a friend's house. It was the day it all turned. Our mother had been pacing the kitchen, stewing on my brother's disrespect. As he entered, she raged at him for his timeliness and the mud that followed him in. He looked at me in disdain for not saying anything as he calmly kicked off his boots, telling her if she took another step toward him he was going to smash her head in with a hammer while she slept.

He said it all matter-of-fact, like he was ordering an ice cream.

I froze.

And so did she.

The look in Ryan's eyes was one I'd never seen before. A serious intent. A plan already rehearsed. My mother laughed it off in that way she could. A skill certain people can carry in the face of blatant defiance.

It worked.

The tension disappeared in a beat and Ryan went to his bedroom, announcing he wasn't hungry and there was no need for our mother to worry about him again.

He was now a fully fledged "adult".

Thinking back, she never hit either of us again. Ryan always remained distant from that moment on, seeing me as the enemy. The moment still haunts me, because apart from our relationship changing forever, there's a side to me that believes he might well have done it.

We all have a limit when enough is enough.

I had reached my tipping point with Serena and her constant desire to pick faults and argue over nothing. She had worn me down.

I had come to the slow realisation I was in a destructive relationship with only one ending. I'm not going to tell him, but I do agree with Teddy-Boy on one thing. I have porous boundaries when it comes to women. When Rowan asked me to move to Ireland, I entertained the idea for months, knowing from the start it would never work. I eventually plucked up the courage to say as much, and it was then that we went our separate ways.

Ryan's personality is more like my mother's.

It is why they clash.

I'm my father and will tend to let things go, especially within personal relationships.

It's a mistake.

Like stealing Serena's key.

And going back.

And lying to DCI Carter and Teddy-Boy and even to my barrister.

I close my eyes, attempting to find the comfort of sleep aided by my beers.

Serena's face begins to glow in my inner mind.

She smiles.

I smile back.

She flicks her long mane of hair, and it falls to one side, bouncing to a stop. Her eyes sparkle with that mischievous tease, egging me on to do something.

What, I have no idea.

'Hello,' I say. 'You've been missed.'

'Hey Sexy! You too. How you doin'?'

'I'm good. You?'

'I was doin' great until you killed me.'

'I didn't kill you. It was somebody else.'
'No baby, it wasn't. It was you. You know it was.'

I endure the same emotional dip as I approach my mother's front door. It's a combination of resentment and dread, all presented behind a smile of contentment.

I've been roped into cleaning out her attic. It's a task she's been nagging me to do for weeks, guilt-tripping me at every opportunity. I don't have a feasible excuse—like work—to say no. The thing I have at the moment is an abundance of spare time, but for how much longer is a different story.

She makes me a coffee and goes through her criticisms of my dress and timekeeping with an all-too-familiar predictability. I accept it all and then head upstairs and into the attic, and despite my sulky mood, I find solace rooting through our family history. My pending trial has tightened the poignancy of what I am doing into a sharp tip. I discover two dusty photo albums that I decide I'm going to take home as I'm sure she'll bin them given a chance. It makes me realise I haven't thought about my own belongings and what I'll do with them should I get convicted.

I look back at the photos, swelling with emotions. They are mostly of myself and Ryan, taken by our dad as our mother could never be bothered with holding a camera. There are shots of us riding bikes, visiting a sheep shearing fair, of all things, and playing in a dingy in the sea, which I think is Brittany.

They were taken before Kodak went bust, and digital
had pushed everyone's life into a phone. They say
pictures never lie, which is the biggest lie of them all.
Looking at the photographs, I see a happy family unit
and not the fragmented car crash, littered with war-
zone stories that is closer to the truth than what is
being reflected back at me.

I can't find a single photograph of my mother
hugging any one of us, and I think of Serena and her
LavishLondonLashes Instagram account, which was a
catalogue of doctored photographs and images
maintaining an outrageous lie of her perfect world.

I place the albums to one side and bag more
clothes that I'll drop off at the charity shop on the way
to the station. I push back an empty cardboard box to
reveal two collapsible garden-chairs.

I swallowed hard and stare at the frayed
chairs with a mixture of shock and disgust.

I'd forgotten about the whole incident until
now.

My memory floods open.

My mother stole the chairs from the local
garden centre.

She'd gone to buy them, and I remember her
spending ages debating whether to purchase them or
not. She kept checking the price tag, huffing at their
cost, as she moved to the cheaper versions before
returning to her preferred choice. I recall she became
angrier and more irritated at each cycle, and I
wondered if I had done something wrong. She sent me

over to the counter to ask the lady where the toilets were. I didn't want the toilet, but she told me it was a game. I would get an ice cream if I did it successfully. I must insist the lady *show me* where the toilet is and not just point it out. When the lady at the counter would walk me to the bathroom, I had to stay on her left side at all times.

That was the *important* part.

The left side.

The part that would get me the ice cream reward.

I did it, positioning myself as my mother had said, not knowing or even caring the reason why. My only objective was not to get into trouble. Once inside the bathroom, I counted to twenty and once I hit the magic number, I ran outside to find my mother by the car.

Before I could say anything, she bundled me into the back seat as if going to the toilet and playing her game had delayed our departure. As we drove away and the garden centre faded from view, she started to laugh, mumbling that will teach you to rip off customers.

It was the throaty choke of contempt that I remember most, followed by the realisation of what she had done as it registered on my seven-year-old mind, seeing the two garden chairs stacked on the front seat.

I never did get that ice cream.

Instead, I'd become a character in a Dickens novel.

A foil.

An object.

Our family's version of Oliver Twist.

I never told my father or Ryan, believing that I would somehow get the blame.

I've held that painful and stupid secret forever.

Even now, looking at these chairs, believing I was somehow mindfully complicit in their theft.

I have never to this day sat on one. I'm not even going to touch one now. I wonder if that's why I've never stolen anything in my life, not even a paper clip from the office.

On the night Serena died, I wanted to go back.

Confrontation and alcohol were pumping in my veins, but stealing her keys in the petty way that I did filled me with a childish dread. I know I wouldn't have been able to sleep, never mind spend five days in Edinburgh on business, knowing what I'd done. The spiteful theft would have turned into a full-blown bank job, degrading my genuine attempts at fixing our relationship.

It's stupid, I know, to think it and even do it, but it was a significant reason why I returned on that night, something I've been unable to articulate until now.

How can I tell Teddy-Boy, or DCI Carter, or even my barrister that two stolen garden chairs that were taken twenty-odd years before I met Serena partly drove me to return to a problematic relationship?

They will think I'm insane.

Like I'm desperately looking for a place to park my guilt.

Lies beget more lies, I think, as a faint metallic creak taps my attention.

I don't turn because I recognise the noise.

My mother has climbed the loft stairs and is watching me stare at the folded garden chairs.

I wonder what is going through her mind right now.

Does she feel guilt or shame or even remember the theft?

I doubt she even cares, and had I not stopped working, I wouldn't have heard her. She has this way of floating through our house. It was another bone of contention with both Ryan and my dad.

I don't know why I've never seen her creeping for what it really is.

Insidious.

'Have you finished, Kieran?' she says like she hasn't been watching me for all this time.

'Almost there. Do you have any of that homemade lemonade—I'm parched?'

'I do. I'll get you one.'

'I'll come down,' I say, looking back to see that she's gone.

Disappeared in the same way she arrived.

A ghost, as she has been throughout my whole life and especially my childhood. I refuse to hate her. Although I think I could if I allowed myself to wallow in her crimes against our family. She's my mother, albeit the twilight version of the one I thought I had. To the world, she's this loving wife who adores her two precious boys; the divorce and the family split my father's fault entirely. She's socially conscious, fighting for local causes. Sympathetic and empathic to those around her. Her phone never stops ringing with meaningful, gossip-free conversations. Her calendar is full of lunches and evening events to celebrate her worth to society.

Nothing could be further from the truth.

She's a walking lie.

She flits from one friend to another, cancelling plans at the last moment. Her successful business-woman persona is as fake as her orange tan. She's never run a company or held down a job for longer than two months. She's been sacked from every position she's ever had. She's a walking catalogue of unfinished jobs, both professionally and personally. A litany of failed relationships trails her like the exhaust from a car. Everything and everyone is levelled down to luck.

Respect is an alien word that never leaves her lips.

Envy is chronic in her system, as is the criticism and anger that lace her every word.

I hate Teddy-Boy for being parachuted into my life. But he's proved right about one thing and something he nailed from our first session.

Serena and my mother are one and the same, and it's taken a murder trial and a set of stolen garden chairs and some keys for me to see it for what it is.

Chapter 18

Dad hands me his breakfast special: sausage, bacon, and egg sandwich, non-organic, with a large dollop of ketchup. He's been on a low-carb diet for as long as I can remember. But not today. When Ryan and I were kids, he'd used to make these every Saturday morning if he wasn't working. We'd stuff our faces, then go out and play, two satisfied kids, feeling like kings.

I glow with the memory as we tuck into our doorstop-size sandwiches, chatting between mouthfuls. We flip topics with the speed of a croupier: the weather, crap politicians, the rising cost of food, the return of COVID, skilfully ignoring my plight and his weight loss. He jokes how he's going to regret eating all this bread in a couple of hours when he bloats to the size of a whale.

We laugh.

It's like old times.

The future is full of hope and not dread.

I finish first, letting out a sated grin and a small burb behind a closed fist. My dad smiles back, proud of his cooking efforts. He gets up to make a fresh pot of tea, and I watch him fill the kettle as the inevitable silence falls. When I showered this morning, I caught sight of my naked body in the mirror. In a matter of months, my stomach has gone from ripped to muffin top. My shoulders have slumped, and my arms are flabby at the back. I became transfixed by the person in the mirror, mercifully saved by the steam misting the glass.

It wasn't me.

This isn't me.

I don't know who I am any more.

My dad wants to stay with me until this is all over. He's concerned about my state of mind and overall health, something I want to highlight back to him, but I don't. I have politely pushed back on this request, mostly because I don't want to risk our relationship. For all the stress, this is oddly the best it's ever been between us. If the trial turns against me, I want to keep these memories intact.

These visits and bacon sandwiches are full of boundless joy.

We've settled that he'll stay for the duration of the trial.

It'll start on Monday 18th October and is scheduled for three weeks. It was confirmed yesterday, and hence the surprise visit and old-school sandwich to make sure I don't fall into a black hole of depression.

It hasn't worked.

'I'm scared, Dad, and it's getting worse,' I say, breaking the heaviness in the room.

He says nothing, keeping his back to me as he puts the milk into the fridge. He turns smiling, returning to the table with the fresh pot of tea and two clean mugs.

'The way you're thinking is only natural,' he says, sliding a mug toward me.

He fills the cup, slowly and purposefully.

'I spoke with your barrister yesterday, and he tells me you're standing tall, standing like a king. He's seen people fall apart, and you're nowhere near that point. You're stronger than you think. Don't forget that part of yourself. You are going to need your inner citadel, and only you can find it.'

'Can I say something... between us... between these four walls?'

'Always, son. Always.'

'I'm scared I killed her. That I did it. That my memory is deliberately cutting it out because of the horror of what I did.' I look away, tears rolling down my cheeks. I continue. 'Or, at the very least, I'm somehow responsible for her death. This is all at my feet.'

My words sit above us.

Mustard gas waiting to burn.

My dad nods, then cups his mug and takes a long, loud sip.

I wipe the tears from my cheeks with the back of my hand.

'You didn't do it, son. If you keep torturing yourself this way, it will find a way through and become a self-fulfilling prophecy.'

'But I went back.'

'And you left.'

'I think I left.'

He sighs, and shakes his head, angry.

He leans in and continues. 'If I was sat here with Ryan and he said what you've just said, then I would be worried. He has that nastiness within him. That switch that can be flicked to push him to a place of no return. That's not you. I held you a minute after you were born and have watched you grow into the person you are today. You couldn't have made me more proud if you had tried. You are the most authentic person I have ever met. Too honest for your own good at times. I'm telling you, you're not a killer. And you didn't kill that girl.'

I nod.

We stare at each other, the tears streaming down my cheeks once again.

'Remember that time I pushed mum, and she fell back and banged her head on the corner of the coffee table, and...'

'...Son, you have to listen to me. REALLY LISTEN. You didn't kill this girl. If this cheap, low-grade Sigmund Freud is getting into your head, then you have to block him out. You were trying to protect your brother, and he pushed you into your mother, who fell backwards and banged her head on the coffee table. It was a bad accident. That's all it was. An accident.'

I don't remember it that way, but I say nothing.

'What about that leather jacket... you know... the one I bought in Brighton. The one I never wore because mum made me pay for the petrol when we got back.'

'Your mother was wrong that day, and you rightly got upset. But it's the same story. Ryan provoked your anger to get back at your mother, and you got caught in the middle. When it comes to emotional confrontation, you freeze. You always did. I wasn't there on that night with Serena but I know my son. Even if you lost your temper, you wouldn't strike out. Whatever you're thinking is wrong, and your memory is playing tricks with you. I understand you feel guilty that she is dead. That doesn't mean you did it. Or even had anything to do with it. You have to separate the two.'

I dry-wash my face with my hands. Images of my life falling apart continue to dominate my mind. I hear the scrape of a chair and, for a split second, think of DCI Carter before I feel my father's arms wrap around me as he gives me a hug.

I return to the moment, breaking into more tears before I start to laugh.

'Sorry,' I say.

'For what? For being human!'

'Can I ask you something?'

'Sure.'

'Why did you stay with Mum for so long?'

'Honestly?'

'Yeah, honestly?'

'Because I was scared. Scared to leave. I got too wrapped up over the money and house and the car. I should have guarded my time and my mental health more than my possessions.'

I smile and nod.

He continues.

'It was hard for me to accept that she wasn't the person I married. I fooled myself into believing that I had to protect you and Ryan from her moods and whims. The truth was, I wasn't there anyway because I was working most of the time. I hoped that she might meet someone else and make the decision for me. I was weak.' I nod. He continues. 'Her real problem was jealousy. She wanted someone who could supply the life she fantasised about, but in the same breath, she hated having her own inadequacies highlighted. I should have left her and taken you and Ryan with me. I'm sorry. I didn't have the inner fight for it.'

'You don't have to apologise to me, Dad, ever.'

'Maybe I do. I was nearly sixty before I worked it all out, and it took a bitter divorce and being in the gutter to open my mind. Anyway, you didn't kill that girl. Don't waste your life contemplating a nothing. I wouldn't swap my two boys for anything, especially you. I wasted much of my prime life trying to change your mother. Trying to fix her problems. Trying to fight pointless battles that I was never going to win. Even the occasional ones I won got me nowhere. Pyrrhic victories.' He takes a deep breath and stares long and hard at me. 'I've kept my silence on this because I've been hoping you'd come to the conclusion yourself. Serena wasn't good for you. I'm sorry she's dead and that she was murdered and died in the way that she did. Nobody deserves that. But the person who did that to her wasn't you. This is uncomfortable to say, but her death is a blessing for you. People waste their whole lives in pointless relationships, filled with resentments that they carry to their graves. You were infatuated with her, and she was a bad person. You're not.'

I'm nodding because it's my dad talking, but I'm recoiling inside at his words.

They hit me like punches—jab, jab, hook.

Bruising my ego and changing my perception of him. I've seen the same callousness when he talks with my barrister, like the truth is unimportant.

It flickers on my tongue to tell him I love Serena.

She was a nice girl, albeit a touch high-maintenance, whose life was cut short.

I then return to the thought that maybe she was toxic.

I met and fell in love with a replica of my mother.

It's all too weird.

Too confusing.

So I nod, like I agree that it's better for me that Serena is dead.

'By the way,' I say. 'Whatever happened to that leather jacket?'

'Your brother sold it for fifty pounds. I told him he had to give you half.'

'He didn't.'

'Of course, he didn't,' my dad says. 'That's Ryan, for you!'

Chapter 19

My intercom buzzes, making me jump.

I mute the Netflix show and stare at the time, listening to the noises outside in the street. It's gone seven, and I'm well into my curfew. On Tuesday, I was spat at in the street as I headed for the station. People have started to stare and point, and I'm not being paranoid. The word is out that a killer lives on the road. It's meant I've retreated further into my shell, something I didn't think was possible.

I debate whether to answer or not until I hear a man shout my name from the street below, and a smile creases my face.

I get up from the sofa to see Dan and his wife-to-be, Hatti, pushing their faces into the camera of my intercom, selfie-style.

'Surprise… surprise,' Dan screeches into the mic, holding up several brown takeaway bags. 'I hope you're hungry?'

I buzz them in, knowing he's bought Indian takeaway with Cobra beers. There's a local Tandoori nearby that's been our go-to ever since I moved here. Dan's been threatening to drop by for weeks to do takeaway. It's a date in the diary I've been avoiding. I don't want the inevitable conversation about my predicament and pending future. It's a conversation I do my best to avoid, yet it is me who starts the topic, unable to stop myself once I get into the flow.

'DU... DE,' Dan yells as he barges in, hugging me like we've conquered Everest. 'I hope you're hungry. If you're not, tough shit! We're starving, so you can sit and watch us eat. It'll give you something to do, right? I mean... how much porn and wanking can one man do in any given day!?'

Hatti gives me one of her sweet smiles and kisses me on the cheek.

'Ignore him,' she says. 'He's a pig.'

I close the door behind them. They know my flat as well as myself, having helped me move in and having been here dozens of times. Dan bounces his energy into my kitchen and rummages for plates and cutlery. He switches the oven on to keep the food warm and to take the chill off the plates. I haven't eaten since breakfast with my dad yesterday. Partly because I can't be bothered to cook and mostly out of vanity. Not eating is the only way to lose weight when you're housebound.

Hatti waddles over to the dining table and lowers herself into the chair. She's eight-months pregnant and looks ready to pop. She laughs at me watching her, blowing hard, her ankles bloated and looking painfully sore.

'I've ordered the Vindaloo, extra hot! I need this little fella out. A heatwave and pregnancy are no fun. Next time I jump his bones, I'm going to be more cunning and plan for a winter baby. I'm never sacrificing my summer holiday again. Selfish, but I don't care!'

'Can you time it so the second one is born on the twenty-fifth, then I only have to buy one set of presents,' Dan says, as he laughs from the other side of the kitchen.

'I married a cheapskate as well as a pig,' Hatti says.

'If we have two, I'll be working until I'm seventy... wow... this smells good. Those chillies are going to make him kick for England.'

'The overnight bag is packed and in the car,' Hatti adds, looking at me with a serious frown. 'We even checked Google Maps before we left. It's only fifteen minutes to the hospital from here, and that's with traffic.'

I smile, and we all sit and chat and eat, Dan ignoring his cutlery to go the full ethnic experience. I say little, listening mostly, deeply thankful for their gesture and more their company. This is a monumental effort from Hatti, forever the trooper.

Dan grabs two more beers and burps as he returns to the table, Hatti giving him a playful, disapproving look.

'Remember, you're driving,' she says.

'Uber,' he winks back.

We've all been friends long enough to let those comfortable silences fall between us, but Dan is in full over-drive for it not to happen.

He tells an old story we've all heard a hundred times when he and I travelled through Goa in South West India. One night, we called the hotel reception for a taxi. We went down expecting to find a tuk-tuk to be greeted by a guy and his elephant. We took the ride. Dan's recount of the night gets further and further from the truth, but we all go with the flow.

I'm about to add my own colour to the events of that night when I rattle badly from a sudden internal thought.

Dan knows I took Serena's keys.

I told him.

When I turned up at his place that night she died. I poured out my pain of that night and the stupidity in taking her keys in the heat of the moment. There's no way he would forget that conversation. But if Dan mentioned it in his statement, then DCI Carter would have been all over it. Or is that why Carter asked me the questions about the keys?

Dan's either forgotten to mention it, or he's decided not to go there. Does that mean he's lied to the police on my behalf? I stare at my long-term friend, unable to square off my thoughts. If I did kill Serena, his exclusion of the facts would make him complicit. He'd be aiding and abetting, at the very least. He'd be risking everything he has for me. I love him to bits, but it's something I wouldn't do for him if the situation were flipped.

It doesn't make any sense.

And does Hatti know?

'You okay?' Hatti says, catching me staring at Dan.

I nod.

'Just thinking.'

'It's bad for you, dude!'

'Someone spat at me as I walked back from the station. Called me a few choice words.'

'Wanker,' Dan says.

'That was one of the words!'

'The world is full of ignorant people who want to believe what they want to believe. Forget it. The truth will find its way out. You're going to be fine.'

'Can I ask you something?' I say to Hatti.

'On no… here we go…' Dan says. 'The serious CEO voice.'

'How did you ever end up with this immature idiot,' I say, nodding at my best friend.

'Technically, it's your fault for introducing us.'

'I didn't tell you to get serious with him and to have his child.'

'I'm clearly not of sound mind. He obviously knows how to control me, which is somewhat annoying.'

We laugh, and Dan high-fives me.

Then it happens.

The silence that Dan has been working so hard to keep out of the room squeezes itself into the pause.

Maybe it's this flat.

My fears and pains have been seeping into the walls for weeks and months, and there's nowhere to hide.

'You hated her, didn't you?' I say to Hatti.

She snatches a glance at Dan before letting her eyes rest on me.

She's naturally calm and thoughtful, the antidote to Dan's hyperactivity.

She returns to that spot within herself.

Her place of comfort, something I wish I could do.

'Hate is a strong word, Kieran, and I don't hate anyone. I thought you could have done better. I nearly said something to you once, but I backed off. I wish that I had because that's what friends are for and who knows, I might have somehow protected you from what's happened. She flirted with my husband to be in front of me and in my own home. I'm allowed a little bit of contempt towards her.'

'She didn't flirt with me,' Dan says.

'She did.'

'I didn't encourage it.'

Hatti looks away, and the silence falls again.

'I was in love with her or thought I was, so it was the right thing to do to keep quiet. It might have spoiled our relationship if you had said something.'

'Thank you for that. I appreciate it. Especially considering the circumstances.'

'I did love her, which I know sounds stupid.'

'We know you did.'

'When I look back on it, we argued all the fucking time, and I didn't see her that much, either. I honestly thought she was the one. It's so stupid when I phrase it like that, but it's how I felt. Dad came over yesterday, and I forgot that he only met her twice. We went for lunch at the beginning of our relationship, and she joined me for breakfast with him one morning. He took an instant dislike to her. He said she was bad for me and that I had a lucky escape. From two meetings. I can't believe how blind I was to it all.'

Dan and Hatti stare at me, smiling, keeping their thoughts to themselves.

I gulp back my beer, then top up my glass from the bottle next to me, deliberately belching to break the moment.

Dan joins in the Salvo with a double whammy.

'You two are disgusting, do you know that!'

'One question, and then let's move on?

Hatti smiles for me to continue.

'Dan tells me you thought Serena knew diddley-shit about marketing?'

Hatti throws her husband-to-be another annoyed look.

'Dude, you could have framed it without throwing me under the bus.'

'Sorry... that's what friends are for, right!?'

We laugh, and then I continue.

'Seriously, I'm interested to know why. She went from one freelance assignment to the next. This girl was busy and doing well.'

Hatti throws me a shrug.

'It doesn't matter any more,' she adds.

'Come on, I'm curious why you thought that.'

'I don't want to speak ill of the dead.'

'I get that, and we're not. I'd seriously like to know why you think what you do about her profession. I won't take it personally. I promise. She did a great job of marketing that Instagram account. Over eight-hundred thousand followers before... you know... she died.'

Hatti looks away, and I'm suddenly sorry I've pushed it.

'I don't know what she was doing outside of that Instagram account other than she was lying to you about her profession. She'd never worked in an office in her life. It seemed obvious to anyone... but you.'

Hot and sweaty, I take a seat in my barrister's cavernous chamber. The brickwork is too reminiscent of a cell for my liking, but it keeps the room at a constant temperature and is a relief from the blistering heatwave outside.

A few minutes later, David joins me, coffee cup in hand.

He's both hyper and relaxed. One of the many enigmas of his personality. His teeth are bleached, and he glows with the skin of a man who has prepared his body and mind for the day's challenges ahead. I used to be like him, but that part of me has disappeared, locked into a maze of crippling anxiety and a pending murder trial.

He places a report on the front of his desk for me to take. The pleasantries dropping from his act as the folder hits the wood. He sits and waits, and I hesitate, taking the document like I would a loaded gun. His style is to let me read the news before he wades in with his sixteen-hundred-pounds-an-hour advice.

I brace myself emotionally for more painful disclosures from the prosecution, no doubt driven by the incident at the *Line Caught* Restaurant.

Or is it another twist involving the keys?

My Faustian handshake with the Devil.

A while back, David asked me if I wanted to hire a private Investigator for what he called "additional materials". I said no. I trust in the law and the legal process, something I'm slowly unlearning. It was my dad who insisted I do it. His reason was simple enough. His love-sick son is unable to make a sound judgement by himself when it comes to his ex, dead or not. I'm Samson to Serena's Delilah, and she's cut off my hair, or another part of my anatomy.

I read on, Hatti's words about Serena having never worked in an office, rising from the ashes and frothing before my eyes.

I turn another page and glance up at David.

He stares on.

Waiting.

Impassive an understatement.

Serena Jane Brown is or was Angelina Morgan Cavalla. She was born in Canada, Montreal, to a French-Canadian father and an English mother from Luton. It's how she obtained her English Passport and, ultimately, full citizenship to the United Kingdom. Two-years ago, she changed her name by Deed Poll to Serena Jane Brown. She had no Criminal Record. An American Express credit card debt of eight-thousand, two-hundred pounds and twenty-six pence. She had no assets. She had never been married. Never had children. Her father died eight years ago of cirrhosis of the liver, and her mother died a year later of bowel cancer. Serena, or Angelina, is an only child. She never went to university or college, dropping out of school at seventeen. Her career from that moment on until she died in London was chequered at best, chaotic at worse. She modelled for a short time—swim-wear and lingerie. Bar work. Waitress. Croupier. Cruise liners. Secretary. Gym instructor. Even a stint as an air stewardess for Air Canada. The house she was murdered in was an Airbnb rental, as was the place she lived before that and the one before that. We met when I was thirty-one and she was thirty-nine. Serena told me she was twenty-eight. When she died, she had close to nine hundred thousand followers on Instagram. Her one traceable source of income.

I scan back to make sure I haven't missed any salient points.

The closest she had to a marketing career was a stint as a team secretary in a digital media company in Covent Garden when she first came to London. It lasted a month. Four months seems to be the average length of employment anywhere.

I remember when we first met, we went to a French restaurant in Hampstead, and she spoke fluent French to the owner. She told me she'd worked in Paris as an intern at a boutique marketing agency. She mentioned the name like I should have been impressed. It was another lie. Like her learning Russian and her gift for languages. Her ability to speak French is a direct result of her growing up in the French-Canadian environment.

I read on.

More lies.

More bullshit.

More white-noise that I have to endure and filter through.

I close the report and drop it on David's desk, the paper toxic to the touch.

'It's your copy,' he says.

I ignore him, looking away, attempting to focus on my own disorder. There's a vast emptiness within that I never thought could be expanded further. It's an emptiness that has been ever-present for as long as I can remember. When I met Serena, it was the first time those feelings had come close to shrinking and getting filled.

I'm beyond angry or even disappointed.

I've been cheated.

Not sexually.

Worse.

Emotionally.

Teddy-Boy's words about my mother flood in, and I see another blatant comparison between the two people. A non-existent career is presented with the front of a seasoned trickster. My mother is the successful entrepreneur of an unspecified business. It's amazing how she never seems to get questioned or pinned into the corner by her own lies. Serena was a marketing executive constantly in demand, her insights into the industry a breath of fresh air.

I took it all at face value, sucked in by her style and presentation.

'Was she seeing someone else?' I ask.

David shakes his head. 'The private investigating team found nothing. It's one of the first things they look for.'

'And that phone number in Camden?'

'They've not been able to trace it, either.'

'What's with the Airbnb?'

'You didn't know?'

I shake my head.

Of course, I didn't, I want to scream.

'I thought she was house-sitting for three-months. On the day she died, she told me she'd signed up for a year. That's what started the argument that night and why I stormed out. You know the rest.'

'You didn't know it was an Airbnb?'

'Absolutely not.'

'Okay,' he says with a nod.

'Does this help me?' I say, pointing at the report.

'I don't know yet. I need to think on it some more.'

'Do the prosecution get to see this?'

'That depends on if we use anything and want to submit it as part of our final disclosure. Let's break it down. She wouldn't be the first partner in a relationship to lie about her age. It's not a criminal offence. You hadn't known each other that long, relatively. You weren't married, you didn't live together, and you had no children, or joint assets, or business ventures. You were two single people on the dating scene. Living in an Airbnb isn't illegal. In fact, it has economic benefits over a longer-term commitment if you are thinking of moving around, which it looks like she did. She had an itinerant life-style. Again, her choice. Perhaps you didn't like that life-style. That's your problem, not hers.'

I let his words sink in, wondering if his last statement is a question or a fact.

'She's presented a completely different person to who she was?'

'You killed her because of it?'

'Fuck off.'

'She's a good-looking, single woman who meets an ambitious, career-minded man. A man she both fancies and admires. However, she's nervous about the relationship. She's slightly older with a chequered career history. She doesn't want those things to interfere with what she thinks is her dream relationship, her last chance to maybe settle down and have a family she so deeply wants. The Instagram gig is interesting, but can she really compete with the Kardashians? She hides certain facts because she's scared you'll leave... I mean, what's a few white lies that she hopes can be ironed out. It may be irrational on her part, but then people do irrational things all the time. Like murder.'

He let's that one hang in the air, and I say nothing.

He continues. 'It's not like she's living off you, although I admit you were generous with your money towards her. One day, you find out the truth. Yes, she shouldn't have lied, but she did, and she regrets it. Your fragile ego is hurt. You lash out. The short history between the two of you is one of a tempestuous relationship. She falls. You decide to finish her off because you're pissed that she's taken you for a ride. The prosecution has all the motivation it wants.'

'None of that is true. I thought she was someone else.'

'If you'd known the truth from the beginning, would you have stayed with her?'

'That's not a fair question. How can I answer that?'

'It's not a fair world, Kieran. It never was, and it never will be. If the prosecution ever asks you that question, the answer is simple. *Yes, I would have stayed*. None of what you heard is a surprise. She joked she was older. You admired her maturity. It didn't matter she had eight-grand on a credit card. She could earn a thousand pounds a day by blinking those eye-lashes. She was an independent person. That's what attracted you. You liked the fact she stayed in Airbnb's. You got to see different homes all the time. It was fun. In fact, her gipsy lifestyle gave a freedom into your relationship you had never experienced. You accepted her for what she was. You loved her, and you didn't kill her.'

'I did love her, and I didn't kill her,' I shout back.

'Good. It's about time I heard you say it with some conviction. But it's not me you have to convince. It never will be. Don't fucking forget it.'

I knock and enter Teddy-Boy's office to see him stood by the open window. He's gazing into the street below. I realise he must have watched me arrive. It squeezes at my insecurity and lasers in on the potential power this man has over me.

He greets me with a tense smile and then thanks me for coming.

He says it like I have a choice, adding how much he's appreciated the efforts I've made during our time together.

I wonder if he's having a laugh at my expense.

His coup-de-grâce to my "fuck you" Edward Carrington-Smythe Jr II.

If his words were meant to bring a slither of joy or a moment's respite, they don't. I will continue to sweat over his final report until I've read it. I hear myself thanking him for his professionalism and his understanding of my plight, none of which I believe. I will never trust this man for as long as I live.

I settle into the comfort of the client chair.

It's the first trap in Teddy-Boy's office and one I've taught myself to bypass.

I stare at him and wait for him to speak. The secret of Serena's newfound history festers and threatens to breakout in a confession-type rush. After a long debate with David, we decided not to leak the private investigator's findings—for now, anyway.

'How do you feel?' Teddy-Boy asks.

'About what?'

'You have a confirmed trial date. This is our last session. Tell me what that's bringing to the surface right now?'

I've had a floating ambivalence towards the pending date. On one level, there's the obvious anxiety but there's also a deep denial of the event. Even now, I sometimes believe this is a dream and it isn't happening.

But it is.

The date is set for the second Monday in October, and we're at the beginning of August.

Which makes it near, yet far, and knowing the date has parked a distracted hesitancy into everything I do.

'Preoccupied,' I say. 'If that's a feeling,' I add.

'I would say it's more a state. Can you elaborate?'

I dwell on it some more, sensing that he may genuinely care.

'I'm tense in the middle of my stomach. A heaviness that never leaves. I'm concerned about the future, obviously. I feel everyone is watching me, and it adds to my nervousness. I'm also concerned about your final report. I shouldn't be, but I am. I don't want to become paranoid about my situation, but it's hard not to be. Someone spat at me the other day and called me a "coward" and a few other choice words, mostly beginning with C.'

'How do you feel about that?'

I shrug. 'It worked,' I say. 'It hit home. I'm the outcast. It's bullshit that you're innocent until proved guilty because everyone thinks the opposite. That's the harsh truth of it, even though nobody admits as much. It's hard when you're on this side of it.'

'I don't think you're guilty.'

'Do you think I'm innocent?'

He smiles, non-committal. I know he's not going to answer my question, so I don't push it.

'I think the feelings you have are both understandable and not unreasonable. If this helps, you've never shown any signs of being paranoid. That should give you comfort. I'm sorry for the incident in the street. Did you report it to the police?'

I shake my head.

'Perhaps you should have done.'

He says it like he's sat here and has to live in my mind with all that I'm going through. He'll never know the vastness of my fears that visit me each morning, followed by each night as I enter and leave the little sleep I can steal. The constant thought that I'll be left to rot in a cell on my own and by the time I leave it, everyone I cared about would be dead. The world an alien place to what it is now. Technology and attitudes beyond my comprehension.

'You know what I really feel,' I say with a sudden spark of energy. 'The dread of being invisible. Like no one is seeing me. Even here with you. My voice is an echo that only I can perceive, and everything I say and do is misconstrued.'

'You're scared of being abandoned?'

'Maybe, maybe not, but isn't everyone scared of being left alone?'

'Some people are, yes. Some not.'

'Since all this happened, I've lost my ability to take responsibility for who I am. I can only see it getting worse. It's like I've become a puppet for everyone else's strings.'

'Is that what you did when you went back to Serena's? You were looking to take responsibility?'

His question hits me as a betrayal of what little trust we just shared.

For a split second, my guard was down, and he's abused me.

Like my mother.

Serena.

DCI Carter.

Even my own barrister to a degree.

I disagree with him on his last statement, even if he is the professional in the room.

His room.

Who wants to be abandoned, other than a fool or a schizoid? It's the same old Teddy-Boy. A snake in the grass. A spy for the prosecution. Watching me from his window. Watching me from his chair. How do you know about my trial date, I think, because I didn't tell you. It might as well have been him who spat in my face and called me a cunt.

I tug in my disgust towards him and what he represents as I debate the implications of my answer. Something I'm getting good at.

My barrister is finally rubbing off on me, I think.

'I've spent a lot of time on my own. Single and happy about it. Yes, I went back to see if I could resolve our differences. I was sorry that it had come to what it had come to. My sense was it had reached the end of the road. Our relationship was over.'

'Did you ever feel abandoned by Serena?'

'No.'

It's a lie.

'Did you ever feel abandoned by your mother or father?'

I want to lie again, but I change my mind.

'There were periods when I only saw my dad on Sundays. You know, he'd work all week until late, occasionally Saturdays. If we missed a Sunday together or Saturday breakfast, then I'd miss him because it would be another week before I saw him. Mum was different. She had a permanent busy schedule. She was always in and out, doing her stuff. She was there, but she wasn't. Engaged, but not. That's her all over. All you ever see is the ghost of the real person. She's the same now.'

He nods, thoughtful, then makes a note.

'When you went back to Serena's on that last night. Had she let you in, what was the conversation you were hoping to have with her?'

'Her refusal to give me a key told me the truth of our relationship. I wanted to make sure I was understanding the signals correctly.'

'You wanted to hear her say that it was over?'

'I'm not sure I would phrase it like that but… yeah… maybe.'

'How would you phrase it?'

'I thought our relationship was in a better place. That it had foundations, and despite everything, it was progressing. I was confused.'

'So you felt lied to? Misled by her?'

His question hits me like another personal attack.

My paranoia kicks in.

I see Serena's face. Her smile. Her mischievous twinkle. I miss her. The laughter. The uninhibited person. The sex. Our weekends away. I wish she was back in my life. In many ways, she is. Indelibly printed on my mind. An image that will stay with me forever.

I settle my mind and come back to his question.

Even before the private investigator's report, Serena had become a catalogue of broken promises. Many of them small throwaways, like the restaurants she never booked, or the coffees she never bought. A nothing, if you look at them individually. Forgettable and unimportant in the moment. If extracted and examined, they each became another brick in her skyscraper of lies.

A giant, immovable building.

My mother.

Serena.

My mother.

Serena.

One and the same.

My poor father building his life around my mother: thinking and believing one thing to discover he was operating in a parallel world with his wife functioning in another.

I'd stepped into the same matrix.

Our arguments weren't two people working each other out that would eventually lead to mutual understanding and workable compromises. They were two people operating on different plains.

Poles apart.

Each wanting a small victory and control more than a meaningful life with a reciprocal partner.

I contemplate the winds of hell I'd unleash if I told him about my mother and the coffee table.

Or the fact that I stole Serena's door keys on the night she was murdered.

I wonder if I'm the person I think I am.

Like I've been looking at a stranger in the mirror for all these years. I've been thinking someone else's thoughts for most of my life. I'm now being slowly unpicked by Teddy-Boy's expertise and a retiring DCI who's determined to go out with one more feather in his cap.

Mine.

'Are you okay, Kieran?'
'I was thinking about your question.'
'Did you feel misled by the relationship.'
'Not one bit. I loved her, and she loved me.'

I climb off my road bike and gulp water from the plastic drinks container I've carried with me.

The sun is hot on the back of my arms.

My neck damp with sweat.

I pop my bottle back into its holder as I stare at the house across the road from where I've stopped. My bail conditions are as clear as polished silver. I can't go near anything Serena related, or I go straight to prison, where I will remain until the trial is concluded.

The court even listed addresses that were off-limits.

Except this one.

My dirty secret from the eyes of the law.

It was the first place I had sex with Serena.

I was pumped for action on the night and couldn't wait to taste her, but it wasn't what I had expected. I remember it being familiar, nothing strained. Old lovers, comfortable with each other's bodies and moves. Like so many elements within our relationship, it became inverted. As time went on, we seemed to know each other less and less, rather than our relationship deepening. We became distant strangers masquerading as intimate partners. Maybe we always were.

I look back at the house.

I only came here once.

Serena told me it belonged to an old girlfriend from school. Looking at the house with my newfound knowledge, I can't believe I didn't see it before. It has house-share written all over it, and Serena only rented the room.

I was a student once, I remind myself.

I recall seeing a mixed-race girl on the landing when I went to the toilet in the middle of the night. She huffed at my presence and was deeply unimpressed. I thought I'd woken her as I'd stumbled in the dark. I apologised. I wonder now if I was just another guy coming out of Serena's room? The girl was pissed at having to deal with the risk and the noise, and the general inconvenience that churn can bring.

Clarke Lott.

That was his damn name!

It's been on the tip of my tongue for days.

The Formula Two Racing Driver Serena constantly talked about, usually at the end of a pleasant evening or directly after sex. Clarke was the ex-boyfriend who supposedly knocked her about, and I suddenly realise he didn't make an appearance in the private investigator's report.

I open my phone and Google his name.

Four pages of hits, but nothing related to Formula Two racing or racing cars in general.

There's a dedicated website for Formula Two. I click in and search for his name. Nothing current or past, and I instinctively know I'm wasting my time.

These drivers look like ten-year-olds, and although
Serena didn't look her age, I don't see her playing
cougar or second fiddle to one of these boys. If this
racing driver did exist, he's a washed-up wannabe by
now.

I'm not even sure I believe that.

What I'm starting to believe is that he was a
figment of her imagination.

Another lie designed to get under my skin and
to squeeze the screws of control.

I shake my head at my own stupidity and take
another sip of my water. I can't believe I allowed this
fictitious person to have such a hold over my emotions
for the best part of ten months.

I stare on, my relationship with Serena
tumbling through me in bite-size chunks. We became
serious around the September after we met. It felt
serious for me from the moment I left this house, if
not the first day we went for dinner. Christmas was
apart, and it was why we went to a hotel in Yorkshire
to have our own festive event. It was gothic and wild,
slightly dark wherever you went. If haunted had a
smell, it was locked into those rooms of musk and
oiled teak. It was where I cemented my appetite for
champagne and dangerous sex. By the end of January,
the bickering had become a habit, escalating through
the rest of the winter and into the Spring.

Clockwork.

Nothing ever resolved.

No-one ever apologising.

Then she died on the fifth of May.

Almost ten months to the day of us meeting.

I dwell on those months, hearing a hotel door click shut within the recesses of my mind.

I'm hungover again.

It's nothing new.

We take the stairs down to the reception.

Gargoyles threaten to attack as we pass by.

Serena skips ahead and bounces to a stop on the landing in front of me.

She turns, the temptress smiling, telling me to prepare for the race of my life.

I pretend like I haven't heard as I saunter up.

Then I reach her side and sprint off.

She knows it's coming, and she cuts across me, beating me on the last step, which takes us into the main area of the hotel. Panting, we laugh hard and loud as the receptionist smiles our way.

I pretend to hobble, blaming my second place on my fake injury.

Serena teases me that I'm getting old and slow, veering toward that line between being funny and not. It's probably my hangover, yet I sense more of a bite in her tone than usual. I ignore it, not wanting to spoil the fun as I theatrically continue to stamp out my twisted ankle.

We head for the breakfast room.

'Room fourteen,' I say.

'Anywhere you like,' the waitress says, ticking us off on her sheet.

We head to a table by the window. It has a panoramic view of the Yorkshire Dales National Park. A sheen of snow dusts the ground. Deer trot in the near distance, some pausing to nudge their noses through the white sheath to graze.

Serena chats on about how she loves the snow and that we should go skiing, throwing in that my jumper smells musty. Her comment rankles, and it adds to her tone about my age and health. As it happens, the jumper is an old favourite, a present from my dad, and it was dry-cleaned less than a week ago. At least I packed a jumper and didn't come dressed for summer, I think, keeping my comment to myself. I tell her that I've never been skiing, which I haven't, and that I'm happy to have my jumper back if she doesn't want it.

I like musty, I add.

The waitress heads over, and Serena orders the vegetarian breakfast with coffee and grapefruit juice.

I nod that I'll have the same.

'You ok?' I say, seeing a gloom descend across Serena's eyes as the waitress leaves.

'You're always copying me. It's tiresome.'

'What... that's rubbish. Not even close to the truth.'

'It's not rubbish. If I have fish, you order fish. If I have steak, you order steak. You don't even like grapefruit juice, but I knew you were going to order it the minute I did. I should have ordered your breakfast for you and saved your energy. You look like you need it!'

'We had meat last night, and I admit I'm a touch tender this morning. I wanted something light, nothing more.'

'Hungover or not hungover, you still order the same as me. It's like you can't think for yourself.'

I spark with anger, but I catch it in my throat and swallow it back before it spills between us and spoils the weekend.

Our coffees arrive, and I ask the waitress if the hotel has any paracetamol I can buy.

Serena chuckles, and the waitress joins in on the joke at my expense.

I've seen this behaviour before. It's like we're having a great time and are happy, but it is too much for her, like she can't stand the evenness of the moment. Like the silly, fun stuff that makes life worth living is too painful. She has to add her twist, push it toward the edge of danger to make the moment appear more real.

Not that it isn't.

And I never did get my jumper back, I think, one of the few gifts that I cherished from my dad.

I continue to stare at the house in front of me.

My barrister and Teddy-Boy, in their own ways have asked if people are going to come out of the woodwork and say I was a bully, or a lech, or even a predatory monster.

My answer has always been no.

I'm none of those things.

Dan always said I'm too generous and too stupid when it comes to women.

He could be right, I think.

The mixed-race girl I bumped into on the landing all those months ago leaves the house.

I can tell she's a student, not the owner.

I wonder if Serena and her were even friends.

I doubt it.

I'd come to speak with her.

To take the risk and ask a host of questions about Serena that are burning me up on the inside. But I know all the answers to my questions. Serena's life was a fantasy that had become a reality, but it was still a fantasy, propped up by me and no-doubt many others. She was a blank canvas on which I painted my own pictures about who we were.

She even encouraged it.

And the truth is that was my problem and not hers.

It's why I'm stuck in this position.

It's why I'm going to court to be tried for murder.

This is all my fault.

I have nobody to blame but myself.

Chapter 23

The little sleep I managed last night was broken by my barrister's call.

It went something like: *'Kieran, it's me. I need to see you as soon as possible.'*

Disconnect.

Sleepy-eyed, I had to check my phone to confirm that it was him and that I wasn't dreaming, unsure of even the day. On edge, I climbed out of bed, washed the sleep from my eyes and immediately called him back.

He wouldn't or couldn't take the call.

I'm going with the former. To make matters worse, he woke me at six-thirty, and I can't leave my flat until nine because of my curfew.

It was a painful few hours with myself.

A person who is no longer my friend.

I turn up at his chambers panting and close to epileptic. He points to his client chair with an annoyed flick of his wrist. His arm muscles look huge, and the veins in his temples throb as if he's dead-lifted three-hundred kilos in his workout this morning. I suspect that he contacted me from the gym and knew exactly the emotional state his call would leave me in. Control is his key motivation.

I see that his usual cherubic glow has been washed out by a simmering irritability. There's a snap in his voice that I don't like and I've not heard before. I wonder if this is the real David about to come out. The corruptness that lurks beneath the polished veneer and the one I'm going to need if I'm to climb out of this mess of my own making.

He takes a sip of water from the glass on his desk and blows out his tension, and then returns to his sophisticated self.

If I hadn't guessed already, I'm in deep water, without a paddle and probably without a canoe as well.

'Thanks for coming at such short notice,' he says. His voice silky but tight.

'My diary is fairly clear these days,' I say in a vain attempt at making a joke.

He says nothing, and my gaze falls onto his wooden desk.

I see a pile of papers with my name versus the Crown in black bold across the front sleeve. I'm guessing he's had the final disclosures from the prosecution.

'What's-up?' I ask as casually as I dare.

'One of the main strengths of our case is the prosecution's inability to prove you re-entered Serena's property to kill her. So what that couples argue? It happens all the time. It doesn't mean they kill each other, even if one or both lose their temper in the heat of the moment. There's inconclusive CCTV footage and doorbell cams around the time of your return. The police lack evidence you took her mobile phone. Their case, in my opinion, is weak. Extremely.'

I hear myself gulp.

'What's changed?'

'Please allow me to finish.'

I say nothing, crossing my legs and then folding my arms.

The back of my neck hot.

The taste in my mouth salty.

'DCI Carter has known for some time that Serena changed her name and was originally from Canada. They have continued to investigate that route. The eighty phone calls she made are a weakness in his case. In my experience, people who let's say, "reinvent" themselves often have a history to hide.'

'And does she?'

He holds up his hand for me to be quiet. He then leans across the desk and picks up an A5 hard-backed envelope from between my file.

"Do Not Bend" is printed in large red ink along one side.

'Due to Serena's nomadic lifestyle, she had an ongoing account at a storage facility. I'm assuming you didn't know about it?'

I shake my head.

He continues.

'Our private investigator missed it too. About a month ago, the police uncovered this.' He taps the A5 envelope. 'I'd be keen to get your thoughts?'

He finally hands me the envelope.

I take it and stare at the front, the sensations in my stomach flicking between heavy and hollow.

I open the lip and slip out several photographs. They come out white-side up. It suddenly doesn't matter, as my memory haunts me. I can hear the click of the camera on Serena's phone echo deep within my ear. I turn the photos and stare in a moment's disbelief, my world swirling into a vacuum of its own creation. I have to fight against the ensuing panic that threatens to consume me.

I look up at my barrister, and he shrugs, eyebrows arched as in, "talk to me".

A mixture of confusion and 'what-the-fuck' dances across his eyes.

'For the record, I take it that's you in those photographs?'

It's clearly me.

I don't even bother to nod.

I look back at the pictures.

My face is twisted in both pain and pleasure.

They were taken in the dead of night in a St Ives Boutique Hotel.

It started like so many of our weekend trips away. A long drive out of London in a rented car. We would chat non-stop, like old friends. We would arrive at the hotel tired but hyped, our adventure well under way. Once checked into the room, I'd bend her across the bed, and we'd have a quickie, followed by a drink in the bar. After dinner and more wine, we'd find ourselves magically transported back to the bar before heading to the local pub. We'd return to the hotel. Another bottle of champagne, if I could take it, before we giggled and stumbled our way back to the room. Then, the door would close. The side lights would go on, and it'd be another escalation in our sexual journey.

Or for me, anyway.

I'd become addicted to our trips. I was planning the next one before the one we were on had finished. I desperately needed to facilitate another hit in our upward spiral. The weekends in London were low-key and mundane in comparison to our weekends away.

I'd never thought of it before as I gawp at the pictures of Serena penetrating me with a strap-on, but our relationship re-set itself after each trip.

Zero-to-one, then back to zero again as we drove home.

A zigzagging of aimlessness that I energised and kept moving forward. We never progressed emotionally. We never moved to another level. We never had meaning. She somehow convinced me that we were riding this wave of an A-grade relationship that was going to take us to the happily-ever-after.

But I was the only one on that journey.

Alone, in a world of my own creation.

If Serena's life was a fantasy, then so was mine.

A figment of *my* imagination.

And she led me into the blackhole of shit without ever trying to stop me.

Without committing to anything.

All she did was receive.

Take.

My emotional and financial supply draining into a bottomless pit.

'Kieran, I need you to confirm that it's you in those pictures?'

'Of course, it's fucking me.'

'Why didn't you tell me about these before?'

'I'd forgotten about them?'

'You'd forgotten about them!'

'Yes. I was drunk, it was late, and I'd thought she'd deleted them from her phone. It never once crossed my mind that these existed.'

'You let her take these kind of pictures, and it never crossed your mind that they even existed?'

'That's right. Now what?'

'This is what's going to happen. Your relationship was on the rocks. You had discovered she wasn't who she said she was. You discarded her. You wanted the pictures back. She refused. You felt these photographs endangered your career. Something you are obsessed with and over protective of. You went back to get them; you argued; it escalated, and you killed her to protect your reputation. You stole her phone to destroy the pictures, but you didn't know about the copies. That's now their case. It's no longer weak.'

I look at the photos, remembering the night they were taken.

Remembering the moment I heard the camera click, but forgetting it almost immediately as I entered a new sphere of sexual pleasure.

One I enjoyed.

My liberation pried open by an artisan.

Fucked then and fucked now.

I slip the photographs back into the A5 sleeve and gently place them on David's desk.

'None of that is true,' I say.

'You still have time to change your statement. We can enter a plea of manslaughter on the grounds of diminished responsibility? You'll be walking the streets within five to eight years—with a bit of luck.'

'I don't need luck. I have you.'

'You do realise how this is going to look in court?'

I stand.

We're the same height, but he's wider and ten times stronger.

I step in close, raise my finger, and deliberately plant it into the centre of his chest, which is hard as cement.

'You've had over fifty grand from my old man. I don't care how the prosecution spins this. It's how you spin it that matters. Your job is to get me off like you do with the rest of the scum that keeps coming through your door. Earn your money.'

I turn and leave.

Chapter 24

I wake from a set of uneasy dreams to the sound of my phone vibrating from the next room. These days, the only people who call are my barrister, my dad, and occasionally the police, which translates into a sixty-six per cent chance of it being bad news.

Even Dan has stopped calling.

I push back the sheet and pad into the lounge where I left my phone to see it's Ryan, my brother. It's four in the morning in the UK, which makes it early evening in Sydney. I flush with excitement and can't answer the phone fast enough, scared I'll cut him off. He won't pick up if I have to call him back.

He's fickle, like that.

The moment gone.

'Hi stranger,' I say.

'Hey, pip-squeak... did I wake ya?'

'Of course, you fucking woke me. It's four in the morning.'

He laughs long and loud.

Memories of him flood my mind.

He was my hero growing up.

My older brother who could do no wrong. My protector at school and at home, especially when Dad wasn't around. It's been a while since we spoke, over five months and well over four years since we last saw each other in person. I was in Hong Kong for a work-cum-tourist trip, and I caught a last-minute flight down to Sydney after the conference ended. I stayed for three days, and for the life of me, I still don't know why I didn't extend my visit. We were getting on and having fun. I remember how melancholy I felt when I boarded the plane, desperate to get off, but it was too late. We had started to head for the runway. I still kick myself over the whole affair.

He's happy on the other side of the world, and I have long respected his choice, although it's been emotionally difficult for me to accept. He tells anyone who will listen how the Australian culture is a natural fit for his personality. His regret is that he didn't emigrate sooner than he did. The part he misses out is that the reason he skipped town was that he hates our mother and, to some degree, myself and our dad. Australia is about as far as he could get before geography started to veer him back.

'How you doing?' I say.

'Same old, same old.'

'Still a wanker, then!'

'Totally.'

We laugh.

He continues.

'If you're wondering about why I'm calling, it's not about money. I'm flush at the minute.'

'That's just as well because if you haven't heard, I'm not working.'

'Someone did mention a sabbatical.'

'Fuck you. What's up? What's with the early-bird call? You desperate to hear my dulcet tones?'

'I have news?'

'You're getting married?'

'Close... you're going to be an uncle... Uncle Kieran. Sounds like a Christmas movie, no?'

His words hang in my mind.

My brother.

A dad.

Mr Irresponsible having the same pending joy as Dan.

'You serious? I didn't think you were dating anyone?'

'I wasn't. More the joys of a drunken, one-night stand.'

'You're joking?'

'It's not my fault I have a high sperm count, and you fire duds.'

'I take it she's not there?'

'It's what you could call a modern arrangement.'

'So she's going to sue your ass for the next eighteen years. Kayne has a great song on it.'

'Little Bro, she's not that type of girl. We've decided not to live together. For now, anyway. We are going to co-parent from the off, and if that works out, then who knows what will happen. My job is off the scales stressful, and she's better off with her mum and her family. You know how it is?'

'I don't, actually... but congratulations. You sound thrilled and committed. You've really sold the unprotected drunken-sex new man to me. I'll recommend it to all my friends… that is… if I had any.'

'You're missing the point. Our DNA chain is going to live on. And those ancestors who hacked it out of the Savanna a few million years ago weren't wasting their time. We're the survivors.'

'I'm sure they'd be thrilled to know you're keeping the Neanderthal line alive.'

He laughs that fake but infectious raucous laugh he's manufactured since emigrating.

'Have you told dad?'

'"Granddad"—as he'll be known going forward—is my next call.'

'He'll be thrilled.'

'He always was too sentimental.'

Then, the pause hits.

The one that hangs heavy and compressing between people I talk with who try too hard to be happy around me and who want to ignore the facts of my situation.

I hear my brother take another gulp of his drink.

'How you keeping… you know… with everything that's going on? The sabbatical?'

He laughs nervously, his tone changing, the Australian twang filtering back, stronger than I remember from when we last met.

'It's keeping me on the toilet.'

I hear him gulp again. I imagine him drinking a beer, wearing shorts and a t-shirt, looking at the ocean

and the white sands and a blue sky. I suddenly wish my
only issue was pending fatherhood from a one-night
stand.

'You didn't kill her, did you?'

'Fuck off, will ya!'

'Calm down. Calm down. Just asking. Weird
no, but if this was going to happen to any one of us,
you'd have bet on me getting stung with a murder
charge.'

'For what it's worth, Dad said exactly the
same.'

He forces another laugh. It's his way of
covering up his embarrassment at the lack of contact
between us.

'What's the old dragon been saying?'

'Not much. One of her sons getting dragged
through the courts blows her image somewhat.
Anyway, she's your way right now.'

'You're kidding me?'

'If only. She's got a new boyfriend, and they
headed off to the Galapagos Islands to swim with the
penguins. It's going to play havoc with her fake tan. I
thought she'd be back by now, but no sign. So unless
she was eaten by a shark, she mentioned something
about the Cook Islands and then onto Australia.'

'If she lands in Sydney, you've got to text me.
I'm on the first plane to Thailand.'

'Why don't you make Thailand, London?
Come and see me and Dad. It'd be great to see you

again, and Dad doesn't look too good at the moment. I could do with my big-bro support.'

I hear him take another gulp of whatever it is he's drinking.

'Is that a dig?'

'Yes, it's a dig?'

'You've got to be the squeakiest, cleanest guy I've ever met, even if you are my brother. You don't need an idiot like me cramping your style. You're going to be fine.'

'If it's money. I can pay for the flight, and you can stay here.'

'Don't hit me with the guilts, pip-squeak. I have my career to think of. I'm in the police force, remember—and it won't look good, me taking time off to go to a murder trial, even if it is thousands of miles away and family. I've had to officially declare it. Then there's this girl and all. I need to be present even though we're not living together. You get it, right?'

'Whatever. Your call. I thought I'd throw it into the ring.'

'When you've beaten this shit, then we can meet up. Maybe you come here, 'cause I'm betting you're going to be needing a holiday from all the stress. What-da-say?'

'Sounds like a plan.'

'Sorry, bro.'

'It's okay. You can't help being an asshole, but I still love ya.'

The hum of thousands of miles of digital airways filling the hole that was once our relationship. He doesn't even video-call any more, and I wonder what he looks like.

'I'm going to call Dad, so catch up later, yeah?'

'Say "hi" to him for me and make sure you ask if he's okay. He looks like shit. Really, he does. And some advice... miss out the drunken-one-night-stand part. At least give him the illusion he's been yearning for.'

'Good shout. Will do. And, bro?'

'Yeah.'

'Good luck in court. If anyone has it covered, it's you.'

'Let me know if it's a boy or girl?'

I'm not sure if he says he will or not, as my emotions fall into the silence, hoping he'll change his mind and catch a flight to England, hoping to somehow recapture the brother I once had.

My hero.

My best friend.

It's never going to happen, and I have a fact confirmed, something I've secretly known for a long time.

In his own way, he's dead and gone.

Just like Serena.

October

David is adamant that I don't wear a suit in court. Only the guilty and the rich wear a suit in the dock, and both are prone to alienate the jury. Anyway, as the prosecution will be pushing hard that my blinding ambition was the driving factor in me murdering Serena, anything corporate is going to send the wrong subliminal message.

David even hired a style guru to tell me what to wear.

I stare back at my reflection.

Like most of the last few months of my life, I feel coerced into something I don't want to do. My court-designed uniform is not me. We've gone dark-blue casual trousers. A neat, slim cut and dark-blue socks and dark-brown shoes.

Neutral.

Neutral.

Neutral was David's mantra and my style guru's one instruction.

It's the top half of my dress code that is giving me the real issue.

We've gone white shirt with a neat collar and cuffs that sit snugly under a blue V-neck jumper. It makes my muffin-top stomach stick out, pregnant style, and I'm acutely conscious of the extra pounds I've piled on waiting for this day to arrive. My suit hides those extra pounds and gives me a small return on some much-needed confidence.

I look back at my suit splayed across my bed and debate whether to wear it or not.

Even I know that trying too hard will be a fatal mistake.

And the opposite: too casual will be read as cocky.

I've even cut my hair shorter than usual. Schoolboy style, parted on the right. My designer stubble has been shaved off. I took the style guru's advice and had a facial and skin peel to complete the fresh-faced approach.

We've gone full "boy-next-door" instead of up-and-coming aggressive "CEO".

Neutral in navy blue.

Young.

Innocent.

And I think about the word.

In...no...cent.

Ten working days from today to make it a reality. Then, I can rid myself of this electronic tag and the accumulated baggage it has dragged with me since I was charged.

My intercom buzzes, making me jump as it has since my arrest. The car isn't booked for another hour to take me to the Old Bailey, and I wonder who it can be as I walk out of my bedroom and press the intercom button.

'Package for Kieran Harrison.'

'Leave it outside.'

'It needs a signature.'

'I can't come downstairs, you have to bring it up.'

'What-evs.'

I buzz him in and open my front door as I hear him gallop up the stairs. It's a UPS driver, all dressed in brown, young and eager. His eyes immediately drop to my ankle, and he smiles like he gets why I can't come down.

I sign his portable device with the tip of my finger, looking long and hard at the brown A5 envelope he handed across. The stamp in the left corner is from *Brown & Hubble Solicitors*. They are based in Richmond and are my mother's choice of weapon. They were the firm that sliced my father into a thousand pieces all those years ago.

I thank the driver and head back inside.

I've not spoken with my mother since I cleaned out her attic. I've had two updated emails from her since she left for the Galapagos Islands with Henry. A one-liner saying they were heading to The Cook Islands before going to New Zealand. I did wonder if she was going to surprise Ryan, but I got another one-liner saying they had travelled to Japan. Nothing since. When she does resurface, assuming she's alive, I'll be blamed for my lack of interest in her travels.

Projection at its best.

Secretly, I'd hoped she would return for my trial. Once she'd notified me she'd landed in Tokyo, I knew she was staying away. That was the real reason behind her trip. I'm not surprised, but her behaviour has again caught me off-guard. I don't know why it does. It's a block in my thinking, even a misguided belief that a different outcome will materialise—one that never does.

The truth remains the same.

A catalogue of broken promises that fuel the continuous cycle of disappointment between us. The behaviour has underpinned our relationship at every junction.

I tear open the envelope, pulling out a copy of her will, along with a sealed letter and a compliment slip from her solicitor.

Attached is a handwritten note from *Brown & Hubble* wishing me a successful outcome at my trial.

A bunch of wankers, I think.

I walk into the kitchen, aware that my heart is trying to leapfrog out of my chest.

I make myself a coffee before tearing open the letter.

It's handwritten in my mother's cursive style.

She does every task with a rushed, impatient approach, fuelled by a never-ending irritability.

Except when she writes.

It was one of the few activities that slowed her down.

Ryan always said thinking was too hard for her, and you only witnessed the neurones struggling when she had to commit her thoughts to paper.

Ryan is often right when it comes to my mother.

Dearest Kieran,

I hope this letter finds you fit and well, and that you are well prepared for your challenge ahead. On that, you have no idea how painful all this has been for me. My star son is determined to ruin everything I have worked for with a single selfish act. The trauma you have caused me has been beyond anything that I could have imagined, and I didn't want to tell you at the time, but I was forced to go to the doctor and was prescribed anti-depressants. Pills that I am still taking. It is the only way I can cope with the shame that you have heaped upon me, my friends, and our family at large.

In the few times you have bothered to visit me before my trip, I honestly felt that you were being deliberately aggressive. Your refusal not to remove, or at least hide your electronic tag was extremely spiteful and hurtful. My neighbours commented on it twice, even posting a comment on social media to our local group. I didn't leave my home for over two weeks.

I can't believe how selfish you have become. I would have expected this treatment from your brother, but not you. I had believed you were my last bastion of support. My one true light within our broken family. Ryan has been lost for some time, but your father's constant negative and malicious whisperings in your ear, I see, have finally turned my baby against me.

I'm sorry to write these words, but the pain I've suffered has been beyond bearable, and if it wasn't for Henry magically entering my life and saving me, I can't imagine what a terrible place I would be in right now.

Therefore, I thought it was best to extend the trip and give you the space to deal with the murder of that poor girl. I'm confident they will find you innocent. For her sake and her family, I hope justice is done and that they find the killer or killers in due course.

You may be wondering why I have decided to stay away for your trial. Apart from the shame already mentioned, I have been unable to shake off the image of that fearful day all those years ago when you shoved me into the coffee table, and I was knocked unconscious, spending three days in ICU. Luckily for the family, I made a full recovery. The similarities to your current situation are frighteningly familiar, and I thought it best I keep my distance in case I inadvertently hindered the rightful course of justice. An intelligent man like yourself will fully understand my reasoning. It is the best support I can think to give you.

Henry has really been a true knight in shining armour. A Romeo to my Juliet. Therefore, it felt only fitting to accept his hand in marriage, which we sealed on a beach in New Zealand last month. A truly romantic setting as the waves crashed upon the rocks in the background. I'm not sure when we'll return, as we're doing what I should have done with your father thirty years ago—travelling the world to enjoy its delights.

Please find enclosed a copy of my will, which I decided to re-issue before my trip. It's self-explanatory, but I would like to draw your attention to Clause 5 on Page 2.

I do wish you all the best for the trial, but should the worst happen, I'm not sure my fragile constitution can take the riggers of a prison visit. It is something I would need to discuss with Henry, but hopefully, it won't come to that, and we can all move on.

Good luck, and I may send you an email from either Hawaii or San Francisco; we haven't decided where to drop next, so do watch out for my next update.

Yours faithfully,

Mum.

I reach for the will and turn to page two.
Clause five is halfway down the page.

*"I have intentionally omitted my son **Kieran Philip Harrison** from this my Will because of his years of ill treatment I have endured and his despicable attitude towards me."*

In one of our sessions, Teddy-Boy told me that "shame" was the easiest way to control someone. If that's true, then I've been bayoneted in the guts. It's ripped open my soul, tumbling me into a trance, the edges of my vision blurring into a vicious spin. I'm falling into another panic attack that not only threatens to consume the rest of my day but deeply impact my first outing at court.

I force myself to stand, knocking my mother's will from the table. I watch it float through the air. The paper slaps against the cold tiles of my floor, and the soft noise somehow pulls me back from the abyss that I am about to enter.

I reach down and pick up the will, tearing it into four and then eight before throwing it into the bin. Half of my attention has switched to the front door. I'm momentarily terrified that DCI Carter and his SWAT Team will smash into my flat and have their moment of glory. My mother's letter acting as the smoking gun they've sought since Serena's murder. If they add it to the photos, the Judge is going to give me 'a whole life term'.

I rummage in the drawer to my right and find the lighter I use for candles.

I rasp the metal against the flint.

Once.

Twice.

On the third attempt, a stubby flame dances in front of my eyes. It's more than enough for my needs.

I edge the corner of my mother's letter towards the golden flicker. The flame leaps. I angle the paper for maximum effect and watch the flame grow as grey ash flakes into the basin below. Within seconds, the reference to my history and a coffee table and her days in the ICU are swallowed into oblivion.

I rinse the rest of her damning voice down the waste with a blast of cold water.

Gone, I think.

Like my mother.

Serena.

Ryan.

And Dan, from what I can see.

Physically at least, but never absent from my inner voices.

Without hesitation, I turn from the sink, stripping off as I walk and step straight back into the shower.

I don't know why, but I'm hit with the urge to masturbate.

I think of the time Serena stripped for me in a hotel room, and I come to the sound of her sighs as I slam the palm of my hand against the wet tiles before switching the water to cold. It stings my skin, and I refuse to move until it feels normal.

I begin to calm and focus my mind.

I don't care about the will. I have everything I need financially. Despite what some people think, I've never been driven by money. It's a hollow goal to chase. Henry's welcome to the Richmond House. It's never been our family home, and I have zero sentimental attachment to it. My mother has always held it as her own, like she'd found it, funded it, and restored it to its current glory. The quirks of the divorce laws and a sharp barrister allowed her to weasel it from my father and get it logged in the records as a fair settlement. Nothing could have been further from the truth.

I step out of the shower and towel dry, feeling better.

Somehow more prepared for my day than I have ever been since this started.

I finish getting dressed and decide not to mention any of it to my dad. Truth is, I would have always been anxious of her presence in court. Unsure why she was making me nervous, her attendance a distracting liability. I would rather take the hit of the letter than be worried she'd echo her thoughts within the four walls of my trial.

I don't trust her.

I never did.

She can turn on anyone in an instant, unpredictable to her core.

My dad calls her capricious.

But she's not.

She's strategic with revengeful intent; ten moves ahead of everyone else, yet positioning herself as the wounded party. It's a manipulation of time and perception that borders on genius.

My uncertainty about that last night with Serena has sat across my shoulders like a yoke. My mother's read it better than anyone. She's convinced herself of my guilt. I finally see through the perverseness of her mind. My dad said nothing after the event that saw her end up in ICU. Ryan and I ultimately went unpunished. Thirty years on, she can get the revenge she's hankered after for that night's injustice. Should I get convicted, all her crimes against our family will be washed away in one fell swoop.

Vindicated, her slate wiped clean for eternity.

Henry will revel in his part as saint and saviour, until she turns on him and sinks his life as she did my father's.

I hope he has money hidden away.

My buzzer hums.

I take a deep breath, grab my house key and head for the door.

It's time to walk my barrister's game.

I wonder if it's taken a letter from my mother for me to see the truth of my situation.

This is no longer about the law and justice and principles and the murder of a woman. It's merely a moment in time that can define my next twenty years or go down as a minor inconvenience that will be forgotten in a month.

It's all about what I choose to recall and what I choose to ignore.

Serena's been dead for close to six months, and nothing is going to bring her back. I'm not sure it's going to matter to anyone if I'm convicted or not because the only person who loved her, from what I can see, is me. I don't ever recall reacting when Serena or my mother lost their temper at me. In my darkest moments, it's been my saving thought, despite the anomaly of the coffee-table incident all those years ago. If anything, I froze while both of them let loose. I did nothing but listen on and waited until the moment burnt itself out. The real thoughts were around resentment at finding myself on the receiving end of another injustice.

Like now.

My empathy and generosity torn from me and laid bare.

Something that is about to happen again if I don't get my mind focused on surviving.

Serena's face flashes in my mind's eye.

Happy.

Sad.

Dripping in blood.

Mine or hers, I don't remember.

My buzzer hums again.

It's time.

Time to face the truth.

My truth.

Chapter 27

Under the shadow of St Paul's Cathedral, I head toward an Italian deli to meet my dad.

I turn into a narrow side street and see him stood by the door, dressed in a suit plucked straight out of a 90's Hollywood Movie. He doesn't see me approach, and I catch an unguarded sadness dancing across his milky eyes that compounds my own fears for the days ahead.

I enter the deli and he greets me with a hug and a forced show of energy. We sanitise our hands and head to the counter, and order coffee and croissants. I tell him he needs to remove his necktie, joking that it's me on trial and not him. Another forced laugh has him tugging at the knot as he stuffs the necktie into his pocket. There's something childlike within the action. An innocence I don't often see, and it drops my guard enough to ask him if he's lost weight.

He shakes his head and smiles like I'm an idiot, and he has no idea what I'm talking about.

He's lying.

I don't push it.

We take our food and stand at one of the high tables near the window. The energy from a few minutes before dissipates, and we don't say much. My mother's letter cascades through my mind, distracting my thoughts further. Our silence begins to dip into the uncomfortable zone, and we decide to head out. Our croissants and coffees mostly untouched.

We turn into Paternoster Square and head for the main road at the opposite end. Up ahead, The Central Criminal Court of England and Wales looms high.

The Lady of Justice impossible to miss.

I'm being tried in Court Room 14, one of the newer courts that David believes gives me a small advantage. Once inside the courtroom, it will look and feel much the same as any other Crown Court in England. The Old Bailey address will lose some of its historical presence.

We enter through the main security gates, and I remind myself that I'm at least not coming up via one of the many underground cells.

I'm a free man.

Entering the buildings is the same process as if I'm boarding a plane. I'm asked to remove my belt. I put my house key and phone in the tray and walk through the metal detector, my electronic tag triggering the alarm.

I'm patted down and then waved on as the central lobby, with its mosaics, paintings, and chequerboard floor, threaten to crush my resolve with its foreboding presence. I force myself to concentrate on the wall ahead so I'm not swallowed by the enormity of what's coming.

We carry on along the brightly lit corridor, finding David loitering near Court Room 14. It's the first time I've seen him dressed in his silk robe and wig. It suits him, like he was born into it, his destiny pre-set from an early age. It's probably the same for all of us if we care to look closely enough at our patterns.

I wonder what patterns of mine got me here today.

David sees me approach and eyes me somewhere between a first date and a job interview. Finally, he nods, more to himself, that he approves of my attire, unawares of the emotional trauma it caused as dawn broke.

We shake hands, and he acknowledges my dad, and I see in that instant they've spoken already, which pisses me off. This is not some exclusive club that I don't have admission to. I'll address it later, as I have enough on my mind for the morning.

David gives me the debrief of the day, a repeat of our call on Friday. Today will mostly be a formality, but he stresses the importance of me giving a good impression from the off. I probably won't speak other than to confirm my name.

I nod.

The doors to Court Room 14 open, and an usher tells us we can enter.

It seems surreal, like I was expecting something else, something more dramatic and high tension.

But it's all calm.

A routine that has its own motion and is out of my control. A conveyor belt that I accidentally stumbled upon and now can't get off unless twelve people chosen at random allow me to carry on with my life as I know it.

I follow David and the usher into the court.

The chill from the air-conditioning hits me first. There's a barrenness to the room that is framed by the use of the light wood and hard wooden chairs. There are no windows, and even my thoughts seem to echo off the panelling.

It's all as I expect.

The Judge's seat is leather and set at the north end of the room. He's sat high and is the lord of all that he sees. The prosecution will be sat to his left with the jury on the same side. My defence is on his right with me square in the middle, the dock raised on a small plinth, in case anyone wasn't sure of who's the one fighting for his future.

David had insisted I go to another Crown Court to witness proceedings, something I did. It was a burglary with aggravated assault, being heard at Snaresbrook Crown Court in East London. I had intended to do a couple of days, even the whole trial, but the connotations were too painful, and I barely managed the morning session.

However, it was good advice, and even that short stint is helping take the sting out of the intimidation which pumps through me.

I'm led to the dock and take the seat that is going to be my home for the next week at least. A security guard appears from another door and sits nearby. He's six-four, three hundred pounds, and grunts something that I assume was a *hello*.

I ignore him and continue to watch the rest of the courtroom fill.

Ushers, solicitors and clerks scurry around.

Everyone slowly becoming more intense, more hyped.

The British judicial system grinding inevitably forward.

I glance behind me and up at the public gallery.

Dad has taken a back-row seat, and I can see Hatti, Dan's wife-to-be, sitting next to him. I give her a smile, realising I never sent a card, or even a present, for the birth of their firstborn, so wrapped up in my own woes. It's why Dan hasn't been in touch. I can't believe I missed the occasion.

She smiles back at me.

It's full of worry and fear and uncertainty.

There are a few other people I don't know, but I'm guessing they must be Serena's friends, perhaps even family.

I don't know why, but I find myself hoping to see my mum. It's a stupid thing to do to myself, especially as she's probably sipping a cocktail somewhere on a Pacific Island. Despite my parent's animosity, I had secretly hoped they would park their differences and be united to support me in this crucial moment of my life.

It wasn't to be.

Another abandonment to add to the already formidable list.

I turn back to see the prosecution for the first time.

Patricia Elmhurst is early forties, with auburn hair streaked with natural grey. She's slightly overweight with a plump, jolly face and large, intelligent eyes. She oozes a work ethic and a sense of right and wrong. I'm sure each victory is her small way of putting the world to rights. She looks the type who will die with no regrets.

I look to see if she's wearing a wedding ring.

She's not, and it bothers me.

She glances my way as she unpacks her files and lifts her laptop free of its case. I sense a taunting smirk bounce into the dock. She then glances toward David and gives him a wry smile and nods, which he acknowledges with a polite smile back.

Apart from the feather in her cap for nailing me, she wants his scalp, too. It's a double win, especially as David's reputation is based on being "Mr Unbeatable". He has a hundred per-cent record he's maintained to date and one the Crown Prosecution Service is wanting to change, I'm sure.

We are told to stand.

I'm the first to my feet, making my security guard jump.

The judge enters, and like the prosecution, he glances across at me before he takes his seat. The look is more neutral and routine than Patricia's. More a courteous reminder of who's in charge. The scar-like frown which sits vertically between his eyes has seen and heard it all before. I get an unexpected beat of comfort from his presence. I was expecting a ruddy-faced, eighty-year-old more interested in red wine and cheese than my personal fate and the law.

We sit, and the jury is ushered in.

This is my first moment on show to the twelve that really matter.

David's been explicit that I watch them enter the court but that I keep my gaze just above the head of the tallest person. My eyes are to remain smiling. My face is neutral and relaxed. My hands by my side at all times. I'm never to look anxious or too relaxed.

It's the median I'm to maintain, no matter how heated any moment might become. Hopefully, those hours spent practising in front of the mirror are about to prove their worth.

The judge leans forward in his seat and waits for the silence to grow. He then breaks the spell by telling the jury it's his job to run the court and to interpret the law. Their task ahead is simple enough. They are here to decide if the evidence they hear proves me guilty or not. He reminds them that the onus is on the prosecution to prove my guilt, and if there is any doubt in their minds, then they must find me not guilty.

The words echo in my mind.

Not guilty.

Not guilty.

I wonder if I look it because I don't feel it.

Chapter 28

A silence descends upon the court. It fills me with a crisp anxiety, and I have the urge to say something to fill the uncomfortable space within and the silence around me.

Then, the delicate scrape of the prosecution's chair catches everyone's attention, the echo scratching across the enamel of my teeth and scarring itself into my mind.

Patricia Elmhurst stands.

It's both slow and poised, and she tugs at the front of her silk robe for both self-assurance and regal effect.

Despite the angle between us, she manages to catch my eye, confirming the taunting smirk I caught when she first entered the court. Her game is clear and has been spelt out by David on numerous occasions. She'll do her best to bait me from the off with the hope that when I take the stand, I'll be primed with annoyance and, therefore, susceptible to being tetchy under examination.

My apparent tetchy personality is why I'm here.

The next time she stares across, I will gently but purposefully look away.

Non-plussed.

Indifferent.

I've failed the first test of not letting her get under my skin, but I can start to cleanse myself of her invasion. I still have plenty of time before I take the stand. I remind myself of the man I was before my life became derailed by the relationship with Serena.

One of hope.

One of mostly joy.

One in which I was in control.

'Ladies and gentlemen of the jury. My name is Patricia Elmhurst, Queen's Counsel for the prosecution. On my right, I would also like to introduce my learned friend, David Goldenberg, Queen's Counsel, for the defence.'

Patricia moves her hand in the direction of my barrister, and in unison, the jury turns to see him semi-slouched in his chair, with his left arm hung across the backrest, gold cuff-links reflecting the white light of the room. His left leg is stretched out under the table, his foot resting loose and nonchalant on its heel.

He's like an Orca.

Graceful power, full of unpredictability.

He acknowledges the jury with a polite nod before turning to Patricia and throwing her what I'm sure is a *Learned Smile* of perfectly timed court etiquette. If I was sat amongst the twelve, I'm confident I would resent the entitlement that seeps from him like the smell of a gangrenous wound.

But I trust him.

I have to.

His record is impeccable to date with an ego that I can leverage to my advantage.

Patricia taps a key on her laptop and brings her screen to life, before letting her stare rest back amongst the jury. She throws them a grave smile, her head tipped in deference. 'As already mentioned and, in accordance with British law, it is the prosecution's responsibility to prove beyond reasonable doubt that on the night of the 5th of May this year, Kieran Philip Harrison forced his way into Serena Jane Brown's home at Bexley Mansions in London's Nothing Hill area and unlawfully killed her in a premeditated act.'

Patricia pauses.

Her voice calm and precise, bordering on the slow.

She taps to the next page on her laptop.

'The prosecution will show that Kieran Harrison and Serena Brown had a highly-charged sexual relationship. The intensity within the dynamic was a force Kieran Harrison's fragile ego couldn't manage. It ultimately drove him to commit the act for which he's charged. We will demonstrate how Kieran Harrison's only concern was his career and his self-image. That he had a complete disrespect for the needs and well-being of Serena Brown, as well as others in his life. Kieran Harrison's self-image was so central to his personality that his narcissistic tendencies meant he used intimidation and violence as mechanisms of control, something that he established early on in the relationship with Serena. The prosecution will further demonstrate that Kieran Harrison's testimony on the night in question was a calculated attempt to distance himself from his actions of that night. We will present evidence to show his motivation was to destroy sexually-explicit photographs of the defendant being anally penetrated by a sex toy. Pictures that the defendant had convinced himself would be made public and ruin his career. A notion based on nothing more than his own skewed view of himself within the world that he operates in.'

She pauses.

The silence hangs in the air.

Thick.

Heavy.

I keep my stare high and wide and as neutral as I can.

Patricia gently coughs, clearing her throat.

David stares on, looking a mix of both unperturbed and perplexed. A cartooned frown of disbelief at every point laboured by Patricia. I see for the first time that his nonchalant teenage approach is part of his core act. Every sentence. Every breath that is uttered from the prosecution's mouth is going to be labelled with as much disbelief as he can slip under the judge's nose without getting wrapped across the knuckles.

'We will show how once the defendant had forced his way into Serena's home, he then deliberately and callously smashed the back of Serena

Brown's head into the corner of a wooden coffee table. Once she was unconscious, Kieran Harrison sat on her sofa and watched the life ebb from her as she died from a cerebral haemorrhage. This wasn't a crime of passion. This was a premeditated act of evil. Kieran Harrison sat down and watched her die. He had a window of choice to call for an ambulance and potentially save Serena Brown's life. He chose not to, having determined her fate. Once he was sure of her death, Kieran Harrison stole Serena Brown's mobile phone in the belief it housed the photographs he so feared. He then calmly left her apartment and ordered an Uber to take him home. He then packed a suitcase to fly to Edinburgh. By the end of the evidence presented to you over the course of the next few days, you will have no doubt in your minds that Kieran Harrison is an accomplished liar and made a clear and conscious decision to kill Serena Brown. The prosecution rests its opening remarks. Thank you.'

I watch her sit.

David curls his upper lip and gives a subtle, contemptuous shake of the head.

It catches the judge's attention, but he says nothing.

I think of Serena.

How sexy and fun she could be that could be equally matched to how spiteful and easily offended she could become over the smallest remarks.

I've never been called narcissistic before, or not to my face, anyway. I'm not really sure what it

means, and people seem to use it all the time,
especially on social media, tossing it out like confetti.

Grandiosity.

Self-obsession.

Lacking empathy.

I'm not sure I'm any of those things. But I do
have aggressive energy, which I've channelled into my
work. It's what good athletes do. Channel their
aggression. And I've often seen myself as a corporate
version of that person. A focused corporate athlete. If
that's grandiosity, then I'm guilty as charged, but I
don't think it is. I'm channelling a negative into a
positive, and I have big ideas and dreams. That has to
be a positive, too. I don't think I'm superior or that I'm
somehow unique at the detriment of others. These
last few months, I've descended into self-absorption,
consumed by my own future. I see most of my current
self-obsession as post Serena's death and not before.

'Your Honour. The prosecution would like to
call Edward Carrington-Smythe Jr II as its first witness.'

An usher opens the door to the court, and I
watch the empty space.

Waiting.

Unsure.

My mind suddenly a crowded space of
desperation.

The "report" is here.

Chapter 29

For a split second, I wonder if I'm looking at the same person I know as Teddy-Boy. The man I met for those eight painful sessions is entering the court with a pronounced limp and needs the aid of a walking stick to move and balance.

David glances across like he's wondering why I never mentioned it.

I shrug my surprise, unsure if this theatrical entrance will have any bearing on the day's events.

It shouldn't, but I sweat that it will.

His limp seems to frame his vulnerability and expand my predatory charge.

There's something spellbinding about his tap-and-shuffle approach. It's in keeping with his brown-checked suit and red dickie-bow, which radiates the pomposity I always thought he had. I can't shake the idea he continues to play a role he deems fit for his status, and I'm his current sacrificial lamb.

He acknowledges the judge with an over-show of servitude before taking the stand, where he's sworn in.

He doesn't make eye contact with me. Not that I expected he would. He sits, fusses with his trousers and then his walking stick, taking an age to get comfortable, all the time avoiding my stare and enjoying the silence he's brought with him into the arena of law.

He finally settles and requests if he can read from his notes, taking the opportunity to open his notebook before being given permission.

'Your Honour,' David says, snapping out of his seat and ramping the tension in the room. 'Mr Carrington-Smythe has had many weeks to prepare his report, and any additional information that may accidentally come into play would be against the disclosure rules and could prejudice my client.'

The judge ponders the point and then agrees.

I grew to detest that notebook, and watching Teddy-Boy forced to return it to his pocket warms my numbed insides.

Both the prosecution and Teddy are visibly irritated, and David makes no effort to hide his first victory and set the tone for what will come.

I stick to our game plan and keep my smile internal as a new silence befalls the room.

Patricia uses the pause to stand, and her presence reins everyone's focus. She thanks Edward for making it today. He smiles back, his professional vanity getting a full airing, as well as another fee slipping into his bank account. Patricia asks him to introduce himself. He takes a sip of water before spewing his credentials like a teenager fighting to find his adult personality. I'm relieved to find he comes across as dry and analytical, falling immediately into spaghetti jargon, something Patricia is unable to extract him from.

For a psychoanalyst, he's a terrible listener.

He babbles on, eyes closing occasionally, as he searches his mind for his words. I always sensed he was insecure and vain—even jealous—and watching him perform does nothing to prove my suspicions wrong.

Patricia slowly begins to rein him in and, as she does, subscribes her own narrative to his report. I've read it twenty times and can recall it verbatim, but under her expert slicing of the salient points, it begins to turn against me even more than in its original content.

I'm the product of a white middle-class family, every advantage laid at my feet on a silver platter until a bitter divorce disrupted my world. A broken home that spiralled into anger and resentment, impacting my life in such a way that I've never fully recovered. Its consequences reverberating into every adult relationship I've ever had.

I glance to my father in the public gallery, who smiles back reassuringly, the pain of our exposed family cutting across his face.

He's a deeply private man, a product of his generation, and I throb with shame that he has to endure this public exposure so late in his life.

Patricia pushes on.

The blame and aggression I've shown toward my mother became the blueprint of my future relationships with the opposite sex. A model Teddy-Boy was unsure about at first. He contemplated if I had become trauma-bonded. A relationship attachment style formed in the war zone of the environment I grew up in. There's a paradox in such relationships that the trauma-bonded individual finds it harder to leave an unhealthy relationship than they would a healthy one. It's a painful behavioural pattern that is difficult to break.

He dismissed this idea when it became apparent I had NPD.

Or Narcissistic Personality Disorder.

A disorder that had become more acute in my personal adult relationships. My modus operandi is to continually push and test the personal boundaries of those I date. I bond via sex and not emotions. Arguments are resolved via escalations rather than resolutions—something he had personally witnessed. I'm envious of all those I date. An expert at isolating partners, demonstrated skilfully through the endless trips away that I obsessively organised. My love-bombing is effectively "grooming" a partner for the controlling relationships I crave and develop within my sexual relationships. They give me narcissistic supply to my narcissistic needs.

A propping up of my false self.

Serena was the type of personality who counterbalanced the image I maintained for myself.

I fantasise about being in a celebrity-style relationship. It matched my high-status job and compounded my grandiosity. I'm emotionally immature and was unable to handle Serena's confidence and superior maturity that was manifested in her entrepreneurial lifestyle.

The problems in our relationship always stemmed from the same point.

When Serena expressed her own needs and desires be met, I would erupt in what is termed "narcissistic rage" having suffered a "narcissistic injury" from not having my own needs continually met by her. I demanded and expected a one-way traffic of affection. I'm ambivalent when it comes to sex and use it as a tool of manipulation, deriving little pleasure from the act.

'Objection, your Honour,' David says, casually standing from his chair. 'Could the witness please show me in his report where it states my client is ambivalent toward the act of making love?'

Teddy-Boy picks up his report and begins to turn the pages.

The flick of paper dusting everyone's attention.

'Apologies, your Honour. It was a mistake on my part. It's why I needed my notes.'

The judge ignores the jibe and tells the stenographer to remove the comment from the court record.

I glance across at the jury, catching a middle-aged woman staring back at me. I'm not convinced its removal matters, as Teddy-Boy has let the smoke into the room, and the damage is done.

Teddy-Boy returns to his report, tripping effortlessly back into his monologue, finally concluding I'm a malignant narcissist who harbours revengeful fantasies on partners who stop supplying my ego with the satisfaction it requires.

What you see in me is a "false self" and not a "true identity".

So I'm not human is what he's just told the court.

Patricia lets that one hang in the room before thanking the witness.

Teddy-Boy might as well have said I'm a paranoid sociopath with homicidal tendencies.

It's all fucking bullshit, and I want to leap across the dock and ram his walking stick down his throat.

I don't.

Instead, I wait for David, who, for a split second, I think is going to pass on his cross-examination.

Then he slowly stands.

His dumbfounded frown is now a permanent fixture.

'For the record, my client was requested to visit your practice as part of his bail conditions?'

'Yes.'

'You were aware of his charge?'

'Objection, your Honour,' Patricia says, standing. 'Mr. Carrington-Smythe is a highly respected consultant psychiatrist and psychotherapist with many years of academic and clinical experience. The defendant's bail condition is accepted procedure in cases like this and should not be drawn into question.'

The judge nods and looks at David with a firm stare.

'Counsel, please keep your cross-examination relevant to the contents of Mr Carrington-Smythe's report.'

David smiles and nods that he will, making a show of turning a page on Teddy-Boy's report, chewing on his bottom lip as he does.

'You state that my client has narcissistic personality disorder or NPD?'

'He does.'

'A disorder that is recognised by the World Health Organisation's International Classification of Mental and Behavioural Disorders?'

'Correct.'

'Currently, there are ten main categories of Mental Disorders?'

'Correct.'

'NPD is one of those?'

'Correct again.'

'To diagnose narcissistic personality disorder, an individual must demonstrate at least five of the nine general traits that are associated with the disorder?'

'That's correct, too.'

'For the benefit of the court, could you list my client's NPD traits that led you to your diagnosis?'

'Certainly,' he says with a sigh of professional indignation. 'Kieran Harrison has a sense of entitlement; he's interpersonally exploitative; he lacks empathy; he has fantasies of being a celebrity; and he requires excessive admiration at a constant level.'

'Very negative traits?'

'Extremely.'

David frowns, glancing towards the jury before looking back at Teddy-Boy. 'Those traits haven't seemed to have hindered his career, which I find unusual for a man lacking empathy, who needs excessive admiration, and exploits people?'

Teddy-Boy rolls the question through his mind, visibly irritated.

'The primary focus of our sessions was on his personal relationships, so I can't comment on his professional relationships and career.'

'So your analysis didn't cover the full spectrum of my client's personality?'

'I didn't say that?'

'What did you say?'

'That the main focus was on his personal relationships, not his professional ones.'

'So you can be a narcissist in your personal life but not in your professional life?'

'If you have narcissistic personality disorder, it will affect all your relationships.'

David smiles.

Teddy-Boy tenses his jaw.

'Mr Carrington-Smythe, does "malignant narcissism" appear in the World Health Organisation's classification of behavioural disorders?'

Teddy-Boy searches his mind for the answer.

'Could you repeat your question? My hearing isn't what it used to be.'

'Is "malignant narcissism" one of the disorders *listed* in the World Health Organisation's list of ten?'

David's voice booms in the courtroom.

Teddy-Boy looks across at Patricia, like he's wanting a lifeline.

'Mr. Carrington-Smythe, I asked you a question.'

David's voice noticeably louder than a moment before.

'No, it's not one of the ten. It's not a medical term as is narcissistic personality disorder, more a term used within the profession to help us categorise NPD.'

'What is the "professional" understanding of a "malignant narcissist"?'

Teddy-Boy scowls, glancing across to me for the first time.

I know what's coming.

I think he does, too.

'If an individual has been diagnosed with NPD and then has a cluster of other negative behavioural patterns, such as anti-social behaviour, paranoia, sadism, then we would class that individual as a "malignant narcissist".'

'And you would agree with this non-medical classification—as a fellow professional within this field?'

'Absolutely.'

David suddenly waves the report like a red flag and says. 'Could you point out in your report where it states my client has anti-social behaviour, sadism, or paranoia?'

'You clearly haven't read my report correctly.'

'Even more reason to highlight to the court and myself where you mention those additional negative behaviours?'

'It's the tone of the report. The overarching picture that is important.'

'You said that NPD affects all relationships?'

'It does.'

'Yet my client has an exemplary career with demonstrable successful professional relationships. In fact, he was voted as one of the up-and-coming CEO's of his generation less than three years ago. His sexual preferences would certainly indicate masochism but not sadism. As by your own admission, your hearing isn't what it used to be.'

David ups his voice again.

It's almost a shout.

'Therefore, you cannot be relied upon to know what you did and didn't hear, and the "overarching picture" you have presented is based on a one-sided analysis that doesn't take into account the complete character of my client. He has both a "professional" and a "personal" life. The report you have presented today is frankly nonsense, is one-sided, and my client is as much a narcissist as I am.'

The judge looks across, eyebrows raised.

I'm sure I hear a chuckle in the court, but whoever it was, it wasn't Patricia.

Chapter 30

Half asleep, I catch my electronic tag on the frame of the bathroom door. The silicone housing snaps back and hard-pinches my skin. I cuss, rubbing at the pain point, the sudden soft snore of my dad filling the darkness around me. The earthy sound sends an immediate spark of urgency for me to check on him.

I walk toward his room, silent as I can. I need the fix of the visible; the emotional surety that it's him and not an intruder who has crept into my spare room and fallen asleep.

I reach for the door and push the panel with the tips of my fingers. The door creeps open, and my vulnerabilities that have come to haunt me each night since my arrest ease as I watch him peacefully in the shadows of the night. It doesn't seem that long ago when it was he who stood in a similar spot, keeping sentinel over me.

If it's true that we become the parents to our parents, then I've let him down.

Terribly.

He sleep-groans, like the snippet of light from the corridor has disturbed him, and for a split second, the word "Dad" enters my lips as I think he's going to wake.

He doesn't, settling again, like a newborn.

But he's not.

He's entered his golden years and is slipping into old age, exacerbated by the weight loss. The youth he'd clawed back through his rigorous diet, yoga sessions, and long walks along the beach have been blown away by the stresses of my trial.

It's like he's the one on the dock, not me.

As much as I'm trying, I can't seem to protect him from the fallout. I'm too wrapped up in my own misery. My own narcissism, maybe, and if the next few days turn against me, I'll never spend another quality minute with him again.

He'll be ninety-plus, more likely dead before I'm released.

Shame and guilt ravage me, welling from my gut and into my eyes and skating across my cheeks in the form of heavy tears.

I hate Serena Brown.

I hate having ever met her and allowing her into my life.

I had a hundred opportunities to walk away and date other women and take a different path, but I didn't.

I stayed with the poison.

My own personal drug of choice.

My dad met her twice and never liked her. It was more what he didn't say rather than what he did.

It's his way.

It's the same today.

He didn't say much after we left court, even when we went for a quick pint to wash the first day from our bodies, other than he thought David had a positive start. I nodded and agreed, but I'm not convinced, close to heartbroken that he had to hear our family history recorded into the court records for anyone to read. The only real upside of the day is that I will never have to see or endure Teddy-Boy again.

My thoughts toward him bordering on the evil.

Projection, I guess.

Because the truth is I missed a trick, and it has the potential to tear my life apart. I never trusted him and detested how he'd been imposed on my life. I went against David's advice and played it too guarded, only giving Teddy-Boy the bare necessities about my life in the hope of throwing off his scent. Teddy-Boy even gave me a way out. Presented it on a golden platter, surrounded by sparkling jewels. He probed to see if I was *trauma bonded*. I didn't even bother to Google the phrase or think about it with any real depth. I just locked myself down, counting off the eight sessions, like minutes in extra time, wanting them to be over, and in the process, missed the chance to define my rules of engagement.

Idiot.

Had I played into Teddy-Boy's vanity, I may well have come out as the victim rather than the sadistic narcissist, prone to rage attacks on those I view as objects.

I doff my hat to Patricia for how she twisted his report and threw me under the feet of the jury as the narcissistic killer in waiting.

Twelve pairs of eyes rested on my soul, making it hard to breathe.

The truth is I never thought of myself as a narcissist.

I wonder if anyone ever does?

The accusation comes out as a cheap shot. An easy finger to point, one that keeps the trolls out there busy, puts me in a box and makes it simple for the doubters to hang a decision on.

So what that I'm ambitious, and I get a touch jealous, and I think of my own needs at times. If that makes me entitled and interpersonally exploitative, then everyone I know is in the same boat. The idea of being a celebrity and recognised in the street fills me with as much anxiety as this trial. Seeking fame is a fool's paradise and something I've never done. I've always looked to gather feedback to improve my life. If my friends are a reflection of who I am, then I don't see a grandiose monster waiting in the wings like some Jekyll and Hyde. My arguments and debates are never about gaslighting or control. I'm guilty of losing my temper with Serena, as I have with my mother on occasions, but they are extremely rare events and not reflective of my relationships as a whole.

It's just not.

No matter what anyone says.

I start to close the door as my dad scoffs another gentle snore, and it triggers Serena's voice deep within my mind.

An echo from the past.

Another haunting of the night.

'You snore. It's annoying.'

'What!'

She laughs, and it's a strange mix of embarrassment and annoyance all intermeshed into one.

She finishes getting dressed, slipping into her winter boots.

'How do I look?'

'The overweight and drunks are the only people who snore,' I say. 'And I'm neither.'

'Now you're being weight-est and addict-est as well as a snorer?' She says with the same mixed laugh that has turned toward the aggressive.

'Seriously… I'm not joking. I don't snore. I know I don't.'

'You're asleep… how would you know?'

'Because I know!'

'That's the most conceited thing I've ever heard. I'm telling you, YOU snore. I hear it each night I stay. Which is a lot. And for the record, it's loud!'

'I'm not having this.'

'Darling… how would you know? Is there a secret camera in here that's recording us—which there better not be!'

'Because no one has ever complained about it before. And, no, there's no camera. I'm not some pervert.'

'So you're introducing ex-girlfriends as part of your defence against snoring?'

'I've shared rooms with mates on different holidays, and they've never complained that I snore.'

'That's because you were all too drunk to notice each other, and it was never more than a long weekend anyway. Your argument doesn't count.'

'I travelled with Dan for five months, and he never said a word. And for the record, he doesn't snore either.'

'I certainly can't vouch for that one.'

'This is a crazy conversation that is easily fixed. Record it tonight.'

'Now you're being ridiculous and over-sensitive. You always take the wrong end of the stick. Anyway, I'm not staying tonight.'

'I'm being ridiculous! You're the one accusing me of snoring when I don't. Now we have the opportunity to prove it one way or the other.'

'You're such a man. Everything annoys you. Darling, please don't get aggressive about it. I don't have to prove what I know. Look, it's not that important—I just mentioned it in passing.'

'Aggressive is if I start shouting and jabbing my finger into your face. I'm defending my position. There's a difference.'

'I simply pointed out you snore, and now you want to install spy cameras. You snore. It's loud, and it sometimes keeps me awake. If I can't tell you that, what can I tell you?'

'Serena...'

'Enough... I have to go to work. I'm not a CEO who can take time off when I want. I'll speak to you later. And, baby, don't let the snoring ruin your day. Lots of men snore. Trust me, I know.'

It's the body odour I smell first, turning to see the security guard join me in the dock. He smirks. He did the same yesterday, like my outcome is pre-destined, and he's part of the inner-sanctum of Gods who have already made their decision.

I need to ignore him.

This rent-a-thug is proving more effective than Teddy-Boy at getting under my skin, and it's only the start of day two of the proceedings.

I turn toward the public gallery to make sure my dad has made it in. It's a relief to see him, despite us seeing each other less than fifteen minutes ago. His yellowing gauntness looks more accentuated in the white light of the courtroom. He's sat in the exact same seat as he was yesterday. And he'll sit there every day, making sure he's first in. He'd never admit it, but he veers toward the superstitious.

He gives me his best reassuring nod and smile.

I acknowledge him with a quick thumbs-up.

I turn back into the main court. The shuffle of paper and the hum of whispers being absorbed by the wooden panelling with a cushioned ease. My eyes rest on Patricia, who made a point of not looking my way as she entered the court. Her mind games from yesterday appear suspended for now, no doubt on the back of Teddy-Boy's vanity collapse.

We all rise, and the judge enters. After some preamble and a warning to the jury not to discuss the case outside of the permitted circles, the gears of the day click into action. The coroner who completed the autopsy is sworn in. I can immediately tell he's an old hand at being in the witness box. Patricia is overly polite, and it smacks of routine and hidden rules. I wouldn't be surprised if they've crossed paths on a previous case or even cases.

I listen on, beginning to get a better feel for who she is. Apart from the quiet determination that lurks beneath, she has two qualities she uses to great effect. She has a knack for twisting reports and statements into her own narrative to the point that they come across as completely rewritten to favour her view. Combined with her ability to let the seminal moments linger in the silence she creates, it is a talent I wish I was observing rather than being its central focus.

'Had Serena engaged in sexual intercourse on the night of her death?'

'Yes... there was semen in Serena's vaginal canal that was traced to Kieran Harrison.'

'And there was no other evidence that Serena had engaged in sexual activity with anyone else other than the defendant?'

'No... we looked for additional semen secretions both in the stomach and the vaginal canal, but there was no trace.'

Patricia lets the implication of his statement sit in the empty space above our heads.

David had stressed that on the coroner's evidence, I don't look at the jury, even glance across. I'm to keep my focus above the coroner's head and to stay relaxed and upright. David constantly reminds me of a Martin Luther King quote.

"A man can't ride you unless your back is bent."

Neutral.

Neutral.

Neutral is our mantra.

'In your autopsy, you state that Serena had trauma marks to the back of her neck, upper back, and shoulders?'

'Indeed, she had bruises and bite marks to the rear of her neck. There were deep scratches across the skin of her upper back and shoulders, especially on the right side, which had drawn some light blood. The bite marks on her body matched Kieran Harrison's bite structure. DNA samples taken from the defendant's fingernails matched Serena's skin. Those traumas took place prior to her death and were caused by rough, or bondage style, sexual acts.'

Pause.

I don't move, remembering what my dad had said as we parted and he headed for the public gallery.

That it's *"OK"*.

"Whatever they say, son, it's OK... really it is!"

I'm sure those words were more to himself than me.

But I suck strength from his sentiment.

'The estimated time of Serena's death?'

'It occurred somewhere between 11.30 pm. and 4:00 am. on Sunday, 5th, or Monday, 6th of May.'

'Can you please tell the court how Serena Brown died?'

'She died from a cerebral haemorrhage, more commonly known as internal bleeding of the brain. This was caused by massive trauma to the rear of her skull.'

'And death was immediate?'

'Not at all. She would have been unconscious for around an hour while her brain slowly died and shut down the key organs within her body.'

Silence.

I gulp.

I see Serena in my mind's eyes.

The woman I once loved, alone in a rented flat, desperately fighting for her life.

'In your report, you conclude unlawful death. Can you explain to the court the basis behind your conclusion?'

The Coroner clears his throat and then takes a sip of water.

'In the main living area, there was a rectangular shaped coffee table made from Indian teak, held together with iron plates and flattened metal rivets. The table dominated the area and was close to twenty kilogrammes with four protruding sharp edges. The iron plates covered the four corners.'

Patricia distributes pictures of the table as her first exhibit. The jury members handed them across to each other in an orderly line.

The first time I entered Serena's flat, I caught my shin on the corner of one of the iron plates. The table was too big for the room and low. One of those items that looks fabulous in the shop but never really goes with anything and is mostly in the way.

The coroner continues.

'The deceased had four sets of primary injuries that were directly related to her death. She had a fractured nose, and her central and left incisors were cracked, with additional bruising to the left side of her lips. These injuries are consistent with a direct and forceful punch to the face. A punch most likely delivered from the right clenched fist of an individual.'

'For the record, is the defendant left or right handed?'

'The police confirmed that he is right handed.'

Silence.

Patricia's moment was choreographed to perfection.

I gulp.

The coroner continues.

'The punch was delivered with enough force that Serena fell with her full weight, striking the back of her skull on the corner of the table. This being the second point of trauma and the first of the two head traumas. At this point, she would have been unable to defend herself or even call out for help.'

Another pause.

More choreographing.

'The third set of injuries was the tearing of the front of her scalp. This indicated that someone grabbed her hair and used the leverage to smash the back of her skull into the corner of the table and thereby created the second set of head traumas that ultimately resulted in her death.'

Pause.

I hear the overhead lights hum.

My own heartbeat pounding its fears.

'If I may surmise?' Patricia says.

The coroner nods.

'Serena Brown had five different injuries to her body, which all occurred within a twelve-hour period prior to her death?'

'Yes.'

'The first was to her upper back, neck, and shoulders caused by rough-style sexual activity.'

'Yes.'

'The second set were facial injuries inflicted by a single and brutal punch from a right-handed person.'

'Yes.'

'The third was an injury to the back of her skull from her initial fall. The fourth and fifth traumas were caused by someone holding first the front of

Serena's hair and then repeatedly smashing her skull into the corner of the table.'

'That is correct.'

'Is it at all possible that Serena Brown died by accidental causes or of her own making?'

'No, this is not possible. Serena Brown was killed unlawfully. She was murdered.'

Silence.

'Thank you. The prosecution has finished with the witness.'

Patricia looks across at David as she takes her seat, ignoring me.

He waits, and I'm once again unsure if he's going to cross-examine or not until he slowly stands and grips the front of his silk robe, smiling, kindly.

'My client told the police that he had had sex with Serena at around 8:00 pm on the Sunday evening. And that they regularly indulged in 'rough-style sex,' something Serena would initiate or often encourage. Were you aware of this before the autopsy?'

'Yes, the police had informed me of that information.'

'So the bite marks and scratches you examined on Serena's neck and upper back did not come as a surprise?'

'It was consistent with what I had expected to see.'

'Did these 'rough sex' trauma injuries contribute to Serena Brown's death?'

'No, they did not.'

'My client cut his right hand badly when he climbed the fence into Serena's property. The police took pictures of his cut and bruised hands. Have you seen these pictures?'

'I have.'

'Was there any evidence that my client had struck someone with a clenched fist?'

'The defendant's right hand showed bruising and swelling around the knuckles, which could have been caused by a single punch. However, it is also true to say that these injuries could have been self-inflicted when he climbed the fence.'

'So it's not conclusive that my client punched Serena other than his dominant hand happens to be his right one, which is true for ninety-five per cent of the UK population?'

'That's correct.'

'Thank you for confirming. You also state that the front of Serena's head was grabbed with such force and used as leverage that it ripped the hairline around the front of her skull?'

'That's what I said, yes.'

'Would the assailant have used one hand or two, or is it not possible to tell?'

'The trauma points to a two-handed grip. Probably with the assailant stood spread-eagle across an either unconscious or a deeply confused Serena. The trauma to the back of Serena's skull and the tear at the front of her hairline indicate a strong individual, or one certainly driven by extreme rage. The girth of the grip would also point to a male or a woman with large hands.'

'Did you find any of my client's blood in Serena's hair? You make no note of it in your report?'

The Coroner looks up to his left like he's searching his mind for the answer. The wood panelling creaks gently in the silence.

'DNA samples taken from the front of Serena's hair weren't conclusive.'

David raises his right eyebrow in mock surprise.

'Inconclusive?'

'Correct.'

'Therefore, if I may surmise,' David says, taking a quick glance across at Patricia. 'If my client had grabbed the front of Serena's hair in a two-handed grip, there's no DNA that could indicate it was him, other than the skin under his nails, which we have already established most likely occurred during their session of 'rough-style' sexual activity?'

'Correct.'

'Considering my client was bleeding profusely from his right hand—when he was to have allegedly entered Serena's apartment—would you have expected to find traces of his blood in her hair or anywhere on her clothes, had he committed the act he stands accused of, more so if he was stood spread-eagle cross her?'

'Unless he was wearing gloves or some other form of protection, I would have expected to have found traces of his blood in her hair or on her clothes, yes.'

'That's all my questions, your Honour.'

Chapter 32

'Nice place,' I say. 'Really nice!'

'If you'd called my dress nice, I'd kill you,' Serena says with a laugh. 'But you like? It's good, yeah?'

'Who wouldn't? It's fantastic!'

I step into the compact lounge, heading for the window to check out the view from her third-floor apartment. I step past the ornate fireplace and bang the top of my shin into an iron cover plate that fits over the edge of the coffee table. I grimace, trying my best to laugh off the embarrassment as the hot pain inflames my shin.

'Don't worry... you'll get used to it. I've done it three times since Friday.'

Apart from the stabbing pain, I see that I've nicked my trousers on a metal rivet. The table is made of a thick cherry-brown-coloured wood. I don't like it, but even I can see that it's expensive. The constant shuffling around it to get in and out of the sofa would drive me crazy.

'What does your friend do?' I add.

'He imports exotic furniture,' Serena says, nodding at the coffee table. 'Mostly on a commissioned basis. He has some exclusive clients. He's taking an extended research trip through lower Indonesia to source pieces and to find himself. Tough life, hey!' she says with a large dose of sarcasm.

I nod and smile, unable to focus on anything but the *he* in the sentence.

I'm sure Serena told me it was a friend, implying a *she*, someone whom she currently worked with, and who had gone to live with her boyfriend. It's not the sort of thing I would forget. I've long learnt that Serena can be vague and selective around information. What I want to ask is how they know each other, or if they've dated, or the one burning question—has she slept with him?

Looking around the apartment, my suspicions aren't eased.

We continue with the short guided tour, and despite my spikes of jealousy, it's hard to begrudge the compact and beautifully decorated apartment in this quiet part of Notting Hill. I'm not big on décor, but even I can see the attention to detail is immaculate, and the furniture is a notch up from the usual tourist junk you can get in an exotic location.

I pop my head into the bathroom and see all white wood and Buddha symbols.

There's a calmness to the flat, and I recall my own travels to the Far East.

'Shall we go?' Serena calls from behind me.

I turn and see her searching a glass-scooped bowl that is the centre piece of an oak engraved console. I should be admiring the carvings within the wood and the uniqueness of the piece, but all I see are three sets of matching keys.

I'm piqued that one set isn't coming my way.

We've discussed living together, but it's gone nowhere.

I froth with frustration and disappointment as *he* seems to settle under my skin, replacing the Racing Driver she still drops into our conversations.

We head out, and Serena deadlocks the door. She looks great in dark jeans and trainers and a short summer jacket that cuts into her shape.

I follow her down the stairs, Serena coquettishly looking over her shoulder. At the bottom, I turn for the main entrance, but she whistles me back with a wink to go the opposite way.

I ping with more jealousy, convinced she's been here more times than she's letting on.

We exit the back door into a high-walled communal garden.

It's well-kept, with mature trees and benches dotted around the lawn, creating natural breakout areas and a small oasis of calm. Like the apartment, it's sophisticated and well maintained, exclusivity in the heart of a busy and popular location.

We head for a secret door. It's cut into the bricked wall that surrounds the rear of the block. I wouldn't have seen it had she not pointed it out. It is semi-camouflaged with thick green ivy and painted the same black-red as the bricks. She uses one of the keys to open the lock. Due to the location of the maisonette block and the one-way traffic system that runs around it, I see we've taken a significant shortcut to *The*

George and Dragon—the pub I've booked for Sunday Lunch.

We walk on.

She hooks her arm through mine.

We haven't seen each other all week, and she's surprisingly quiet.

I am, too.

I'm sulking.

And it's a bad one at that.

I'm doing my utmost to break out of it.

I had volunteered to help her move, taking the day off work. At the last minute, she tells me an old friend is booked to stand in. The rejection wrangled. Now I'm sure this old friend is a *he*? Serena and I didn't speak until Saturday morning when she rejected my help for the second and third time, saying she was almost done and she was going to finish off, do some admin and get an early night.

I clock myself and realise I didn't see a single suitcase, or cardboard box, or even a black bag full of clothes waiting to be moved.

'It's like you've been in there for months?' I finally say.

'It does, doesn't it! I thought the same this morning before you came over. I'd already had a big clear-out and a couple of trips to the recycling before packing up, so I didn't bring much.'

'When's your friend back from their travels?' I say as innocently as I can.

Serena pretends not to hear my question as we enter the busy pub. We fall into a single file to navigate the crowd, heading for the dining section off to our right. At a separate workstation, we are met by the waitress who checks my name against a list and takes us to a table by the window.

'It's a good job you booked,' Serena says, squeezing my arm.

We sit, and Serena orders a glass of red wine, and I order a pint of Guinness. The waitress takes our order and leaves. Serena and I are unexpectedly left in the hole of our silence. I feel like I'm waiting for the answer to my question, but then I remember she mentioned something about three months. It could be three years, I think. Then it strikes me that we seem more like adversaries than lovers, and the idea we could be long-term partners seems nothing but a distant dream, hovering on a deluded joke.

Our drinks arrive, and I'm glad to have something to do with my hands.

'How was Paris?' Serena asks, taking a sip of her wine.

'Hot and sweaty. Eco-Blue hasn't been too successful in raising money in France, so I might take it off the list. It doesn't help I'm not a fan.'

'You're not a fan! I love the place. How come?'

'I don't know. I don't speak the language, or not well enough to do business, and there's only so many times you can see the Eiffel Tower and go wow.'

'We'll go together next time, and I can show you around. Remember, I worked and lived there. I could be your translator.'

She says something in French.

It's too quick for me to comprehend, and I smile back, adding, 'That would be nice.'

The lack of enthusiasm in my own voice is painful to my ears. I should have cancelled today or certainly addressed being cut out of the move before turning up, rather than pretending it doesn't bother me.

Because it does.

Thankfully, our food arrives, giving us a much-needed injection of energy.

We've both gone for roast beef with all the trimmings.

I order another pint, and Serena orders a bottle of Bordeaux and two glasses.

My second drink arrives, and I use it to push past my sulk. Perhaps Dan is right, and I'm being too impatient. I can be prone to wanting to have my own way, which is not always fair to the other person. Serena and I have only known each other for ten months, so is there really the need to move in together right now? What's another few months while she house-sits for her friend on his travels?

I sip at my drink.

The alcohol starts to buzz through me.

The warmth invading my skin and my senses.

The waitress appears from my blindside and pours Serena another glass of red. I decline and order another Guinness while Serena chats on about a post she made on Instagram that had over ten thousand Likes within an hour.

I tune out.

Bored of her light conversation that never seems to include us. The unanswered question of us living together and our weekend-based relationship fades further into the background.

We chat on, but we don't.

It's Serena talking about *LavishLondonLashes*, or herself, really, and me nodding in agreement.

The lame pup I've become.

The bystander in this union.

I'm grateful for the food, which borders on the excellent, and we both opt for apple crumble-and-cream as a dessert. It's unusual for me to have a sweet, almost unheard of for Serena, and I wonder if it's a sign of the strain.

I stick with another Guinness and Serena finishes off the Bordeaux, my mind starting to drift into the zone whereby I can both watch myself and be semi-critical of who I am at the same time.

The chat has turned to one I've heard hundreds of times. It's full of platitudes and relationship endorsements, energised by alcohol. None of it holds true any longer. I want to scream that we can't even share keys, the topic as toxic as incest. If Dan, or any one of my other friends were sat where

Serena is sat now, I'd be telling them to forget this girl. To move on. You're an option, nothing more, and you need to protect yourself against being used. That you have to see past this beautiful outer person who talks the talk but whose actions don't match a single word that drops from her lips.

The inner is empty, or towards 'you' anyway.

It's reality time, buddy.

And it's true.

Her actions don't match her words.

Our weekends are great, but she vanishes in the week. Disappearing like a butterfly in the wind. I've only met two of her friends and none of her family. Even her two friends were a brief encounter at my expense. They were two dedicated party girls whose names I can't even remember, and I'm not sure I want to know anyway. The world is full of people who'll dine on your dime.

We order more drinks, and it numbs me enough for me to park my jealousy.

I seriously wonder, for the first time, if there is someone else in the background, waiting to make his move?

Perhaps he has already?

I'm the Friday-to-Sunday guy. The new man is Tuesday-to-Thursday.

Maybe, after this weekend, I've even lost my Friday slot.

His toothbrush already parked in the bathroom.

I gulp my drink and order another pint, lost to my own thoughts. I miss how we finish our meal and end up in the street, other than once again, I'm folding the receipt into my wallet, a reminder of the one-way direction my relationship has become.

Maybe always was.

Serena puts her hand into my pocket and pushes her fingers deeper than is necessary.

I jump, and we giggle like petting teenagers.

But it's the same pattern unfolding before my eyes.

Meet, eat, drink, have sex, the weekend merging into a haze of mild debauchery.

Progress zero.

She's happy with it.

I'm not.

I want more.

And I'm not sure this girl can deliver it for me.

Serena closes the door and then turns and leans in and kisses me, sucking and then biting my bottom lip in the process.

I taste blood, but I smile. It's the alcohol talking, not me. She does it again. I've seen that look in her eyes a thousand times. It's a mixture of alcohol and her sexual energy that combines and takes her to a place she's never invited me to.

'I want to look out of the window,' she says, taking my hand and pulling me into the lounge...

'Mr Fitzgerald?' my barrister says, bringing me back into court.

I look across at the crime officer who was in charge of the crime scene. His skin is sweaty and pale. It's like being here is a major inconvenience to his life.

He has my sympathies.

'Yes,' he says. 'I was debating your question. Kieran Harrison's blood was on the glass and handle of the outside of the back entrance door. We also found his blood on the garden wall and path. But you're correct in that there was no blood or significant DNA within Serena's apartment that matched his. We did find his fingerprints on the handle of the bathroom door and the handle of the kitchen. There was cotton from his trousers on the right, inside corner of the coffee table. On examination, he had a bruise and small indent in his left shin that was matched to the table.'

'I'm correct in that you found DNA of two different males on the hand towel in Serena's bathroom. Consistent with two separate individuals wiping their hands?'

'Yes, we did.'

'But not the defendant's?'

'No.'

'I put it to you that the fingerprints and DNA found that match my client are consistent with someone who had visited for the first time and spent very little time in the space.'

'Well, yes and no.'

'Why no?'

'The defendant could have cleaned up after the event.'

David frowns, looks deeply concerned, almost offended.

'Cleaned up?'

'Yes... cleaned up.'

David picks up the technicians report.

'I don't see any reference to cleaning products. Or any reference that the property had been sanitised prior to the discovery of Serena's body? So, I put it to you again that although my client fully admits to having entered the property, his DNA and fingerprints are consistent with the story he has given. He had a quick guided tour. He banged his shin and nicked a hole in his trousers on the table. They went for lunch. They came back and had sexual intercourse. A "quicky". Then, my client left. I see nothing in your report that can possibly suggest anything else. Or have I missed something?'

'No, you haven't missed anything.'

'That's all your Honour.'

Chapter 33

'Faster... '

Serena's demand borders on a threat, her voice hoarse and quick.

I comply, disconnecting from our sexual act in a way that disturbs me.

Vicarious.

Uncommitted.

The helicopter view of my own life and the acts within it.

The alcohol in my blood no longer a comforting support, but twisting against me, fuelling a new level of paranoia.

'Faster.... '

I'm panting hard.

Serena has become the blow-up caricature of the real person I want to meet and share my life with.

I've somehow ended up with an inferior copy.

'Bite me,' she whispers.

I'm not sure I can or even want to any more.

'Kieran...'

'Yeah...'

'Do it.'

The bullying command triggers a new surge of anger, a deep pulse from a latent strain. A fragment I've been hiding that has long threatened to wreak havoc with my life. It erupts out in a primal grunt. I tug her hair, then I lean forward and sink my teeth into the base of her neck.

Hard, bordering on the sadistic.

She groans.

It's guttural and full of pleasure.

She tastes like perfume and sweat, mixed with the salty taste of blood that drives me on.

She arches her back, and it pulls me in.

I wrap her hair around my hand and pull hard to the rhythm of my pounding. Her hair the reins to this wild beast below me. My aggression is not enough to sustain the ride, and I'm suddenly out of breath, panting to the point of hypertension, the muscles in my thighs burning unbearably with lactic acid.

She senses my decline and grips her thighs and groans to encourage me on.

But all I hear are the insidious tones of deceit.

I need to stop to protect myself.

My ego lost to another world.

I'm spent.

Thankfully, no one from the street has looked up. There'd be no illusions as to what was happening if they cared to glance our way. And we're stupid, I think. We both have much to lose, or me certainly.

'Don't stop,' she grunts.

Don't stop, I repeat in my mind.

But if only I had.

If only I had walked away when she had overreacted for the umpteenth time. Yet, I was a willing participant. I enjoyed how she treated others as if I was somehow immune to her behaviour.

I wasn't.

That look of annihilation was her ultimate weapon and is why I'm fighting for another kind of freedom, one which is beyond my control.

I dry-wipe my face as I continue to stare out of my bedroom window as the dawn over London arrives. My dad's gentle snores reverberate from the room next door. As a kid, the sound would drive me crazy. So much so that I had to beg my mum to buy earplugs, something she took an age to do.

Now, it's the most soothing sound I could wish to hear.

I let it imprint itself further into the scars of my soul in case I will need to hear it for another time. A memory recall that is going to get me through the next twenty years or more of my life.

No earplugs required this time.

A man isn't born to live in a cage, I think.

'Don't stop,' I hear Serena say again as she comes back to haunt me from the depths of my mind.

Don't stop!

It should be her epitaph.

She could never stop.

She was selfish, unaccountable and deceptively reckless.

The rules never applying to her, only to others. She had an inverted entitlement that was hard to spot unless you spent time alone in her presence. I hope David can paint the picture I have now begun to understand.

'Don't stop.'

I didn't.

I came.

And it hurt.

And I think I knew there and then that it was the last time we'd ever have sex or even see each other again.

She turned to face me, giggling like she always did when her sexual energy seemed to embarrass her.

Or maybe it was just another one of her acts.

I've never thought about it in that way before, but I had unintentionally shamed her at that moment. I had made her feel cheap. A mistake. I pulled up my trousers and tucked myself away. I've never paid for sex, but I'm sure that's the nearest I'm going to get. No emotional connection. A need met with zero satisfaction, accompanied by a waterfall of guilt and a desire to run. She sensed the whole gamut of those spent emotions.

'Kieran...' she says, fastening the front of her jeans.

I get that lump in the back of my throat from the tone. It's like a reverse sneeze is about to block my lungs.

I'm about to get dumped.

"He" is now the new *"Me"*.

Our ten-month relationship ended in an alcohol-fuelled quickie over the arm of a chair, witnessed by the crowd below.

'What?' I say.

'This place.'

'Yeah?'

'I've taken it on a year's lease. I've been meaning to tell you. I think it's best. It gives us more time to work on *us*. Make sure that it's right. We're both too busy to live together anyway, and I know how much it annoys you when I'm on my phone all the time. This way, it gives you time to sell your place. Make sure you get the right price. We can spend Christmas here, mostly naked... what do you say?'

I hear my father's snore.

Two separate men had wiped their hands on a hand towel in Serena's bathroom. My blood was smeared on the handle and glass of the outside door but nowhere else.

'I've taken it on a year's lease. I've been meaning to tell you.'

Her words cut through me now with the same hot intensity as they did then.

Was she breaking up with me?

Was I being moved on?

Our last two months of conversations about being more of a couple, nothing but a running lie that had sucked me in. Conversations I'd started to build my future life on, yet were meaningless to Serena. I'd put my flat on the market. She knew what I was doing. We'd agreed.

Or had we?

Serena never committing to anything, but always sounding like she had and she was leading the charge.

It's a skill I don't have.

Yes is *yes,* and no is *no* in my world.

There's no ambiguity.

And she's pointing and shouting and blaming me.

I'm not taking responsibility.

I'm immature.

I'm a bully.

I'm selfish.

I'm cruel.

I can't be trusted.

She could do better in a heartbeat.

I'm listening and agreeing, and all I can think is that she said "one year" and not "three months".

One-year.

He.

Whoever *"He"* is.

I'm walking toward the door, wondering if Serena had sex with him yesterday and me today.

Then I'm in the hallway.

I'm staring into the bowl on the oak console.

Serena is shouting.

'You fucking coward. You fucking coward. Fucking stay here and be a fucking man.'

The door slams behind me, and then I'm out of the front door and into the street with my precious keys.

The one thing I've wanted.

Coveted.

She wouldn't give it to me, so I took it from under her nose.

And it's here.

Pinched between my fingers, and there's not a fucking thing she can do about it.

Chapter 34

I keep having random thoughts about whether I'd pass a polygraph or not. David informs me that the results are not admissible under British law. I'm thankful, as I listen to Mila Sidorov, the Russian waitress cum-ex-ballerina, cut me down to size with Patricia's skilful help.

I reach for my glass of water and attempt to wash the inky taste of what must be guilt from my mouth. It doesn't work, and I doubt alcohol mouthwash could shift this repugnant dew.

Mila is like the eyewitness who tripped into the prosecution's lap, and they can't believe their luck. She keeps glancing across at me as she goes through her statement, nuancing on the points. Her darting eyes make me think she's viewing me like I'm a Russian gangster sent by Putin himself who's going to poison her and her family to exact my revenge the moment I get my chance.

Apart from her natural beauty, tucked behind delicate feline features, her innocence, combined with her palpable fear, is firing the sympathy gene in everyone except myself and David. She's a twenty-year-old beauty telling the truth. She's as convincing as convincing gets. The problem is she didn't see the reality of that night. She saw a blinkered version, myopic, filtered via the heat and the noise. The entitled crowd she waited on all wanting to feel important and noticed has impaired her view.

Her naivety is a dangerous step toward my undoing, and Patricia's kid-glove handling is adding the pressure.

It's the first time I've seen David take notes.

I listen on.

Mila's version is compelling even to me.

It's like she was sitting on my shoulder for the whole night, having unprecedented access to my intimate conversation with Serena. If I hadn't experienced it personally, I could believe this young woman's version of events.

But what she didn't know is that I'd left the conference in Geneva a day early. I should have stayed for the gala event on the Friday night. It was a networking haven of willing financiers I'd left behind to have dinner with Serena, a dinner I could and should have had on the Saturday.

I didn't.

I made all sorts of weak excuses to leave.

An oversight on the days. Flights. Another meeting. My aunt was unwell.

All lies.

I was so on the emotional hook that I could barely get through my presentation, imagining Serena in the audience, watching me perform, smiling me into her bed.

The ache to get home burnt white-hot inside.

And not just in my groin.

It had infected my whole body.

I'd landed at Heathrow and had come straight to the restaurant, not even bothering to go home. I had my carry-on in one hand and my passport in the other. I sat at the bar for nearly an hour like the tamed puppy I'd become, waiting for Serena to grace me with her presence.

I couldn't have been less cool if I tried.

Thinking back on it, I was the only guy in the place who was wearing his suit shirt and trousers, jacket crumpled across my knee.

Serena entered wearing that summer dress, the one that had caught my eye on Tinder. No bra. Almost see-through, but somehow staying away from tacky. Turning heads as she glided in. Pushing those boundaries as she always did. The behaviour ingrained into her DNA.

Patricia asks a question, and Mila backtracks and comments that she recalled Serena entering and that I'd been sat at the bar, visibly irritated at being kept waiting.

David objects, saying it was impossible for Mila to know my state of mind.

The judge agrees, and Patricia changes gear.

I wasn't irritated, not even close.

I'd long got used to Serena being late, and I couldn't wait to see her.

We drank and ordered tapas. The food was great, fresh and clean, but it came too quickly. Mila was trying to force us on to get another couple in, but I assumed that was the policy of the restaurant and nothing to do with her. Although, I do remember asking her to slow down, which she looked offended at.

I'd forgotten Serena and I had decided to carry on drinking in a hotel bar a three-minute walk from the restaurant.

Serena loved her long bars.

High stools and a place to be seen.

I ordered the bill from Mila.

As I think it.

She says it.

And to my surprise, Mila tells the court that she heard Serena accuse me of checking her out.

Admiring her legs and bum.

Mila blushes.

It's a fucking lie.

I was on the hook for Serena.

I'd flown nine hundred miles and had not gone home to shower or change so I wouldn't risk missing or even being late for my date. I'd cancelled dinner with serious players, some of whom could make a difference to the causes we at Eco-Blue were trying to fund. I wanted to rip that dress from Serena's body and take her there and then on one of the tapas tables, which I'm sure she'd have been up for.

'And did Kieran Harrison continue to look at you in a sexual manner? One that could be seen as inappropriate?' Patricia asks.

Mila glances across at me.

As do most of the jury.

'Yes,' she says. 'He'd been checking me out since he'd stepped into the restaurant and did at every opportunity. It was a bit creepy and made me uncomfortable.'

I gulp.

She's a kid.

Who's sunk me.

'And what happened next?' Patricia asks.

'I went to get the bill and the card machine. It was then that Phil—another waiter working the same shift—nodded at Serena and the defendant. They were arguing. I knew what it was about.'

'And what was the argument about?'

'That this man had checked me out.'

'Which man?' Patricia asks.

Mila points at me. 'Him over there.'

'The defendant?'

'Yes.'

'Thank you for confirming. Please continue.'

'I was scared. I could see the argument getting more... how you say... big. So, I asked Phil to take over the bill and get payment. That was it. I move on to my work, then I hear all this noise, and I see the defendant run out. But it was different run out.'

'Could you explain what you mean by "different run out"?'

'Sorry, my English not so good.'

'No, it's very good. Please continue.'

'We have lots of people who run off without paying. You can tell the type. They always sit near the door, and they look different. It's a different run, too. His wasn't like that. His was angry. He was chasing after her, and she was running away. Then he hit her, and she fell to the floor. It was over quickly, as the waiter near the door, a man called Jake, stepped in and pulled him off the lady and wrestled him to the floor. That was it. It was all over quickly, and then the police come. I see it all with my eyes. Definite, I see it.'

I'm living her words as she speaks, overlaying them with my own events.

There are points at which they cross.

I wasn't running out of the restaurant to avoid the bill, but I was chasing Serena.

I was angry at having my evening ruined for something that I hadn't done, annoyed that I'd been unprofessional in regards to my job and career.

'Thank you,' Patricia says.

I guess I'm in trouble by the speed in which David stands, the nonchalant schoolboy act immediately dropped. He likes to attack the person's credibility. Creating doubt for the onlookers.

He's good at it.

Expert.

But not today.

Picking on the quality of her English and its interpretation is misguided and gets us off to a bad start.

I want to tap him on the shoulder and tell him to sit down and let her go.

A twenty-year-old ex-dancer and natural beauty with the face of an angel has fingered me for the malignant narcissistic killer in a way Teddy-Boy, with all his credentials, couldn't get close to.

Then, that question that haunts me returns with its full force.

Am I...

A narcissist.

A murderer.

Or both?

Chapter 35

Myself and my defence team — David and my Dad — head for a quiet spot in one of the side streets near St Paul's. It's the first time David's made space in his diary for anything resembling social. It's been strictly business all the way. Anything friendly disappeared the moment we had our spat.

We walk on.

I get the sense there's an unwritten pact between barristers that the defence head to the right of the Old Bailey and the prosecution off to the left to keep the warring parties apart.

We find a small bistro, sanitise our hands, and then head to an alcove toward the back for even more solitude and a light lunch.

I don't know why, but I suddenly feel like a gangster.

The waitress comes over immediately, and we order sandwiches and non-alcoholic drinks without looking at the menu.

I watch her walk away, thinking of Mila's evidence and reliving that night in Soho—something I've done endlessly since I had to give my retrospective statement.

'Don't worry about this morning,' David says, loosening his tie. 'After lunch, we'll win the momentum back. She's a kid who doesn't know her ass from her elbow.'

I nod, glancing across at my dad, whose skin looks yellower by the day. It's like he's become nicotine-stained before my eyes. I'm starting to worry for him in a way I don't even want to contemplate.

The waitress brings over our coffees and sandwiches, and I make a point not to watch her leave before picking up on David's last comment.

'Any chance we can get Mila off the stand? Just get rid of her?'

'You telling me how to do my job?'

'I'd never do that. You're right that she's a kid, and if you can put doubt into her credibility without bullying her then great. But she looks terrified, and the more terrified she looks, the more plausible she comes across. Serena made a fucking drama and a heap of trouble out of thin air on that night. That's the story, and not this ex-dancer's version of events.'

He nods.

Smiling.

He knows the point I'm making, and I can see he's thought about it.

'A client asking me not to defend him in court is definitely a first.'

'That's not what I'm saying.'

'I know what you're saying. But as my client, I'm telling you that I'm not letting her off the hook because she looks terrified. That's first a tactical, and then it becomes a strategic mistake. If we go back and I tell the court I have no more questions, that's going to stink of defeat and do you no favours now or as the trial unfolds. However, I'll change my tone. Point noted.'

'Thank you. And by the way, you're doing a great job.'

'It's early days, but we're in the driving seat. They don't have a case, or it's weak at best.'

'Patricia's good,' my dad chips in.

'She is, and she's been around for a while, but I'm better.'

It's my turn to smile.

David believes it.

Inside out, upside down.

I wish I had his confidence; maybe I did once, but not any more.

My dad starts to ask David technical questions about the law and this morning's events.

It's the first time I notice my dad's voice has changed. It sounds old, having lost that youthful lilt he's carried for all of his life.

I tune out.

My mind needing the rest from the worry of my father and my pending future. I need my mental strength for the afternoon session ahead.

In the mid-distance, the waitress is serving another customer. She's young and pretty and Mila-like, and it triggers Serena's voice deep within my mind.

'I've taken it on a year's lease. I've been meaning to tell you.'

I've never told David, or anyone, for that matter, how devastated I felt in that moment. I was crushed by the letdown. The curtain in front of our relationship finally dropping. I've carried this fear that the prosecution are right and that I lost my temper and killed her in a fit of rage.

I didn't.

I was shocked at what she'd said and its implications for our future and my life.

I was blindsided.

Like being t-boned in a car.

I just didn't see it coming.

I'm pulling up my trousers, and she's zipping herself up after frenzied, drunken, emotionless sex. I'm thinking about "*He*", and she drops it in like she's asking if I want a cup of tea.

I said nothing.

The shock clamping my mouth.

I stepped away to go to the bathroom or to get a drink of water, anything to give me the time to compute what I heard. Then I saw the front door, and I thought *fuck it*.

Let's get out of here.

Let's stop this now.

I'm sure that's what I did and what I was thinking at the time.

I don't always remember.

But I'm sure she was screaming at me.

Calling me a *coward* and *pussy* for not facing the truth of our relationship. I didn't want to argue any more. I was hurt and offended, and I wanted the space. The pain of her words had unpicked the deception of our relationship. The truth crashing into my life with a force I couldn't hold at bay at that moment.

Then I did it.

I took the keys and didn't look back, the door slamming behind me as the surge of victory spiked my adrenaline.

When my emotions calmed, I was at Dan's, playing the *c'est-la-vie* card.

Move on, I'm telling myself. I'm still young. I have a good job and a nice place. There's plenty of fish in the sea. Dan's taking my coat, and we crack open beers. I tell him I'm convinced Serena's done someone else behind my back, and it's why she didn't want me to help her move. He tells me to chill, that I don't know for sure. That I shouldn't let my mind take me on a wild ride of hell.

He slips into the mate talk.

He's good at it.

Some things are just not meant to be.

I mention the keys.

The victory.

He belly laughs, and I join in.

I'm sure he tells me to throw it away, or if I do patch it up with her, that I pop it back in the same place as if it was always there. Then he gives me one of his "big-bro-man-hugs" that he does to everyone, reminding me of the story when we dated the twins back in the day. How we'd gotten drunk, and the girls had laughed about swapping and how the pair of us didn't have the nerve to pick up on the conversation.

We laughed, and Dan kept reminding me there's a life out there, but it's up to me to take it and to make it work. You can't push a rock up the hill your whole life. Don't become Sisyphus. There are enough stupid people out there wanting to be him as it is.

I agreed with everything he said.

It's why I went to see him.

I wanted to hear that talk.

To tune into the playbook.

He was right about one thing which I had been ignoring. You have to be able to talk in a relationship. You have to trust you can have those big conversations and be safe.

Dropping the bombshell the minute you've stopped having sex is not a conversation.

It's manipulation.

I leave Dan's to go home.

To pack my carry-on for Edinburgh.

But I don't go home.

It's why I'm here listening to Mila crucify me in her cute, broken English.

Then David does what's inbred into him.

He goes on the attack.

It's vicious and nasty and full of intellectual spite.

He can't help himself.

Mila does what she has been threatening to do since she took the stand.

She sobs.

Now I'm the monster again.

The malignant type.

The man who fucks his girlfriend and leaves, stealing her house keys in the process so he can return to smash her head in because he can't stand the idea that she slept with another man and enjoyed it.

Chapter 36

If the simplest plans are the best, then Patricia has laid this one out in baby steps from A-to-Z. She's kept an easy line for the jury to follow: I'm the malignant narcissist prone to rage attacks if my ego is remotely slighted or I'm not given the attention I crave. I have a legacy of problematic relationships, coming to its ultimate flash-point the night I murdered Serena Brown.

Patricia has elegantly laid out the crime scene and the body and got everyone puking into a bucket before returning to my volatile relationships to hone her point.

It's now the turn of the heavy hitters to finish me off and sink me into the abyss of forgotten time.

First up is DCI Simon Carter.

On one level, it's no surprise to see him enter the courtroom, but in the same breath, I'm close to slack-jawed and rubbing my eyes in disbelief that he's finally made it today to nail me once and for all.

He has no problem holding my stare, and I return the compliment.

We are, after all, proxy friends via Serena's death.

He takes the oath and then settles into the seat like a relaxing walrus, shuffling his weight to find a comfortable position. He glances my way again, and I recall the first time he entered my life. The door to my cell opened, and he filled the gap like a bespoke plug, but all I saw was his jovial face and flushed cheeks. I didn't realise his seniority at the time and thought he'd drawn the short straw to tell me the police had made a bumbling mistake and that I was going to be let go, even getting a ride home to placate my annoyance.

I couldn't have been more wrong if I tried.

Carter marched me to an interview room on the next floor. I spent hours there under interrogation. It was my dad who miraculously discovered David; paid his fee, and, between him and a street lawyer, got me out. I'd never thought of it before now, but had my dad not been in London that week and had reacted with the speed and foresight he did, I'd have probably convicted myself through a process of naivety and some latent guilt I've never been able to shake.

I even asked him if he and this was for real.

He smiled, leaning in nose-to-nose, fully aware that the interview recording had stopped.

'You're fucking cooked, you evil bastard,' he said through a tight smirk before leaving me to stew in my own panic.

He's been my nemesis ever since, cloaked in this polite, cordial friendship we've developed.

Patricia continues to play mother hen, holding his hand and walking him through the steps of his investigation from start to finish.

Serena's flat wasn't the leased apartment I had been led to believe, but an Airbnb she'd rented through the website. A fact that is twisting against me.

She'd rented the apartment for two months with an option for a third. Part of the agreement was that a cleaner came bi-monthly, always on a Monday. The owner wasn't a *"he"* but a *"she"* who lived in Singapore. The flat an investment property and nothing more. The cleaner was a Polish girl who had arrived on the Monday morning to find Serena's body. The cleaner screamed on finding Serena. So much so that the owner from the flat two floors above had come down to see what the commotion was all about. It was him who'd called the police. Patricia has already put the Polish girl through the filter, and the girl gave the jury a full account of the horror she'd witnessed. It was a compelling recall, and David dismissed her without questions. A dead body is a dead body, he told me later. A space filler for a desperate prosecution.

I hope he's right.

I have my reservations.

Carter moves on to say his team was called shortly after the police had arrived, and it soon became apparent that there was no forced entry, so the assailant either had a key or was known to Serena.

I pulse at the mention of a key, shifting in my seat.

The wood creaks beneath me.

Carter explains that the crime scene had all the hallmarks of a known associate. Patricia is quick to backtrack and make sure he isn't making assumptions that could come across as a dereliction of duty.

I listen on, anticipating what is coming next and seeing a different man to one I had got to know, or at least professionally. He'd scared the life out of me. Countless nights kept awake as his shadow sat in my psyche. It was my uncertainty about that last night with Serena, combined with a childlike fear of the police.

Watching him perform now, I'm struck by how insecure and robotic he comes across. He has small, shifty eyes, and his skin is sweaty and pallid. It's like he's out of his depth. The courtroom and the judicial system an alien place.

I'm either concentrating too hard or his voice is starting to grate, but the 5th May begins to white flash through my mind.

I left Dan's place with the right intentions. I'm heading for the station. I'm heading home. I want to pack. Get some sleep, if I can, before I have to get up at four am to catch my flight to Edinburgh. I look up from my seat on the train to count the number of stops before I get home when I see I'm heading in the wrong direction.

I'm going back to Serena's.

I'm angry but not crazily inflamed.

Just pissed at being used.

Pissed at being lied to.

The trust we had developed blown up forever.

I have the keys, I tell myself.

I'm going to let myself in and then hand it to her like the mature person that I am. The one she has managed to suppress within me. I'm going to tell her some home truths. Some of her bullshit lies I've been avoiding that need calling out. When I've finished, I'm going to leave the key and tell her we're done.

It's about time I had my say.

It's about time I reclaimed my agency.

I remember feeling sad at my decision but confident it was the right move.

Carter's robotic tone interrupts my thoughts.

'Kieran Harrison quickly became our prime suspect.'

'Why was that?' Patricia asks.

'The resident of the top floor flat and the person who initially called the police, Fredrick Olson, had seen him return at around 11:30 pm on Sunday the fifth. He had heard the defendant calling out to Serena from the street. The defendant had been shouting and getting agitated. Mr Olson had called out to the defendant to be quiet and had been told to "fucking mind your own business, you bald cunt"'.

Heads turn to look my way.

I don't react, waiting for Carter to continue.

He does after gulping water from his glass.

'We had found blood on the door, handle and glass at the rear entrance to the block. The entrance that leads into the communal garden and is only accessible to residents. At the rear of the communal garden, shielded by a high brick wall and dense shrubbery, is a secret door that is keyed and gives direct access to the street. Blood was found on top of that wall by this secret door. The blood was later confirmed as Kieran Harrison's, as was the blood on the handle, door, and glass at the rear of the block. The blood came from a deep cut to the defendant's right palm, sustained while he illegally climbed the wall and entered the residents' communal garden. It became clear early on that both Serena and the defendant had a tempestuous relationship that we believed warranted further investigation.'

More closed thinking.

More lazy investigation from Carter and his team.

What about the mobile phone number they couldn't trace and the eighty-six calls?

What about the two DNA samples on the hand towel that weren't mine?

I want to sigh and shake my head, but I keep my gaze soft, my mind flipping back to that awful night.

I jogged from the station to Serena's place, my impatience carrying me forward. I'm relieved I'm there. Fired up to say my piece and get it all out of me. Cathartic. I search my pockets for those damn keys, and I can't find them. They're gone. I pat my pockets harder, checking my jeans over and over, not wanting to believe my own mind. I can still feel the lightness that overcame me, driven by my disbelief at not finding it. The hollowness growing inside. The nausea and irritation building.

I shouted up to Serena's window.

The light is on.

I see a shadow moving around.

I wonder if *"he's"* returned?

I rage inside, shouting her name, and I'm thinking that I have this responsible job and this big title and a functioning life and here I am, the hurt teenager locked outside my girlfriend's flat screaming abuse.

Serena suddenly looks down at me from her window.

I can see her mouth moving, but I can't hear her other than I'm convinced she's mocking me.

She's enjoying my pain.

My humiliation.

The window to the right and two above opens, and Fredrick Olson sticks his head out.

Carter is right.

I told Fredrick what he could do with himself and that his balding head offended me.

My anger at Serena needed an outage.

He gave me that pleasure.

'You became certain of the motivation after your detailed investigations?' Patricia says.

'That's correct. Sometimes, the death of an individual, particularly in a domestic situation, can be the consequence of a loss of control within the moment. But this wasn't the case. The crime scene was ordered, indicating premeditation. Having interviewed the defendant, it became apparent that he was sensitive to criticism and was particularly defensive about his career. When the photographs came into our possession, we were confident that we had the motivation behind the crime.'

I gulp.

More embarrassed for my father than myself. I would do anything to protect him from this moment, glad my mother and Ryan are half way around the world.

'Your Honour, I'd like to submit eight photographs belonging to Serena as Exhibit E, items one-to-eight. They clearly show Serena having penetrative sex with a sex toy on Kieran Harrison.'

The photographs of that drunken night in St Ives get passed to the first juror and then the next and the next.

Pornhub at my own trial.

My eyes drop to the floor, the shame crushing and too heavy for me to hold.

I don't need an expensive barrister to tell me I look guilty as charged.

Chapter 37

The last time Serena and I spoke bolts through my mind. It's like a foreign language I can't understand. Her voice is dancing across Carter's monotonous tone and Patricia's crafted questions like a three-part harmony.

I'm hit with an unexpected snow-blindness that blurs my vision. I've had this happen to me before. The heat in my body making me tug at my shirt collar. I push at my temples, attempting to ease the pain as Serena's outline appears on the peripheries of my mind. She looks beautiful, sexy, too, in a casual way, lounge pants and a baggy top. It's all soft grey cotton that smells of fresh laundry. Her body is warm like she's been wrapped in a blanket. And she's laughing with me at a joke we've just shared. I can't remember what we were discussing that triggered the moment, but it's followed with a hug and then she mumbles something which I can't decipher, like she whispered the name of a man.

My name, maybe?

Or was it the Formula Two racing driver?

Then she's gone.

Vanished within my next blink before "he" is pushing her against the sofa, ripping at the back of her tights in that way she liked and encouraged. I watch as he takes her from behind, and she turns and smiles that it's okay and that I should relax and enjoy the show.

Join in, maybe?

Why not?

It could be fun.

She turns from me and descends into a personal bliss of pleasure that echoes my pain.

"He" doesn't exist as the owner of the apartment, but "he" does exist in another form.

Carter knows it within his heart.

I know it.

Everyone connected with the case knows it except the twelve people in front of me who matter.

"He" should be easy to find. He's at the end of the phone number the police couldn't trace. A number Serena repeatedly called in the last weeks of our relationship. "He's" out there somewhere, watching, maybe even sitting in the public gallery for my ultimate humiliation.

I cough and squint and palm the front of my forehead.

Through my blurred vision, I spot the judge, and two members of the jury glance my way as I take a stern look from David.

I'm doing the opposite of our game plan.

The hours spent on my court demeanour crumbling away.

I sit back and upright.

Sweat beading down my forehead.

I take a deep breath in an attempt to slow my heart rate, which has begun to beat at an irregular pulse.

I remember telling Fredrick Olson I was going to kick his teeth into the recesses of his brain if he didn't mind his own business. Thank God he'd shut the window. Hearing that threat bounce through the walls of this courtroom, elegantly framed by Patricia, is going to sink me quicker than the Russian waitress.

My concentration, as well as my composure, starts to return as Carter drones on.

I notice he uses the collective —The Team— when he's unsure and then refers to himself when he's confident of his point. Like Teddy-Boy, he hides behind procedural jargon and a monotone delivery. His bluster is designed to hide the truth that he never looked for an alternative option to Serena's death. I fitted into his narrow view. I put the automatic into his workload. His Sherlock Holmes moment was when he worked out that Serena and I had a "fuck-and-fight" relationship. His words, not mine, which told me all I needed about his attitude.

In my more positive moments since my arrest, I'm convinced his investigation against me borders on an injustice, but hearing it now, twisted into a simple idea and run through the prism of Patricia, it has an unquestionable credibility.

His half-hearted attempt at detective work is all propped up by a system that has a diabolical record of prosecuting violent crimes against women and is looking to claw back some ground.

Carter and Patricia go over the moment my blood was found on the wall from climbing the fence, something Fredrick Olson has miraculously caught on camera.

I have a permanent scar that runs diagonally across my palm.

Combined, it's the smoking gun.

But it's not.

Carter is wrong.

It's nothing more than a deep cut that came about from a moment's immaturity and a loss of myself.

That loss only extending to climbing a wall.

Not smashing Serena's head to a pulp.

If you choose to, Olson's footage can be seen in a hundred different ways.

Serena had turned away from her front window. I had waited, expecting her to come down and let me in while I continued to search my pockets for the keys I stole.

'We'll be submitting footage from a personal mobile along with CCTV footage at the end of DCI Carter's evidence,' Patricia tells the court.

A movie trailer leaving the jury wanting more.

The silence tightens the noose further.

I waited outside the front communal door, looking up at the window like a begging dog, slowly realising that Serena was ignoring my pleas. I felt the stab of the insult, and I jumped over the wall at the front of the property. Hot with rage, I ran along the main street and around to the rear of the maisonette. I remember it took an age, like the building had swelled to twice its size. I found the secret door and climbed the wall nearby, ripping open the skin of my palm on the broken glass, which had been cemented into the top ridge as a crude security measure.

My blood was sticky and hot, which should have brought me to my senses.

It didn't.

All it did was enrage me further, and I'm running across the lawn. I reach the rear of the building and peer into the block, my nose pressed hard against the glass of the door. All I see is the empty corridor. No lift. Stairs off to the right. A racing street bike propped against the wall. I call Serena's number from my mobile. It goes straight to voicemail. I'm banging on the door. Banging hard. Fredrick is right. I'm shouting Serena's name, and my blood is streaming down my sleeve and along my arm.

'Serena,' I shout.

'Serena!'

She appears, and it's then I know I've gone too far. Lost something within myself in the craziness of our relationship. Who I am and the values I stand for have been sucked out of me when I wasn't looking. It's identity theft in a way that they never tell you about.

She's standing on the top of the stairs.

Dressed like she's about to go out.

Looking radiant.

Sexy.

She shrugs at me.

Laughs at me.

Then turns.

She turned.

She turned.

I see her in a pool of blood.

It's my blood and not hers.

It's the blood smeared across the glass, and the shadows, and the angle that makes it look like she's smeared in death.

But she's not.

She's alive, and she's walking up the stairs.

Away.

Disappearing from my life in the same way she appeared all those months before at the conference.

'I didn't kill her, you lazy bastard,' I shout across the courtroom, pushing up from my chair as I jab my finger in Carter's direction.

Everyone turns.

The Judge is banging his gavel.

Order in the court. Order in the court.

There is order.

There's no confusion.

It's clear.

Crystal.

I didn't kill her.

The security guard is up and pulling me back into my seat, twisting my neck and arm as he does.

His dream moment of glory handed to him on a plate.

Carter watches on, smiling, and it's hard not to see the smirk creasing Patricia's plump face.

The jury is dumbfounded at what they see.

They're wrong, and so is Carter.

It's the blood that has haunted me for all these months. Serena is coated in it. Death dripping from her. But it wasn't her blood. It was my blood smeared across the glass and not her carpet. The glass door was the barrier between us.

To make the difference between life and death.

I glance across at David.

He's sat motionless, staring into his laptop, waiting for this moment to pass.

I look up and across toward the public gallery, and my dad is mouthing: *it's okay, it's okay...* as the girl next to him gathers her belongings. She stands and heads out, and I realise I've seen her before.

She was blonde then and not a brunette.

She was one of the two girls who gate-crashed our work drinks with Serena.

It was the only friend of Serena I had ever talked to.

Chapter 38

My phone rings. I wished it hadn't woken me, sleep, a luxury that has long departed my life. As I reach for my phone, I know the time and who the caller is going to be.

It's 5 am.

It's David.

I'm right on both counts.

'What's up?' I say.

'I want you to ask yourself a question.'

He sounds like he's in the gym.

'Sure. What is it?'

'I'd like to frame it further before you answer because, to be honest—blatantly honest—I don't fucking care about your answer. The reason I don't care is because it has no direct impact on my life, bar a possible dent to my record, which is going to happen at some point anyway. Are we on the same page?'

'Thanks for the clarity. What's my question?'

'When you get out of bed for the next twenty years, what view do you want to see from the window?'

The phone goes silent in my ear as my father appears in the doorway, yawning and wondering who I'm speaking to at this time in the morning.

'*David,*' I mouth.

I listen back to the call, but David's disconnected.

'Everything okay?' my dad asks.

'He was confirming the morning's agenda. Court starts at nine-thirty. No pre-meet this morning. Nothing to discuss.'

My dad nods, asking me if I want tea.

I'm not sure where the rest of my morning goes. I see David in the courtroom, and he's sulking. My dad looks terrible, and he's clearly sick. I wish Ryan was here. I'm more pissed at myself because apart from taking a severe warning from the judge about my conduct in court, I've gifted the jury a reminder of my anger issues which had been neatly highlighted by my telling off before the proceeding started.

Carter continues where he left off yesterday, Patricia content and happy to be able to drag his evidence into a two-day marathon, giving him the kudos he doesn't deserve. She's doing what she does well. She's making him recap his key points from yesterday, and it somehow comes across as net-new news.

Headlines for the day.

It's beyond tedious to listen to and even more tedious to hear the responses through his robotic drone. But I know Patricia's game. If you say something loud and enough times, it becomes real. Not only to you but to the listeners, and that's the real game she's playing.

Carter and Patricia have long convinced themselves of my guilt.

This is their affirmation love-in, but it's the first time I sense the jury swinging their way.

David has stayed mostly quiet.

He's interrupted Patricia on a few points, but he's let Carter keep the central stage. I wish David would get back to his more aggressive, nit-picking self. I hate it when he does it, but I hate it more when he doesn't. He's sulking at my future's expense.

Patricia breaks my thoughts when she asks for the TV screens to be brought in. There's a sudden flurry of action, and it's like the court is taking a giant stretch and yawn, numbed by Carter's personality. I look behind me to check on my dad. He gives me his customary nod of approval, but really, I was looking for the girl who has been sitting in the public gallery from the beginning.

She's not here, and I wonder why.

I turn back and wait, and then the lights in the court are dimmed, and the position of the TVs gives the jury and the judge a perfect view. I've seen the clips a dozen times in David's chambers as part of the disclosure. The first clip is from Fredrick Olson's phone. It's dark and grainy, but despite the distance, the clarity is more than enough to see it's me climbing the wall, the flinch as I check my sliced palm before I climb down and sprint across the lawn to the back door of the maisonette block. The whole clip is less than forty-three seconds. The longest section is when I pause to investigate my sliced hand. I've often wondered what it really proves. Yes, it's me. That's it. It doesn't show me enter Serena's apartment, something I have always denied. Until yesterday, I've been unsure of my innocence.

Not any more.

As the footage is being played in open court, the image of myself magnifies and takes on a new narrative. I look demented. Determination and anger forcing itself through every pore. Patricia has hit the jury with first impressions, and I see now why David is so angry at my outburst yesterday. It's turning into a multiplier in front of my eyes, and I'm not sure how Carter milks thirty minutes of stage time from a forty-three-second clip.

Patricia moves on to the CCTV from the front of the building. The maisonette itself didn't have any cameras. I was picked up by two independents. One was from a 24-hour Turkish mini-market on the opposite side of the road, and the other was a traffic control camera from the adjacent street. Like Olson's footage, I've seen it more times than I can remember, and again, it takes on a life of its own in the confines of the court. The black-and-white night footage somehow adds its own slice of menace as it shows me arriving and searching my pockets for the keys. I give up and pull out my phone to call Serena. Even David didn't pick up on what I was doing, and I wonder if any of the jury are thinking anything more than me searching for my phone.

I flush with guilt at the real intention that was going through my mind on that night.

I watch on.

I'm getting more agitated, which turns into the anger Patricia is keen to highlight.

Thankfully, you can't see Fredrick Olson appear, although you do see me shouting up at him.

I'm even more thankful that I turned a quarter circle, and it's enough of an angle so I couldn't be lip-read by an expert.

I push at the front door. Rattling it against the lock. More frustration and anger clear to anyone watching. I then jump the small wall and trip on the raised garden, like I was surprised it was there. As I work my way around the building and to the rear wall, it's the second CCTV that picks me up. It's a shorter clip, but it strikes me as the most damning. I'm clearly looking for the route to take me to the rear of the maisonette block. There's an intention and wilfulness that radiates from the screen and screams:

Manic madman with murderous intent.

The clip finishes, and Carter takes a long drink of water like he's toasting his victory in the local pub.

This pause has been deliberately staged to let the footage continue to play in people's minds.

Patricia gets another fifty minutes out of Carter on the two clips. Then they backtrack to show me leaving for the first time at 8:32 pm.

It looks normal, just a man leaving an apartment. I know myself better now than I did a few months ago. I'm full of sadness and anxiety, and I see something I've not seen in the clip before.

A bewilderment in my soul.

A deep loneliness.

A regression into a place of pain I've been hiding from for a long time.

Patricia has the footage fast-forward in pre-defined blocks. It shows another five people arriving at the front door of the maisonette block. They've all been traced and ruled out. Two were residents. One was a Deliveroo Driver dropping off a pizza, and the two others were guests for different residents who were buzzed in and stayed the night. The next person to enter the block was the postman at 7:16 am, who was let in by Fredrick leaving to get a pint of milk from the 24-hour mini-market.

Patricia asks Carter why there's no footage of me leaving. It's a forced question delivered with a natural tone. Carter tells the court that they found my blood further along the wall, where a bench had been dragged across the garden.

He's right, although my memory drops into a hole of blankness from this point on. I vaguely recall using a branch of the nearby tree to help circumvent the security glass, but that's it. I have a total loss of memory from that point on, so I guess Carter is accurate in his painting of the picture. He tells the court how I dropped back into the street. How I used the blind spots from CCTV coverage to help conceal my departure. I was arrested in Edinburgh the following morning as I walked into the terminal after disembarking the plane. They'd already found my bloodstained jacket in the collection bin outside my flat. He makes it sound like I was on the run and not going to one of several meetings that had been in the diary for months.

Patricia thanks him and tells the Judge she's concluded with DCI Carter.

The judge looks across at David, who gives his customary nonchalant pause before slowly standing.

'Good morning DCI Carter.'

There's a bite in David's voice that I've been desperate to hear.

I sigh a moment's relief.

My predator is back.

Chapter 39

'Could you please tell the court how long you've been a detective?'

David's opening question comes out inquisitive and friendly. I immediately spot the shadow tone of contempt. Carter picks up on the undercurrent and is visibly annoyed at not being protected by Patricia.

He glances her way but stays seated and he sighs with irritation.

'Let's think… I've been in the force for nineteen-years, plus. A detective for fifteen or so of those years, mostly in homicide.'

'A dedicated service. Thank you. Which means, if my sums are correct, you'll retire in about eight-months?'

'More like five, not that I'm counting. I'll be moving to the coast with my wife. We've had enough of living in London.'

'I'm sure everyone in this room understands that. Therefore, is it safe to say that this is your last ever court appearance and case?'

'Objection, your Honour. How long DCI Carter has been in the police force and when he retires has no relevance to the unlawful killing of Serena Brown.'

'Your Honour, while the defence recognises DCI Carter's track record and dedicated service to the British public, the line of questioning has deep significance to my client's case, which will become apparent if you will allow me to continue.'

I look at the Judge.

He chews at his bottom lip and then slowly nods for David to proceed. Patricia huffs to herself as she re-sits. It's a habit she'd do well to curb, and she's not in David's league when it comes to keeping her frustrations in check.

'DCI Carter, will this be your last appearance in court as an active detective?'

'There's a good chance that it will be, yes.'

'And how many active cases are you working on right now?'

'None. I've handed one over and am advising on a number of different cases to more junior colleagues.'

'Just so the court is clear. The investigation of Serena Brown's death is the last case that you will have personally led?'

'I hadn't thought of it like that, but yes.'

'In your experience, what is the usual length of a murder investigation?'

'I couldn't possibly answer that. Each case is unique to itself, and that determines the length of the investigation. Some cases are never solved, or they get picked up again ten, fifteen-years later when new evidence comes to light.'

'You appeared in this same court fifteen months ago and was asked the exact same question. Your answer was around three months. Let me jog your memory. It was Crown vs. Lawson, and Lawson was acquitted due to lack of evidence.'

'I apologise. I stand corrected.'

'You do, Detective.'

David's response is crisp and knifes its way through the court.

DCI Carter takes a drink of water and sits more upright. I see him reddening behind the ears. He glances at Patricia and then at the clock on the wall. It's an hour and fifteen minutes until lunch, and he's already been sat in the chair for nearly two hours.

He's going to be hungry by the time David's finished, I think.

'Serena Brown's body was discovered on 6th May at around 8:00 am by the cleaner. It was Fredrick Olson who called the police at 8:14 am after he heard the cleaner screaming hysterically and came down to investigate the disturbance. Mr Olson told the police that he had heard Serena arguing with a man he believed to be her boyfriend on the night before. A man the police soon identified as my client. My client was then arrested as he stepped off the plane in Edinburgh at 9:40 am that same day. You interviewed my client the following day, and charged him with Serena's murder seventy-two hours later. An average three-month investigation condensed into three-days. You must have been fairly convinced of my client's guilt?'

'We were.'

'Were there any other suspects considered during that seventy-two-hour period?'

'No, none.'

'Did it even occur to you that the murderer might be someone other than my client?'

'Yes, of course, but the facts pointing to Kieran Harrison were compelling.'

'Compelling?' David says, shock resonating out of his voice like a sonic boom. He continues. 'Like his blood-covered jacket found in a plastic bag in the bin?'

'Very much so.'

'A jacket that had none of Serena's blood on it, if I'm correct?'

Carter doesn't say anything.

'Detective?'

'There was no trace of any blood from Serena on the defendant's jacket.'

'Were the sexual photos of my client and Serena compelling?'

'Yes, they were.'

David turns to his notes and flicks a page. 'You told the court earlier that: "The crime scene was ordered, indicating premeditation. Having interviewed the defendant, it became apparent that he was sensitive to criticism and was particularly defensive about his career. When these photographs came into our possession, we believed we had the tipping point, the motivation behind the crime."'

'Yes, I remember saying that.'

'When did the photographs come into your possession?'

Carter flushes bright red behind his ears as he reaches for his water.

'At the end of August.'

'At the end of August? That's nearly three months after my client was charged, is it not?'

Carter says nothing, looking to Patricia for support.

'Detective. I asked you a question. Do I need to repeat it?'

'The photographs came to our attention after we had charged the defendant.'

'So if the photographs are post-charge, then what other "compelling" evidence made you believe it was my client who committed this offence?'

'It was the combination of information we had available. The DNA, the CCTV footage, eye-witness accounts of their volatile relationship, the defendant's behaviour during interview, and his attempts at distancing himself from the crime scene.'

'That isn't what you told the court. You said that the photographs "were" the compelling evidence. The "tipping point" in the investigation.'

Carter clears his throat.

'It wasn't my intention to mislead this court. The photographs were the icing on the cake. It confirmed the other "compelling" evidence we had before us.'

'Let's traverse some of those "compelling" points, shall we?'

Carter shrugs.

David smiles.

'While the defence acknowledges my client cut his palm while climbing the rear wall then subsequently banged his hands on the glass of the back door to attract Serena's attention, leaving a substantial DNA footprint of his presence—something he's never denied. But beyond the threshold of the rear door, where is my client's DNA?'

'His fingerprints were everywhere.'

'That is a misrepresentation of the facts. My client had been in Serena's apartment for less than an hour on the Sunday, spread over two short visits. He had a guided tour when he first turned up and then returned after their late lunch to have consensual sex. The fingerprints found on the door handles, a wine glass, and a wooden chair are consistent with nothing more than a cursory time spent in the apartment.'

'That's not how we interpreted the evidence.'

David smiles and then continues.

'With the depth of cut my client sustained in his hand climbing the wall, wouldn't you say that it is unusual that his blood trail stopped at the back door?'

'It's our assumption that he wrapped his jacket around the cut, stemming its flow, once Serena had let him in.'

'The crime scene officer's assumption was my client wore gloves?'

Carter says nothing.

'I can have the court stenographer repeat back the conversation if you like, detective?'

'We believe that the defendant either wrapped his jacket around his cut hand, or potentially used gloves, or a combination of both.'

'My client admits that he used his jacket to stem the flow of blood once he had re-climbed the wall to leave the garden. He needed to do this as the Uber driver wouldn't let him in the car. And as you rightly point out, the inside of my client's jacket was covered in blood to the point of saturation, as the jury has already seen. Where did you find his jacket, Detective?'

'His bloodstained jacket was wrapped in a plastic bag and then hidden at the bottom of the collections bins at his residence.'

'Did you find any gloves in that plastic bag?'

'No, we didn't.'

'Did you find Serena's mobile phone in that plastic bag?'

'No, we didn't.'

'And you say the plastic bag was hidden?'

'Yes, it was pushed to the bottom and forced behind another black refuse bag.'

'When was the plastic bag with my client's jacket in it discovered?'

'At about 9:00 am on the Monday morning.'

'The sixth of May?'

'Yes.'

'Was his jacket in a black plastic bag or a see-through one?'

'A see-through one.'

'And when is bin collection day at my client's residence?'

'Monday mornings.'

'At about what time?'

'Around 10:00 am.'

'Is it not, therefore, feasible that other residents had put their black refuse bags ready for collection into the refuse bin, thereby pushing my client's bag to the bottom?'

'The bag was pushed hard into the corner. The photographs that have been shown to the court are clear enough.'

'Clear enough that they don't show any gloves or mobile phone. And if this was the methodically pre-planned murder of Serena Brown as you have tried to portray. It strikes me as a terrible risk to dispose of a bloodstained jacket at his home in a see-through plastic bag when he had the opportunity to dispose of it in a hundred other ways. In fact, you are wanting the court to believe that my client skilfully disposed of Serena's mobile phone, gloves used in her killing, but gleefully left a bloodstained jacket in a place most likely to be searched by any competent police officer.'

Carter stiffens, his jaw locked tight.

'The jacket was clearly hidden. Had it been taken in the refuse collection, we would have never found it. It was a lucky break that a competent officer searched the bins before the collection happened.'

David keeps his smile.

'Two DNA samples were found that belonged to two separate men on the hand towel in Serena's bathroom?'

'That's right.'

'It is your belief that two separate individuals washed their hands and then wiped them dry on her towel. One of the individuals had left a small trace of blood, probably from a nick on his hand or finger. His blood type was O Positive.'

'That's our assumption, yes.'

'So if these two DNA samples didn't belong to my client, then who did they belong to?'

'We don't know.'

'Your Honour, I would like to submit to the court Serena Brown's mobile phone bill for the last month of her life as exhibit thirty-nine: 1a.'

David turns back to Carter.

'For the court, Serena Brown made eighty-six calls in the last month of her life to a mobile number the police have been unable to trace. She spent more time on the phone with this person than she did with her boyfriend, my client, in that period. Is it possible that one of the DNA samples found on the hand towel belonged to the person on the other end of that phone number?'

'Objection, your Honour. That's conjecture from my learned friend. I request that it be struck from the record and that DCI Carter is excused from having to respond to that question.'

The judge nods without a blink of internal debate.

'Defence, please re-frame or move on from this questioning.'

David continues to stand, holding his space, his loose Orca grin locked onto his face.

His giant triceps flexing under his gown.

His eyes telling everyone his mind is churning through its gears.

'Fredrick Olson called in the crime and immediately told the police of the argument the night before with a man he thought was Serena's boyfriend. My client was traced, and the police mistook his flight to Edinburgh as a man on the run. They were unaware that my client had flown to Edinburgh fifteen times in the last year, all on business, and travel is very much part of his normal business activities. The meeting he had in Edinburgh had been in the diary for months. Fredrick Olson made an assumption on an argument he witnessed. The police made an assumption on my client's departure and a blood-stained jacket they found in his refuse bin. That assumption has been followed through by yourself to the point of inventing mythical gloves. However, I put it to you that the truth is very different. The truth is there is no direct DNA evidence to link Serena's death to my client. By your own admission, you have not entertained the possibility of other suspects. While I concede to my learned friend that my question relating to the DNA on the hand towel and the phone number was conjecture; it doesn't negate the fact that you were unable to trace the person Serena called over eighty times. Or trace the persons to whom the DNA samples belong. People who clearly visited Serena's flat in and around the time of her death. I put it to you that you have fast-tracked this investigation to put one final feather in your cap before you retire, creating a deeply flawed and negligent investigation?'

Carter slowly smiles, and I give him credit for taking the hit to his integrity with a calmness I don't think even David expected.

Carter leans forward in the same way he did when he told me I was cooked.

His eyes pinched.

His skin sweaty and pallid.

'There was never any need to waste valuable police resources. Kieran Harrison's body language in the film footage was clear. Everybody who entered that maisonette block after 8:30 pm has been traced and discounted as a suspect. The only person who could have killed Serena Brown and who had the motive and the access is stood in the dock over there.'

He lifts his arm and points directly at me as twelve heads of the jury swivel my way.

Chapter 40

Outside, I thank David for his morning's work.

He shrugs, indifferent.

'It's my job,' he says, reaching for his phone. 'Sorry, but I have to make an important call. I'll see you back in court at one-thirty.'

He doesn't wait for my answer, and I watch him sulk off. We've never really connected beyond the superficial, and we're not going to now. I've grown more comfortable with our indifferent relationship since my trial started. His internal battle for perfection might prove enough to dig me out of this hole. He's welcome to sulk on my watch if he wants.

My dad and I find a small cafe near St Bartholomew's Hospital. We order ham sandwiches and coffee, and then I ask him outright if there's something he's not telling me about his health. He looks like shit. His eyes are bloodshot, and his skin is positively jaundiced.

I tell him he could audition for a kid's bath duck.

He forces a smile and tells me it's a lack of sleep and the obvious worry for his one son.

I tell him he has two sons.

His one son, he repeats.

He seems to have forgotten that he's staying with me, and I'm witnessing his sleeping pattern. Even more so as I'm getting close to zero myself. He sleeps soon after we finish dinner until he wakes in the morning. That's close to nine hours straight. Double what I'm averaging.

I don't push it. I can't today. I have too much to contend with as it is. So once again, I smile and agree and let it go, hearing an old man quiver in his voice rather than the youthful dad I remember.

Our conversation turns to Ryan. It doesn't take a genius to know my dad misses him badly. I tell him he should go see him in Sydney once the trial is over, no matter what the outcome. I make a lame joke that he'll know where to find me if things don't go my way. My attempt at humour falls flat as the duck joke, and I regret saying anything.

We shift gears, circling back to Carter's performance. He's not the polished article he presents, but despite everything, he's had the upper hand so far. The photographs of my bloodstained jacket stuffed into a plastic bag have smoking gun written all over them, and he's won that battle.

Like all of Serena's Instagram photographs, pictures do lie.

We finish our food and head back, the sun high and warm for October.

We go through the metal detector, sanitise our hands, and head back to court 14 in plenty of time.

Being late is not an option.

I watch the jury enter.

Nobody looks at me.

I'm sure they've been told not to.

It's the "solemn crew shuffle", as my dad calls it.

Then, ushers bring in a large model of the streets and maisonette block in which Serena was killed. It takes three of them to carry it. I've seen computer 3D-generated images of the same model but not its physical representation. It's theatrical and old-school. Its size captivates everyone's attention. I admire David's sense of showmanship. It's a natural streak of his personality, as is his aggression.

It's maybe one and the same thing, I think.

The model is painted gunship grey, except for two sections that are painted in fluorescent yellow. The first is a large triangular patch in the garden at the rear of the block. It represents the area that Olson's phone camera captured and a bit beyond. The second is a street to the right side of the maisonette block that bleeds into a thin line which stops outside the main front doors.

I'm sure nobody's noticed the extra thin slither of yellow.

It's the ace in our sleeve.

Or so we hope.

The only other colour is a dotted red line and a red arrow that points to the tube station. There's one figurine on the top balcony. It represents Fredrick Olson. A single piece of string shows the camera angle from Olson's phone and stops in the centre of the yellow section at the rear.

I look across at Carter, who eyes the model with both interest and contempt.

He twitches an uneasy glance towards Patricia, who mouths there's nothing to worry about.

A natural silence falls, and David stands into it.

He introduces the model and then briefly describes the layout to the court. He takes on a new persona, the one I wanted him to use when cross-examining the Russian waitress. He's the parental father and dedicated teacher, patiently explaining a difficult concept to his flock.

He's warm and inviting.

A gentle giant.

David turns towards DCI Carter. 'Detective, I'm going to run the footage we saw this morning and compare it to the model we have here in front of us. If at any point you disagree with what I say, can you please let the court know. I will take your silence that you agree with the statements I make.'

Carter nods.

David takes the remote for the television screen and starts to replay the footage from this morning. At each point, he corresponds what the jury sees on the screen to its location on the model.

I live it all again.

The slow jog from the train station.

The embarrassment at witnessing a person I never thought was me.

The search for Serena's keys.

David occasionally glances at Carter for signs of any interruption.

It doesn't come.

Of course not.

There's nothing to object to, and David is on point. This is a physical representation of Carter's statement from this morning.

Verbatim.

The playback.

If Carter interrupts, he's got to be damn sure he's right. Otherwise, David is going to unpick Carter's Statement and do his best to make him look the lazy detective he is.

Perjury, our end goal.

David moves on to the back garden.

We switch from the CCTV to the footage from Fredrick Olson's phone.

It's the same routine.

The footage finishes.

'Mr Olson is five floors up from the back door. He has no direct sight on whether my client entered the building or not.'

David looks at Carter, who says nothing.

Olson has already made a statement confirming the same.

I stare at the back door of the apartment block on the model.

When Serena came down the stairs, she was dressed as if she was about to go out.

To a party.

For a date.

She had newly applied make-up.

Red lipstick, bright and shiny.

A tight dress, sheer stockings.

It flamed my anger, and I banged on the glass, smearing more of my blood.

Then she disappeared out of sight.

Or did she let me in for a second time?

I used to think that she had.

That thought has left the internal question mark which has hung so heavy across my mind and heart for all these months.

I no longer think that she did.

She had come down for one reason only.

It was to laugh at my helplessness.

It was her idea of fun.

It was part of her spiteful behaviour and one I'd witnessed her commit to others.

It's the same with my mother.

Ryan, too.

I suddenly hear his voice over-lacing Serena's.

My brother is laughing at me in the exact same way. It's the same full-throttle of disregard and disrespect for who I am and what I stand for. My mother has gone to grab him, slap him because he's refusing to do what he's told. He ducks out of her way and continues to bait her. He wants to inflame her anger to the point of exploding. He's pushing me in between as a shield so he can continue his game.

It's his idea of a joke.

I remember I raised my hands in front of me.

Southpaw style.

It's the only way not to get hurt in the war zone that is erupting now my father has left the house.

Then I'm suddenly relaxed.

The pauses in between David's voice have a pleasant warmth as a fresh focus descends within like I've had a solid eight hours of sleep.

That moment all those years ago is clear in my mind.

I'm not the shield.

I'm the aggressor.

I pushed, too.

I did it because I was angry and scared and wanted to protect my brother. I wanted to show him that I cared for him and that we could be the true brothers we had once been. Not the splintered pair we'd become.

I find a surge of strength.

A fearlessness I wasn't used to.

My mum stumbles backwards.

Followed by a thud.

A deep, slug-like sound that is thick and heavy.

I see blood.

Serena has reappeared. She is laughing at me and telling me that history has repeated itself.

A fate my character was destined to endure.

That's why I'm here.

I had it coming.

Chapter 41

'Do you know what the yellow sections indicate?' David asks DCI Carter, breaking my reverie.

'Why would I? It's your model.'

His response gets a chuckle from the court, and the judge gently bangs his gavel to remind everyone to pay attention.

David gives it a beat and then says,

'Thank you for confirming. The yellow sections on this model denote zones where there are no stationary cameras to record any activity. That includes camera doorbells and home security units.'

He lets that sink in, staring at Carter, who must know this as part of our disclosure, but it looks to have caught him off-guard.

David continues.

'I will reframe my statement. If someone were to approach the front door of the maisonette block where Serena lived—from the Green Street side—there is no CCTV that would have recorded their coming or going. The police have traced the five people who entered the block via the coverage we have already witnessed after my client initially left at 8:30 pm. These individuals have been ruled out of any involvement in the death of Serena Brown, which the defence agrees is accurate. However, this doesn't exclude the "possibility" that a person or persons could have entered the property from the Green Street side undetected?'

'That's not possible,' Carter barks out, catching everyone by surprise.

Patricia glances at her witness.

'Why is that, Detective?'

'The front door closes with a heavy bang. It's annoying to the residents and had been reported to the management company for repair on several occasions. We interviewed all the residents who were home on the night of Serena's death, and they all responded to low foot traffic on the night in question.'

David allows himself a small sunshine smile.

'Have all the residents had audiograms to ascertain their hearing ability?'

'Objection, your Honour. The defence is baiting DCI Carter. The police rightly interviewed all the residents within the maisonette block. It's a small residential block and has its own community. It is more than reasonable to ask if they heard or saw anything unusual on the night in discussion.'

'Your Honour, while I agree with my learned friend that DCI Carter and his team are well within their rights to ask the residents if they "heard" or even "saw" anything unreasonable on the night of Serena's death. However, it is unreasonable to expect this court to believe that nobody else other than the five people already discussed could have entered the property based on the hearing of the residents alone and the noise of a broken front door.'

The judge nods.

'Please continue Counsel.'

'Thank you, your Honour.'

Carter scowls.

'Detective, you told the court this morning that my client used the "blind spots" at the rear of the building to aid his departure unseen?'

'That sounds correct.'

'That's exactly what you said.'

Carter shrugs.

'A "blind spot" is a view that is obstructed, thereby creating a space that can't be seen from a particular vantage point. That's the Oxford English Dictionary definition. If we look at this model, that is not the case here. There is no CCTV at the rear of the maisonette block or in the street at the rear of the garden. While I admit this is unusual for London, it is the case here. Therefore, it can't be labelled as a "blind spot". It is, in fact, a mostly open but unmonitored space, as can be seen by the yellow sections before you. Your statement of this morning makes it sound as if my client was attempting to hide his departure by using natural obstructions such as trees or walls. I put it to you that he just happened to find himself in an "unmonitored" zone. If this is the premeditated crime you would have this court believe, then why didn't my client arrive the same way he left or come in via Green Street, allowing him to potentially slip through the front door undetected? Furthermore, why call an Uber? He was effectively calling his own eye-witness to his alleged crime. My client's actions on that night are simply those of a man who was deeply frustrated because his girlfriend wouldn't let him back into her property—a property he never entered.'

Carter says nothing, staring at the model like an envious younger sibling waiting for the opportunity to smash it to bits.

'That's why we are fortunate to have Fredrick Olson's footage,' Carter finally says.

'Detective. My client called an Uber nine minutes and twenty-eight seconds from the moment Fredrick Olson stopped filming him in the communal garden. So, in nine minutes and twenty-eight seconds, you want this court to believe that my client was let in by Serena Brown at the rear of the building. He then went up into her flat, killed her in the manner already described, cleaned up any DNA trace, including blood from a deep wound to his hand, not only inside her apartment but in the communal areas within the block, then left her apartment, unseen, climbed over the garden wall and called an Uber?'

Silence.

The court's eyes on Carter.

He sits impassive.

'That's exactly what we are saying.'

'So where are these gloves my client wore to clean up after he supposedly killed Serena, along with the cleaning products and cloths that he used?'

Carter says nothing.

'I again put it to you, Detective, that they don't exist because my client never re-entered Serena Brown's property. The re-entering of her property by my client is a crucially important fact and one this investigation has not established beyond any unreasonable doubt. No more questions, your Honour.'

I should be happy, watching Carter squirm in his seat. His laziness looks to finally be unpicked.

But I'm not.

It's the first time I've seen the end of Fredrick Olson's footage frozen on the screen. I've disappeared out of view, and Olson has lifted his phone to press stop. All you can see is the empty garden, the wall, and the residential street beyond.

In the grainy black of the frame, there's an outline of a car I recognise.

Or think that I do.

There's a growing nausea at what I'm looking at.

The car is an old BMW Tourer.

And, if I'm right, it belongs to my best mate.

Dan.

Chapter 42

The Judge breaks us for the day with a reminder to the jury not to discuss the case. His tone leaves an unexpected sombre note and adds to what I see as another incremental win in the case for Carter and the prosecution.

I look across at David to catch his eye.

He ignores me, hurrying to pack his files and laptop.

I'm allowed to leave the dock, and I rush out and corner him in the corridor before he disappears through a door I'm not allowed to enter.

He's visibly annoyed.

'I'm sorry, Kieran, I'm working on another case, and I need to make a call. I can call you tonight if it's anything urgent? By the way, this was a good day for us. We might have even clawed back some of your outburst.'

I'm not sure I agree, but my mind is somewhere else.

'I need a copy of the last frame from Fredrick's phone—the one that shows the empty garden. It's the moment before he stops recording,' I add.

David gently frowns, and I can see that he's unsure if he heard me right, semi-distracted by the phone in his hand.

'I can't,' he says. 'It's evidence and currently the property of the court.'

'It's one picture. There's nobody in it.'

He ignores me, turning to walk away as he starts to dial a number on his phone.

I step in front of him and clasp my hand around his mobile device.

'I need a copy of that final clip—today. It's blank. The chances that anyone will even know it's from Olson's phone are next to nothing. It's been shown as evidence on more than one occasion. It's one picture. Of a garden. It harms no one. Please!'

We stare at each other.

It's uncomfortable.

The tension sitting in the pit of my stomach waiting to burst.

He makes a point of looking at my hand. I release my grip from his phone, but I don't move. I can see him thinking that I'm guilty and he's defending a murderer. I wouldn't get too moralistic about it, I want to tell him, as he's going to be making a habit of it going forward.

I don't.

'It's important,' I add. 'Potentially, life-changingly important!'

'Why?'

'Let's say it helps with my memory.'

'There's nothing to see.'

'There's a garden. With trees. I like trees,' I add.

His eyes flick from left to right. He doesn't believe me, and he's right not to because I'm lying through my front teeth. Any hope that I had that our relationship might bounce off the rocks into calmer waters was blown up the second I gripped his phone and blocked his path.

'I'll get it for you tomorrow.'

'I need it now. Charge me overtime. Charge me double. I need it tonight.'

'Okay!' he says, huffing. 'You can pick it up from my chambers in an hour. I won't be there, but my paralegal will have it ready. I'm charging you for it— double rate.'

He walks off, redialling the number of his new client.

My dad stares at me, unsure about what just happened. Before my dad can pry, I ask him if he'll go and pick up the picture from David's chambers. I'm still under curfew, and I can't be certain I'll make it to Lincoln's Inn Fields and back home in time. My dad nods that he'll do it, and I blow out hard as we head our separate ways.

It's good to be outside, and I sense a freedom I haven't had for a while.

I stop for a quick beer near my flat before I go home, my thoughts from the day pounding hard against the inside of my skull.

My dad doesn't make it back to mine until well after eight, so I was right not to do the trip myself. He places the envelope on the table and says nothing, like he didn't even make the journey. I quickly check that the paralegal had printed off the correct frame.

She did.

My dad rustles up a light supper of spaghetti. We chat about the day's event, keeping it surface-level, even managing a genuine smile at Carter's expense. The big man sweating under the court lights and David's barrage was a small joy.

The conversation inevitably turns to my mother and then Ryan. My case has been the great leveller, bringing them back into the fold of conversation in a more open and honest way than they have been for years.

I still haven't mentioned the letter and my mother's amended will. I hint she'll probably get married again. My dad laughs out loud, saying he can't believe that it hasn't happened already and, like the will, I leave it there.

It's the first time he voices that he's scared he'll never see Ryan again or even his pending grandson or daughter.

The way he says it scares me, and I make a promise to myself that if I get off next week, the first thing I'll book is tickets for Australia once my passport is returned.

I head for the shower and then into bed, taking the envelope with me.

I slip under the duvet and slowly pull the image from its sleeve.

The quality is fuzzy, blurred, and black-and-white, the original being in colour.

But it's okay.

It was a rush job, done via a Xerox, but it's enough for my needs.

I was right, not that I doubted myself. In the far corner of the frame is an old BMW Tourer, 5-Series. The car is easily fifteen years old, and I need to check how many iterations of the design have come into place since then.

It's the same year as Dan's car, no mistake.

But is it his?

I stare hard, wishing I had a magnifying glass, although I'm not sure it would make a difference. I can't see the license plate. It's obscured by the car behind. That would have nailed it in one. Life is never that simple. I know Dan's car has a large dent on the driver's side. He let his brother use the car, who took a corner too tight and hit a metal barrier. Dan never did get it fixed. That's Dan. He's not into cars. He'd rather spend his money on travelling and good food. He'd drive a van if Hatti would let him. The angle I have is the passenger side. I recall his pet Beagle chewed the passenger seat headrest one Christmas when he double-parked and rushed into a shop to buy some booze.

Dan joked it would have been cheaper to have gotten a parking ticket.

It's another thing he's never bothered to get fixed.

I stare hard at the picture.

It's me who has the blind spot now.

There's a lamppost that is perfectly placed between the car and the rear garden. It blocks the angle into the passenger side of the car. Even in the black-and-white picture, I can tell the car is a silver-fog-grey, the colour of Dan's car.

I don't want to believe it, but my gut reaction is telling me it's his car.

But it doesn't make sense.

My instinct has repeatedly let me down since Serena came into my life.

Even today, I threatened the one man who's trying to keep me out of prison.

His words about my future seep into my mind again.

'What view do I want to see out of my window when I get up in the mornings?'

I think of the eighty-six calls Serena made in the last month of our relationship to a number traced to the London borough of Camden. That's almost twenty-two calls a week. Dan lives in the London Borough of Islington, which borders Camden. In truth, he's more the Hackney end than the Camden end. Anyway, the number wasn't his, so I don't know why my mind is flipping that way. He loves Hatti. He always has. He chased her into submission, and he's been nudging her to start a family for years. I'd put him at the bottom of the list of guys I know who'd cheat on their wife.

And is that what I'm saying?

Dan was seeing Serena behind my back?

I look back at the picture.

My mind doing its utmost to turn on my friend.

'Do you want to tell me about the photo?' my dad says from the threshold of my door.

'Not really.'

'You didn't kill her, son. Don't ever forget that.'

'How do you know? How can you be so sure?'

'As your dad, I know you better than you know yourself. You're innocent.'

I smile at him, looking back at the picture in my hands.

I'd stake my life that it's Dan's car I'm seeing in the picture.

If it is.

Then why is it parked there on the night of Serena's murder?

Chapter 43

My dad and I enter The Old Bailey, and I watch him slope off to the public gallery. His head is bent forward, shoulders hunched. He looks as miserable and as tired as I have ever seen him. We barely spoke over breakfast or even on the journey here, both of us preoccupied with our own worlds. I'm sure it's my fault. I've still not been able to bring myself to tell him about Dan's car. Or my mother's will, or even her marriage to Henry, for that matter. I don't know why I'm holding it all in other than I'm exhausted, and it's hard enough to contain the stress as it is without adding additional layers.

I take my seat in the dock and look up to get my customary wave from him. I had a text from Hatti this morning to say she'd be wishing me luck from the public gallery. I see her enter and sit next to my dad.

I get two supportive smiles this morning.

I need all I can get.

I look for the girl, who I presume was Serena's friend, but she's not been back since my outburst. The rest of the gallery is a mixture of ages and sexes. I don't know anyone else. Reporters, law students, maybe? No one jumps out at me as Serena's immediate family or friends. I hate to think it, but the lack of outward grieving for her passing is both pitiful and tells its own story. I've never wanted to believe it, but she did have a shadow life, one beyond us.

What that was and who it involved, I've no idea, and I wonder if I ever will.

The one thing I'm now sure of is that the person she presented wasn't the true Serena but a false version of someone else.

I wonder if she even knew who she was beneath the carefully crafted veneer that I had grown to love.

The scrape of chairs starts the same routine and brings me back to the now.

The court goes quiet.

The judge enters.

Followed by the "solemn crew shuffle".

Patricia calls Fredrick Olson as the first witness of the day. He's the prosecution's next big hitter after Carter. Olson is taller and older than I remembered. I first saw him only briefly, in the dark, five floors up. He's bald with no eyebrows, like he's had, or has Alopecia. He has the aquiline Nordic looks that go with his last name. He's dressed like he's going to a high-end nightclub. He drips femininity like it's a badge of honour. There's a jolliness, even excitement, at his moment of fame.

As he takes the oath, I see he's a talker and likes to gossip, and he's not going to paint himself into a corner with jargon and procedural talk. I'm sure he has hundreds of friends, and he's going to dine out on today for the rest of his life with the smoking-gun footage he took to back up his pending Oscar performance. I can hear him now, his story bloating with each new audience: *'These are the moments before that lovely young woman was killed. I could tell immediately he was trouble. I told her to stay away from him.'*

Patricia knows his type and relaxes him in, warming him up and allowing his natural effervescence to percolate through. It's all painfully predictable, or to me, anyway.

He heard me continually ring the buzzer and then start to shout up to Serena. His lounge is two floors directly above Serena's, and because noise travels up, he got the full acoustic version. Of course, he was shocked and offended when I verbally abused him, like he's never heard the f or c-word before. He even thought about calling the police, convinced that had he come down to confront me, his own safety would have been in danger, hence why he stayed indoors.

David objects that Olson couldn't have possibly known my mood, but the judge lets it stand. My attitude and mood are exactly what prompted Olson to take his award for cinematographer of the year, rather than the stroke of serendipity it turned out to be.

A key point that has, for now, been lost on the court.

He talks on.

His excitability growing.

He's a smoker—a habit he's been trying to break—but he went to his balcony to have a quick puff before bed. It gets a laugh, as it sounds like he's smoking hashish, and he laughs at his own faux pax. The judge bangs his gavel to bring back the court's attention, and Olson blushes as he trips over himself to explain he meant cigarettes and not anything illegal.

He apologises to the judge.

Olson gets his thoughts in order. He explains how he saw a man from the corner of his eye enter the street where the garden wall curves. It was the speed and intent that caught his attention, and once he focused, he immediately knew it was me by my outline. It's then he rushed inside to grab his phone and start filming. He adds that I must have been "pumped" because there's glass cemented along the top of the wall as a security measure, and it was clear I'd hurt myself as I climbed up and dropped into the garden and that I looked unperturbed by the pain the glass had inflicted.

David objects again that the witness couldn't possibly have known my state of mind and if I was "pumped" or not or even in pain. But like the first comment, the judge lets it ride, and I feel this poisonous gossip, with his lucky footage, turning the thumb-screws on my life.

He tells Patricia that I ran toward the back door with the speed of an athlete. He then heard me banging on the door but couldn't see me, which is why he stopped filming. He continued to listen hard. He could hear Serena arguing with me from behind the

door, and that's when he heard the door open, and me
enter the block.

Categorically, he adds.

Patricia leaves that one to hang.

Members of the jury glance my way.

I keep my gaze as neutral as I can and stare
on, his venomous words cutting through me.

I want to ask him what we were arguing
about because I don't remember us discussing or even
arguing about anything. I remember her dress. How
stunning she looked. I recall her coming down the
stairs. One foot delicately placed in front of the next. I
remember her sneering at my desperate pleas.

But most of all, I remember her walking away.

I see her image through my blood, which is
smeared in thick streaks across the wired glass of the
communal door.

We didn't talk.

She didn't open the door.

He's wrong, and he's misled the court.

His memory is playing tricks on him, and he
wants to believe his own narrative, devoid of a truth
filter.

'You distinctly heard the back door being
opened, and it was Serena who you believe let him in?'

'Yes. The defendant was demanding to be let
in. I could hear Serena saying something along the
lines of "Be quiet, you'll wake the block". That sort of
thing. I don't remember the exact words. Then the
door opened. I know it opened because the base of

the door swells in the hot weather, and it scratches across the tiled floor. It's fingernails on a blackboard moment. You can ask anyone in the block. It's worse than the front door—and that's bad. The sound echoed up like a bird's squawk, which is why I know Serena had let him in.'

He stares at me, defiant, like he's finally got his revenge because I insulted his ego all those months ago by telling him to go fuck-himself.

He's wrong on all his key points but all I see is a man who is utterly convinced that I killed Serena. He's the prosecution's star witness. It's about lasting impressions and I wonder if Patricia had reservations about Carter and she needed Olson to smash any flickers of doubt out of the park.

Olson takes a large gulp of water, and Patricia allows him his moment in the sun before gently moving on to the morning when the cleaner's screams made him think she was being attacked.

He came running down the stairs, entering Serena's apartment to see Serena's body twisted near the coffee table, blood all over the carpet.

He immediately knew she was dead.

It was obvious, he adds.

Patricia thanks him for being a conscientious and brave citizen. She tells him that her learned friend will have some questions. It comes across as a warning not to be intimidated and to stick to the facts because the facts are fucking gold dust.

David thanks Patricia as he stands.

He lets some of the tension fade from the room and focuses his cross-examination on the moment I supposedly entered the maisonette. He reiterates the point that Fredrick couldn't have seen me. His balcony is fifty metres up with no direct sight. How could Fredrick be sure of what he heard with the street sounds, cars, and a flight path above?

Fredrick's not having it.

He's sticking firm.

He knows what he knows, and he's not some young Russian waitress who is about to break down in tears.

His bitchiness is enjoying the banter.

He's Fredrick Olson.

A gossip with integrity.

I tune out of the spat.

I've lost this one, and David should leave it, but that's not what I'm thinking any more. I suddenly recall that Hatti was away the weekend Serena moved. Hatti had gone to see her mother, and Dan was home alone. He'd been busy setting up his new business and was glad of the space, but he's not a man who likes to be on his own. His high energy that continues to bubble beneath his skin needs an ever-present audience. He'd normally organise a boy's night out or, at the very least, a few beers with me to reminisce over our single days.

He didn't.

I'm wondering why.

Did he have another engagement?

A better offer?

A couple of rounds in Serena's bed?

Chapter 44

I'm agitated and want to speak with David. He's managed to slip out of court before we've had time to discuss Olson's performance and the impact it's had on my case.

'He's on your side,' my dad finally says.

'I'm beginning to have my reservations.'

We head outside to get some fresh air. I want to clear the fog from my mind.

We walk into Paternoster Square, turning south towards the Thames, our silence from this morning returning between us.

'Are you going to tell me about what's so important about the picture I picked up? Or are you going to keep it a secret like you have about your mother's marriage to Henry?'

I'd smile if I wasn't so angry.

At myself.

The world.

Anyone who falls into my immediate vicinity.

It's an emotion I've not been able to shake since my arrest. It's ageing me and frying my brain in the process, fast-tracking me into dementia. I need to break free from the emotion. To get back to the person I was before Serena entered my life.

'I've been meaning to tell you about Henry. Sorry.'

'This isn't the time to start wanting to do things on your own.'

I bring my hands to my face and rub hard at my eyes as we stop at the beginning of Millennium Bridge. I lean on the rail, staring at The Thames curve its way towards Canary Wharf.

I glance back at my father. A man who'd fight to the death for me.

I'm unsure if I'm worth it.

Even if he can help me any more or that I want him to.

Perhaps I've reached that point of no return.

'What's up, son? If you can't tell your old man, who can you tell? I've never judged you, and I'm not about to start now.'

I reach out and grab his hand, and we share the pause.

Our history passing between us in milliseconds, our bonds locking tighter together.

'What I'm about to say doesn't make sense, which is why I haven't said anything. In the split second before Olson stops filming, all you see is the rear of the garden and the immediate street behind the wall. In the corner of the frame, there's a car. It's a car I've seen hundreds of times. A car I've been in hundreds of times. It's Dan's car. Or I think it is.'

Silence.

People pass us by.

The Thames flows peacefully below us.

'Dan? Your friend from university? His car…
parked at the back of Serena's?'

'It looks like his car. It doesn't make sense. Or
it didn't. But it could be. I mean… I don't know what I
mean, frankly.'

'You saw Dan's car at Serena's?'

'I didn't. It's in the picture. The more I look at
it, the more I'm convinced it's Dan's car. And if it is—
what is it doing there? Or, more to the point, what was
Dan doing there? And then it gets fucking weird
because if it is his car, then the only conclusion I come
to is that he was there to see Serena. But what am I
saying? They were having an affair behind my back?
That he killed her? That he managed to sneak past the
CCTV and enter her apartment without being heard or
seen. But why would he do that? Dan's in a great
place. He has the love of his life. He and Hatti have just
had a baby. His own business is doing fantastic. He's
getting married in two months. Dan has always
wanted what he's got. It's what he's worked toward
his whole life. I've known him for fifteen years, and
he's not the type to sneak around having affairs. But…
it's his car. I know how this will sound coming from
me. I'm desperately wanting a way out, and I'm
prepared to throw anyone under the bus, including my
best friend, if needed.'

'You have to tell the police—today.'

'You mean have a power-chit-chat with DCI
Carter? He's going to laugh himself to death if I do.'

'He has to take it seriously.'

'No, he doesn't. The photograph is blurred at best. He's going to do what he's done from the beginning. He'll pretend he's all official and by the book, but his mind is made up. I'm guilty, and that's the end of it. The only thing Carter is going to do is go to the pub for a drink.'

'Speak with David. He'll know how to handle this.'

'He pretty much ignored me since the outburst. He's done with this trial. You've paid him enough, Dad.'

'There's a long way to go before this is over. David can get the private investigator he used to have a look into it. What if he proves it's Dan's car? That changes things. Substantially.'

'The picture's not clear.'

'It's clear enough for you to have these thoughts. You have to raise this.'

'I am… with you.'

'To someone who can make a difference.'

'This is Dan we're talking about. The only friend who has stuck with me throughout this nightmare.'

'Don't put him on a pedestal.'

'I'm not.'

'Yes, you are. What if his relationship with Hatti isn't what you thought?'

'It doesn't mean he killed Serena?'

'Get the picture checked out. You have nothing to lose.'

I nod reluctantly, unsure why I'm being hesitant.

My own guilt at Serena's death, perhaps.

We head back to court, and it's the first time I seriously wonder if I should have pleaded to manslaughter on the grounds of diminished responsibility.

It's not too late, I think.

I could still confess and put an end to all this pain.

Except, I didn't re-enter Serena's apartment.

It was somebody else who came in after I left.

Dan?

A silence falls, the judge enters, and the proceedings start.

Patricia is about to stand when an usher enters and hands her a note.

Next up is Carole Moore. She's a close friend of Serena's. So close, I'd never met her. The police thought she was the recipient of the eighty-six calls. She wasn't. I've read her statement as part of the disclosures. It's more bullshit and white noise. She's going to tell the court how Serena had become unsure of our relationship. How she had become concerned about my temper and controlling nature. I'm genuinely curious to see who this Carole really is. Another Instagramer, from what I can see.

'Your Honour,' Patricia says. 'Our last witness is Carole Moore. She appears to have left the court. We are currently attempting to make contact. Would the court mind waiting for an additional five minutes before we resume?'

The judge looks across at David.

'No objections, your Honour,' David says.

'Five minutes, then we continue.'

'Thank you, your Honour.'

There's nothing to do but wait and endure the constant chattering of my paranoid mind.

Five minutes drifts into ten.

I do my best not to fidget.

The judge looks across at Patricia.

'Your Honour, we've been unable to contact Carole Moore. Therefore, the prosecution concludes its case against Kieran Harrison.'

Patricia sits and looks across at David, who stands, holding the side of his robe, back straight, chin out.

He's a giant of a man, and he's taking all the time and space he wants.

'Your Honour, the prosecution has not presented a single piece of coherent evidence. There is no DNA linking my client to the offence. There is no photographic or direct eye witness that shows my client re-entering Serena's apartment after he left at 8:30 pm. My client is in the dock today because of a flawed and inadequate police investigation that has been based on the fact my client and Serena Brown had a volatile relationship. That does not make him guilty of the crime he stands accused of. Therefore, we make an application to the court that there is no case to answer. We request this case be dismissed and my client be allowed to go free.'

Much to the dismay of the prosecution, the judge gives me a massive leg up. He's going to review the case. I can't decide if it's a masterstroke from David or another ploy that's going to piss everyone off and work against me.

Monday's session gets cancelled, so I now have my own unofficial bank holiday. I'm back to another round of wait-and-see mode. There's nothing new there. It's been my life for the last six months.

We filter out of the court, and I see David reach for his phone. I trot over to thank him, but he looks at me and then at his phone, his eyes telling me he's busy, and I should push off.

'We need to chat,' I say, non-confrontationally.

'I have another case starting in under a month. We're doing okay, and we've had a small victory. You should do your best to relax, and I'll see you here on Tuesday at 9:00 am, Jake,' he says into the phone. 'I got your message, thanks. We still need to discuss your whereabouts between five and six-thirty on the twenty-eighth. I'm around to take your call.'

He disconnects and looks at me with a streak of disgust that I'm still standing in front of him.

'It's important. Can we talk? Not here.'

'I'm going to be busy tonight. Can it not wait?'

'Thirty minutes is all I need.'

I'm polite.

Firm.

We hold each other's stare.

His phone rings, and I see the name on the front of his screen.

Jake De-White.

I recognise it from the news. He's a rich kid. The family is worth several hundred million from selling low-cost sportswear. Jake made the news when the police found fifteen plastic bricks of cocaine with a street value of twelve million sterling on his motor cruiser, moored in St Katherine's dock. He denies all the charges, having lent his cruiser to a friend the weekend before. The tabloids are feasting on the story. They are pushing the theory that Daddy was about to cut Jake's money due to his party lifestyle and that Jake was looking for a financial quick fix. I couldn't care less about Jake's coke problem, but I bet David's hourly rate is enough to keep him distracted from me, and that's my worry.

'Let's say, seven-fifteen at Heron Tower. See you in the bar.'

He disconnects the call and looks at me. The Heron Tower is David all over. An upmarket Sushi Restaurant and a bar full of high-maintenance girls. I entered that world with Serena, and it did me no favours.

'We can walk to the Heron Tower from here and talk on the way.'

'I don't walk anywhere. I've got an hour. Come on, I'll buy you a pint.'

I nod and smile.

He continues. 'I'll tell my paralegal to call the service and say you're with your barrister. Trial's in progress and all that. You can go for dinner with your dad afterwards, but you'll need to be home by ten.'

I'll take the pro-bono offer of his hour and dinner out with my dad.

I ask Dad if he minds if I do this on my own. He reluctantly agrees and heads to my flat while I wait outside The Old Bailey for David to call his paralegal and then get changed.

He comes out looking dapper in a fresh shirt, new jeans, and brown leather shoes that probably cost more than a weekend away. The upside of representing drug dealers and murderers, I guess.

We walk to a pub David knows that's off the beaten track and down one of the many alleys that crisscross the south side of St Paul's.

I take a seat, feeling the stress of the first week ease out of my shoulders, and David returns with two pints of pale ale. He suddenly looks like a good guy. Relaxed, the type you'd want to have a laugh with and share a drink. Within his peer group, I'm sure he's the centre of attention and is great fun to be with.

I push the envelope across to him.

'It's not a bribe, is it?' he says, half smiling.

'I wish it was that easy,' I say, taking a sip of my drink. He opens the envelope and slips out the picture. He looks at me, then back at the picture, then back at me, shrugging.

'You see the car in the far corner?

'What about it?'

'It belongs to Dan King. My best mate. Or so I think.'

David says nothing, taking another longer sip of his beer as he takes a closer look at the picture.

'It's barely recognisable. How do you know?'

'We went to Cornwall once, and I slept in it for two days. I've been in that car more times than I can remember. Is there any way your private investigator can look into it? Maybe get a better-quality picture from the footage. Do some forensics, or whatever it is they do?'

'Why didn't you mention it before?'

'I only spotted it because you froze the last frame of Fredrick's footage after I dropped out of the shot. I would have never noticed it otherwise. No one would.'

'Let me look at the footage again. See if it appears in any of the other frames.' he says.

'Thanks. Appreciated.' I say, taking another sip of my beer.

The pub's getting busier, someone nudges into the back of me.

It's Friday.

It reminds me of happier times.

The end of a long week at Eco-Blue.

The start of a weekend with Serena.

'Can we have an off-record conversation?' I say.

'Don't compromise me now. There're a lot of twists and turns left in your case to play out, and despite your outburst, our noses are ahead.'

'I won't compromise you, but I want to tell you something.' He nods, and I continue. 'I didn't kill her. I was scared that I did. I kept seeing her face in a pool of blood. I was terrified that somehow I'd got in and… you know… that I'd done it… and that I'd blanked it. The blood that's haunted me was my blood. From the cut. On the glass. I want you to know that. It's important.'

He nods.

I continue.

'Why did you take this case?'

'Honestly?'

'Yeah, honestly?'

'I thought you were a good guy. That you were innocent. And this would never get to court. Some pocket money for me. I got that one wrong, didn't I I!'

We share a laugh.

Almost friends.

'For what it's worth, I don't think you did it. But you're a fucking idiot and a liar, and it might still cost you.'

'What do you mean?'

'You should have got rid of that girl from your life a long time ago. Why you persisted, I'll never know. A fella like you can't be short of his pick. That's the problem you have with the jury. They don't get your choices. You're not one of them.'

I think about Serena's keys.

The ones I took from her bowl by the door on the night I left.

'What did I lie to you about?'

David looks left and right, checking there's no one he knows close by.

'Fredrick heard it right. It was a clear night. Serena opened the door to you, and you guys spoke. I'm concerned you've fucked yourself by not telling me about that conversation. It makes you look guilty and, what's worse, the jury feels it's the truth. I know you didn't go up because you'd have bled everywhere, and you'd have never had time to clean it up without being seen—no one would. But that doesn't change the facts. Serena opened the back door, and you guys spoke. You've lied about it. It changes people's perception of that night and your participation in it.'

I nod.

Thinking.

'If she opened the door. I couldn't tell you. If we had a conversation, I don't remember a single word we said—that's the truth.'

'It doesn't matter any more. It's too late to backtrack. That bell has rung.'

'If I get convicted, can that picture of the car be used as new evidence? You know, if I have to do the whole appeal route.'

'That's a long way off. Let's cross that bridge.'

'Do you think this will get acquitted on Tuesday?'

He shrugs.

'This case is weak, but their star witness so far is you. If I were you, I'd prepare for this to continue, and anything else is a bonus. You've got a long weekend. I'd do my best to relax and get your attitude right. You look distracted, moody and, worst of all, aggressive. It's costing you. A death by a thousand cuts. Let's say we're back in court on Tuesday to continue. Then, I want to get you on the stand early and work from there. Can you do that? Can I trust you to change your attitude and deliver?'

We stare at each other.

'Yes,' I say. 'You can.'

I get home just after 8:00 pm to find my dad asleep on the bed. He's fully dressed and snoring gently. He looks so peaceful, child-like, and I don't have it in me to wake him to go to dinner. I love him from the bottom of my heart, but I know he's sick.

Seriously.

I saw blood in the basin as I cleaned my teeth the night before last. I did nick myself the previous morning while I shaved, and it could have been mine, but I don't think it was. He's not going to tell me what's wrong until after the trial.

Any father would do the same.

I turn and head into the kitchen and sob.

The next thing I remember is my dad waking me on the sofa and apologising that he missed our opportunity to go for dinner with my curfew temporarily suspended. It doesn't matter, and we decided to make up for it by going out and having a swanky breakfast.

It's good to be outside, and I am determined to have a memorable weekend with my dad and my one true guardian. We head into Marylebone at a leisurely pace to find a boutique hotel to have our up-market treat. From there, we'll go to Madame Tussauds and maybe a museum if we still have the strength. I'm sure we're going to fit a pint or two in somewhere as well.

I can't help but think we are both on our Last Detail, and I have to fight against the thought so as not to spoil my day.

We find a niche hotel near Regent's Park that'll let us be guests for breakfast. The waitress takes us to our seats, and we giggle like school kids at the cutlery wrapped in hard starched cloth napkins.

We play Hill-Billies on our Big-Town Adventure.

The game lightens our moods.

My phone rings and interrupts our conversation.

It's David.

I answer as the waitress brings over the menus.

My dad orders a latte.

I mouth "the same" as I take the call.

'I thought you'd be hungover and done for the weekend?' I say.

'I know you saw his name. He's a baby and a client and in deep shit. Let's leave it there.'

I can hear the chirp in David's voice. I bet he's the type who waters his drinks when he's out with a client. Stalin would do the same. Careful not to let his guard down while he watched and observed. I could put it down to his barrister training. It's not. It's his nature. He's a complex animal.

We all are.

Serena, too, I think.

'It sounds like you're out. Can you talk?'

'I'm with my dad having breakfast. He gets the full story anyway. What's-up?'

'Out of curiosity, I had another look at the footage from Olson's phone. Let's say through a new perspective. There's two interesting points that jump out. The BMW isn't there when you first come into focus. You can see the empty parking space behind you. As you climb the wall and drop down into the garden, Fredrick follows you, and we lose sight of the road. But as you start to run across the lawn, Fredrick shifts position. It's enough to see the car is there.' My stomach tightens, and David continues. 'In the time you jumped down, whoever it was driving that car pulled into that empty parking spot.'

'Can you see who it is?'

'No.'

I sigh, hard.

'The owner of the car could live in the square. We can check it out, but it's not cheap. Fifteen grand plus with all the work involved. If you want to go ahead, then I need Dan's details. We should get photographs of his car and see if there's anything that can be matched. I want to say that this is a long shot and not your focus. Your concentration needs to be on the next three days in court if that's what it comes to. Nothing else.'

'I hear you. Let's do it.'

'Okay, good, I'll action this today. I'll need a further five thousand on account by Monday.'

'I'll organise it. Question: in the first shot, when the car appears, can you see the passenger-side headrest?'

'Why?'

'Dan has a Beagle, and the dog chewed the headrest when he left the dog in the car.'

'Let's see what the private investigator comes up with. I'll mention it. There's only three, maybe four days left of your trial, assuming we don't get the acquittal on Tuesday. If the investigator comes back with something interesting, we can push for a re-trial. That is going to be much harder once the jury has gone out to start their deliberations. I might not put you on the stand first, after all. If we can stretch this into another week, it'll give the private investigator the time he needs. Question: did you ever suspect anything between Dan and Serena? Any indication they were seeing each other behind your back?'

'No.'

'I'm going to ask you again. There was no deep voice that you were ignoring?'

I think about the time Serena flirted with Dan when we went to their house for a dinner party. His high-energy needs feeding off the fix.

'No. It never crossed my mind.'

'Okay. Let's play this one out. You leave his place, and you told him you were going home?'

'I did.'

'But you didn't. You go back to Serena's. It's pure luck that he parks up and sees you climb over the wall. Then why didn't he drive off? He must know you'd recognise his vehicle, and there's a risk that you could see him?'

'What if he didn't see me? He doesn't expect me to be there, right?'

Silence.

'Let's follow that line. The CCTV doesn't pick him up. He might have got lucky and walked in via Green Street. If he had, he wouldn't have been seen by the traffic monitoring cameras or the one at the 24-hour mini-market. It makes sense to where he was parked and is the most direct route to the block. That still doesn't cover the noise of the front doors. Carter is right. The door slams, and there's an issue with the top hinge. Even the intercom system isn't in a sound-proof casing and chimes out. All the residents had complained. Dan would also have to get through the door at less than sixty centimetres, or the door would have been seen opening at least by one of the two cameras. The police are correct in that the door wasn't seen opened again from about 1:00 am until the postman arrived in the morning. So, if Dan did go to meet with Serena, how did he get in without making a noise? Unless he had keys, which would have helped with the noise issue? And if he did have keys, how did he get them? Did Serena give him one?'

My breath shoots out of my lungs.

My chest tightens.

I stand to fight against the avalanche of emotions that pump through me.

My dad stares on, concerned.

Serena's keys.

I always thought I had dropped them.

Maybe I did.

Maybe I didn't.

Dan handed me my jacket as I left.

He was alone with it while I went to the toilet, and he knew that I had stolen Serena's keys.

I told him.

We laughed about it.

What if he was having an affair with Serena?

What if he took her keys from my jacket pocket?

'Do you think Dan could have had a set of keys?' David asks.

'It's possible, right? Anything is possible,' I say.

Chapter 47

I take my seat in the dock and ache with a desperate hope and a hollow fear. It's a volatile appetiser to the day which crawls through my veins, making it hard to sit still. The security guard sat next me has become nervous, sensing my unease. I don't care what he thinks, but if he can pick up on my vibe, then the rest of the court can, too.

I take another deep breath to help centre my nerves.

David eases himself to his feet to begin outlining our case. He's precise and matinee-idol engaging, losing the factual efficiency and middle-classness of Patricia. It took the judge an extra two days to come to the conclusion that there was still a case to answer. It was a crushing disappointment. David has spun it well, and it's improved our relationship. He's almost convinced me the delay plays into our defence.

Only time will tell.

David moves through his gears, adamant that he's going to prove to the jury, beyond any reasonable doubt, that it couldn't have been me who killed Serena Brown. We are here today because of a flawed investigation.

I nod my consent as agreed between us. I occasionally glance across at the jury as I've been instructed to do. I want to look into the eyes of those who hold my fate in their hands. It's my turn to express how I feel, albeit unvoiced for now.

I will have my say soon enough.

My silver lining from the acquittal disappointment is the two-day hiatus it has given the private investigator. He's working the overtime and blank cheque with full gusto. He's taken dozens of pictures of Dan's car from various angles in the hope of finding enough dents and bumps to make a match. He's even got a couple of Dan sitting in the car. Three hundred pictures have been sent to a forensic photographic lab, and it's going to be a few more days to get a preliminary reply.

David's used the break to swap his order. I'm going to be taking the stand on the Monday of next week. With cross-examination, he expects it to absorb the rest of the following week, and if the jury is sent out, it guarantees I get at least two weekends at home with my dad. The downside is I'm at risk of crumbling under Patricia's venomous attack and thereby convicting myself in the process.

My leg trembles at the thought.

I've rehearsed my testimony enough times in my mind, and I'm as ready as I'm ever going to be. There comes a time in everyone's life when you have to nail your flag to the wall, and mine is ticking closer by the minute.

'Thank you, members of the jury,' David says, concluding his opening remarks. 'Your Honour, I'd like to introduce our first witness for the defence. Dr Harriet Little, consultant psychiatrist.'

I watch the tall and elegant Harriet walk in. She's young and confident and glows with being five months pregnant. She's the psychotherapist David arranged I see to counter Teddy-Boy.

Her entrance lifts the mood in the court, and there's an inherent warmth and naturalness about her that even the toughest of cynics would be hard-pushed not to notice.

She glances across at me and keeps her eyes warm.

I smile back, a friend in the midst of enemies.

We only met twice, for forty-five minutes each, but like now, her openness drops my guard. I felt more connected and understood in those two sessions than I ever did under Teddy-Boy's scrutinous gaze, maybe in my whole life.

She takes the witness stand and is sworn in. David asks her to introduce herself to the court. There's a delicateness to her movements and speech, and it draws you further into her orb. Where she lacks the clinical experience against Teddy-Boy, she trumps him on the academic side. Like Teddy, she's a qualified medical doctor who switched to psychotherapy, but her PhD is in Neuroscience from Cambridge, where she's now a resident. She is being fast-tracked to become one of the youngest ever professors at the University. She has more research papers printed under her name than Teddy-Boy can even dream of, and her topic of choice is narcissism.

'Dr Little, in your opinion, what makes a narcissist?' David asks like he's a kid who'd just heard the word for the first time.

'That's perhaps the first and most common mistake associated with the word. We're all narcissists. It's built into our hard-wiring from birth. It's when it becomes fragmented, or not re-integrated in a coherent way, that the problems begin.'

'Are you saying I'm a narcissist, Dr. Little?' David asks.

It gets a laugh from the court and even a smile from the judge before he throws David one of his disapproving looks and a reminder to keep on script.

'You are,' Harriet says. 'As I am. Having positive self-worth without entitlement could be argued as healthy narcissism,' she adds with a smile.

'You used the words "fragmented" and "re-integrated". For the benefit of the court, could you expand on those two statements and how they relate to my client?'

'With pleasure,' she says, giving another warming smile towards the jury. 'You have "primary" narcissism and "secondary" narcissism. The primary is what we are all born with. You then start the emotional process of understanding that you are an individual who is different from your parents with your own unique abilities. That is "secondary" narcissism or stage two. If stage two is interrupted during the re-integration process, your self-image can become "fragmented". Narcissistic personality disorder is the fragmentation of this secondary process. Negative narcissism is really a person's inability to regulate their self-esteem. It is a form of self-protection and a defence of the "self" is often seen through a number of unpleasant social interactions. Some of them can be quite extreme.'

'Could you describe some of these unpleasant social interactions?'

'If you can't regulate your own self-esteem, it's extremely difficult to think positively about others. You become deeply wrapped up within yourself, having little to no self-awareness. You will tend to see other people as a mere extension of you. In the same way that you might use your arms or legs, you will expect the other person to respond to your needs in a similar fashion. A narcissist sees someone else as "self-objects". Objects or people to be used by the narcissist's self. They are not seeing the other person as an individual with their own life's journey. This is a completely unrealistic way to live. We are neurologically wired to interact with other members of our species. A better way to describe this ability to interact is called "empathy". A deep narcissist has none. They have none because their true self has become fragmented. If you have no empathy for yourself, it is impossible to have empathy for others. It becomes and is a vicious circle.'

'Thank you for that explanation. If you are potentially diagnosing a patient with a narcissistic personality disorder, at what point do you conclude that they have this fragmented self you just described?'

'It can be confusing as there are certainly crossover behaviours from other disorders such as borderline personality disorder, schizophrenia, and anti-social disorder, to name but a few. Someone with narcissistic issues will tend not to lose their sense of grounding in the world despite their behaviour toward others. This is mainly down to the creation of their "false self". The image that they have created to help deal with the fragmentation they are unable to emotionally hold.'

'Could you perhaps expand on the idea of the "false self" for the understanding of the court? I don't believe Dr Edward Carrington-Smythe Jr II mentioned this for the prosecution,' David says, glancing across at Patricia, a sneer hidden in the corner of his eyes.

'I'm not sure how technical you want me to be?'

'My learned friend may want you to go down that path, but for now, could we have the layman's approach?'

Harriet smiles, touching the top of her pregnant stomach.

'In many ways, the views we have of narcissism come from the work of Heniz Kohut, who was a revered psychoanalyst. Kohut gave us the term *narcissistic rage*. When we talk about self-worth, self-love, self-soothing, etc., the word "self" is very important. As a child, once you hit the two-year mark, you begin the painful process of separating from your parents and realising that you are an individual in the world. It's a long and ongoing process, not really complete until early adulthood. When this process of separation starts, it's crucially important that it isn't interrupted. By interrupted, we mean by "emotional trauma". If it does become interrupted, the child "can" but not always create a "false self" in order to deal with the trauma of the separation. This new "false self" is their invulnerable superpower, their protective mask, if you like. And that's when the problems begin.'

David nods, thoughtfully glancing back at me before turning to Harriet.

'How is this process interrupted?'

'You could generalise it into two camps. Some form of abuse: sexual, emotional, or abandonment, as an example, would fall into the first camp. The second is just as pernicious, whereby a child is smothered too much by a parent, which stops the child from developing emotionally. This is often referred to as "enmeshment". Unfortunately, once the "false self" has been created, the ability to self-soothe when you are hit with an emotional issue is profoundly impaired. Often, the only way you can manage these uncomfortable emotions is by constant affirmation or controlling others. You effectively "use" people as a "supply" of energy—self-objects—believing they are there for you and you alone. Even chaotic energy can be used to soothe the "false self". It is, after all, attention on you and it's that supply you require.'

David nods like he's thinking it through and not coming off his script.

'The more drama a narcissist creates, the greater their soothing is?'

'It should be thought of in terms of attention. Whether it's positive or negative, it will generally have the same effect on them. You have to remember that despite what most people think of narcissists, they are not in love with themselves. Their inner worlds have no reprieve from their self-loathing. It's bleak. It's extremely difficult for a healthy person to understand a narcissist's world because a healthy emotional person will naturally self-soothe if they have an issue. They might not do it immediately, but they will get there. A narcissist never gets there by themselves. However, therein lies one of the great mysteries. Narcissists can often drive themselves to great heights. They can be extremely charismatic and intelligent. History is full of such characters, but a lack of self-awareness is the common thread and, ultimately, their undoing. If you look closely, even at the outwardly successful, their lives are deeply tragic, littered with abandonment, which is often their greatest fear. As we speak, there's no cure for being an unhealthy narcissist unless they can develop self-awareness, which brings us full circle to the original issue. You can't be self-aware if you're self-absorbed. The two are not compatible.'

David nods.

'In your opinion, is my client, Kieran Harrison, an unhealthy narcissist?'

'In my professional opinion, no, he's not. He has demonstrated self-awareness and empathy. Although, I would say he has an unhealthy relationship attachment style. To put it simply. He bonds with his sexual partners via negative traits, such as jealousy or distrust, rather than healthy ones, such as kindness and consideration. It's more commonly known as "trauma-bonding" and is most likely related to the relationship he has with his mother. Fortunately, he has a healthy relationship with his father, and that probably saved him from a fragmented self.'

'Is Serena Brown an unhealthy narcissist?'

Patricia's out of her chair, catching her robe on the corner of the table.

She scowls at David.

'Objection, your Honour. Dr Harriet Little has never met the deceased. My learned friend clearly knows that he should not be asking such a question to the witness.'

David looks surprised, incredulous, but he's done what he's wanted to do from day one of this trial.

He's called Serena Brown a narcissist in open court.

More doubt.

More muddying of the waters.

Chapter 48

The judge reminds David that he expects a certain standard within his court.

No exceptions.

David lightly bows his apology, telling the judge it won't happen again.

I know him enough to see he doesn't give a shit.

He's like Serena. He's going to push those boundaries as far and as hard as he can until someone attempts to stop him.

Serena is now the "unhealthy" narcissist in the room.

It's our subliminal message to the court and the one we're going to pursue.

Patricia is pissed as can be that he's slipped it by her, but there's nothing she can do, and she knows it.

I look back at Dr Little.

She appears oblivious to what's just happened as I recall our two meetings with a sense of joy I haven't experienced for months.

I'd never met anyone who listened in the way that she did, running it through her deeply analytical mind. Anything replayed back to me was layered with an abundance of understanding and acceptance of who I am.

It wrapped me in a safety of cotton wool that I miss.

I wanted more sessions. Desperate to tell her about my life. She's booked out for months ahead. David had pulled strings from his Cambridge network to get her onboard. She knew from the start why I was there and that she might be requested to appear in court.

She never once directly asked me about Serena. Something I valued and appreciated. We talked about my childhood, my career, and my deep love of wanting to protect our planet. She poked and prodded at my relationship with my father and mother and Ryan, and my relationship with Serena seeped out of those threads. She understood the dilemma I lived with. Despite my mother's cruel streak; a streak she was proud of, I'd struggled for most of my life to openly criticise her attitude and behaviour to others.

Even an internal comment created enormous shame.

External ones were pure treason.

I ponder my mother's last letter and will, wondering if she drew pleasure in sending it.

I can't help but imagine that she did, and the thought stabs at me more than the contents of either. For years, I've witnessed how her twisted logic worked. Her words and actions forever justifying poor behaviour. It was always someone else's fault. Never anything she did or said. It's easy to blame others. It's projection in its purest and ugliest form. My mother is a world champion at it and a monster in the process.

David clears his throat and takes a sip from his bottle of water.

'Dr Little. I apologise for the bluntness of my last question. I'm certainly not looking for you to pass judgment on someone you've never met or for myself to incur the wrath of the court. Having spoken with my client at great length, you must have formed an impression of the personal relationship he had had with Serena Brown? If you believe it has relevance to why we are all here today, I would like to hear your opinion in relation to my client.'

A slice of tension creeps through the room.

I glance at Patricia, wondering if she is going to object.

I cough, gently clearing my throat, the judge glancing across at me.

Patricia says nothing.

'It is clear I never met Serena Brown. Therefore, I couldn't say if she was an "unhealthy" narcissist or not. Listening to Kieran describe their relationship, there were certainly negative patterns on both sides that could be described as narcissistic in nature. Serena was more dominant than Kieran, both sexually and emotionally. From how he describes their interactions, there is evidence that she sexualised her needs and conflicts through their relationship. This is a negative narcissistic trait.'

'Did my client ever discuss Serena as a narcissist to you?'

'No. It is my professional opinion based on how Kieran discussed their overall interactions.' Harriet pauses to think, touching her pregnant bump as she does. I look across at Patricia, who's perched on the end of her seat, ready to stand. Harriet continues. 'Kieran has a relationship history of being submissive to his partners, who often betray him, creating high drama in the process. Fear of abandonment is a key theme. Viewed in relation to his professional life, it is like he's two different people. He wouldn't behave like that or accept similar kinds of behaviour from his professional colleagues. Kieran was both frustrated and drained by the relationship with Serena. He was also stuck in a paradox. He believed it represented a healthy relationship. It didn't. He knew that subconsciously, but he didn't know how to break the pattern he found himself in.'

'So why did he continue with it?'

'His model for what is healthy and unhealthy in relation to his sexual partners is misaligned. I would say he is drawn to narcissistic personality types.'

Patricia is caught on the edge of her seat.

I look across at David, wondering what his next question is going to be. Harriet is on my side, but she's telling the court I'm a poor partner with a poor relationship model. Patricia is wanting to object, but she doesn't want to emphasise Serena, the unhealthy narcissist, in the process.

I want to give David a hug.

I suddenly look up at my dad.

He gave so much emotional attention to my mother that it sucked him dry. It was an impossible job to fill the void that washed through our mother. It's one he never signed up for in the first place. It took him more than seventeen years to bring that relationship to a close.

I did it in ten months.

'Dr Little, thank you for your time. I'm finished with my questions.'

Chapter 49

Patricia is up and out of her seat a beat too fast for true composure.

It brings a smirk to the corner of David's eyes.

'Dr Little, for clarity to the court, you've never met or spoken with Serena Brown in a professional or personal capacity prior to her death?'

'That is correct. I've never met her.'

'In your professional opinion, you are confident the defendant isn't an unhealthy narcissist? In fact, you say, he's the opposite, he's over empathetic?'

'Yes, in my professional opinion, that is correct on both counts.'

'But you said in relation to the defendant's relationship with Serena, and I quote: *"There were certainly negative patterns on both sides that could be described as narcissistic in nature."'*

Patricia makes a note, but she's really letting her statement hang in the air so it's absorbed to its full capacity.

She continues. 'Surely that's a contradiction? Either the defendant is or isn't a narcissist?'

'It's confusing, I admit. We are all narcissists. It's the scale at which you sit. View it as a scale of one-to-ten. Ten being deeply unhealthy. I would put Kieran in a three/ three-and-a-half range. There are many reasons for this, but for one, he has high levels of self-deprecating humour and an ability to read other people. These are usually good indicators that someone is low on a narcissistic scale. In regards to your question, you can be low on the personal narcissistic side but find yourself in a highly narcissistic relationship. This is the situation Kieran found himself in with Serena. He was effectively mirroring her behaviour as a form of self-protection, and therefore, their relationship could be seen as narcissistic by nature.'

A broad smile breaks across Patricia's face. 'So the defendant moved from his three-and-a-half on the scale to a ten?'

'No. He stayed in his low zone but became narcissistic in "behaviour". That isn't the same as being deeply narcissistic by "nature". You can see this in group behaviour. Individuals may mirror the traits of the leader, particularly at stressed times, but they don't necessarily have that trait themselves and certainly can't maintain it over the long term.'

David smirks again.

'You state the defendant was involved in a volatile relationship?'

'I did.'

'Which is something the prosecution agrees with. You also state Serena was the dominant personality within their relationship?'

'I believe that to be true.'

'You met the defendant twice for a combined ninety minutes. Two sessions spread over four weeks.

From your own introduction to the court, you have multiple projects on the go and pending motherhood on the horizon.'

'I have a busy schedule, yes. I always have done. Two sessions was more than enough to evaluate Kieran Harrison and his relationship with Serena Brown. It was volatile, narcissistic, and dominated by Serena Brown's agenda and not Kieran's.'

'You are aware that the court has heard from a respected psychoanalyst, someone with years of clinical experience?' Harriet nods. Patricia continues. 'He saw the defendant eight times for one hour each session. Based on those sessions, he has come to a different conclusion of the defendant. I put it to you that you would need at least another six sessions to have reached the conclusions you have stated today?'

Harriet holds Patricia's stare, calm, relaxed, unfazed.

'Kieran Harrison describes his relationship in terms he doesn't understand.'

'You've lost me and probably the court with that one?'

'When he discusses his relationship with Serena, what he describes is the cycle of narcissistic abuse whereby he is the victim. This is seen through a combination of "idealisation", "devaluation" and finally "discard". That was Kieran Harrison's relationship with Serena. On the night of the fifth, this cycle was completed. He was "discarded". Most likely, Serena had found a new emotional "supply" to meet her needs going forward. A narcissist needs this newfound energy supply before they can move on. It's fundamental to their emotional survival.'

Patricia smiles.

'The prosecution whole-heartedly agrees with your point on the defendant being discarded. It is why he went back and killed Serena Brown. I put it to you again that the defendant is, in fact, the narcissist in this relationship and couldn't stand the thought of Serena Brown sharing her life with somebody else other than him? Kieran Harrison solved this problem by murdering her in the manner already described.'

Silence.

Harriet frowns for the first time since she entered court, soothing the top of her stomach with the flat of her hand.

The mother-to-be.

'No more questions, your Honour,' Patricia says.

'No… that isn't what happened on that night,' Harriet says.

Her voice soft, almost inaudible.

'I beg your pardon?' Patricia says, stopping herself from sitting.

'That isn't what happened,' Harriet repeats.

'Unless you were an eye-witness, aren't you being a touch presumptuous, Dr Little?'

'A trauma-bonded individual such as Kieran believes he's made his choice of relationship. He hasn't. All he is doing is reliving his negative past experiences in the now with the belief he will be able to resolve his past with this new person. Kieran Harrison has deep-rooted fears about abandonment, especially by the females in his life. What you see in the footage is not a man in a rage, ready to kill his partner. What you see is a repetitive compulsion or more simply put, a relationship-bond built on terror. A bond that is being repeated for Kieran. In this case, the terror and destruction Kieran believes will happen if Serena leaves him. He's gone back to plead with her not to leave him. He's not gone back to murder her. He has done this in a hysterical and highly immature outburst. In that moment, Kieran Harrison would have done anything to be back in that relationship. The last thing he would want is for Serena Brown to die. Her loss equates to his internal destruction. This man did not murder that girl.'

'Dr Little, while the court respects your qualifications, your clinical experience is limited in these matters. You met the defendant twice for what amounted to an hour and a half. I'm not sure the court can accept your explanation based on two sessions.'

Harriet smiles, warm and inviting.

'Any Psychologist with an understanding of trauma-bonded relationships would have spotted the pattern within half an hour of speaking to the defendant. They would then only need to review the footage to prove their hypothesis. It's all rather simple, really.'

I smile along with David.

So does the judge.

If only Teddy-Boy was here.

Chapter 50

'I'd like to call Kieran Harrison to the witness stand.'

Hearing David's request makes the months since I was charged distil into a single moment. Stares burn into me from every angle. I take a long, slow sip of water, hoping it will fill the chasm within.

It doesn't.

It never will.

Whether I like it or not, the accused has to explain themselves. We want to hear their tone. See their eyes. Watch how they pause and react between questions. We're all judging, looking for our own understanding of the truth.

I've practised the walk from the dock to the stand hundreds of times in my mind. But nothing can prepare me for when my name is called. There's a silence within the silence I had never imagined could exist. I hear my trousers chafe against my calves on each step. Even the judge is making his assessment. The prejudices he's trained to overcome, fighting their way to the top. He's made up his mind and is waiting to see if it is the same as the twelve people off to his left.

I take my seat, and I'm sworn in, settling into the same chair that DCI Carter, Teddy-Boy, and the waitress have all been sat in before me. I feel their hate. It seeps through my body, trying to infect my mind and throw me further off course.

But most of all, I see Serena.

Her beautiful face.

Covered in blood.

My mother lying on the floor next to her.

Ryan calling an ambulance.

'You killed her,' he's shouting at me. *'You killed her.'*

'Kieran, good morning,' David says. 'How are you today?'

'As well as can be expected.'

'It's been a trying few months?'

I pause to think, letting the question take hold as we've rehearsed.

'The stress is hard to describe, especially when I don't believe I should be here. It's affected my mental health.'

'You didn't kill Serena Brown?'

'No, I didn't kill her. The last time I saw Serena, she was alive.'

'Why do you think you're here today, Kieran?'

'The police jumped to conclusions based on the fact Serena and I had an argumentative relationship. It wasn't the type of relationship I wanted, and I regret it. But I didn't kill her because of it.'

'Can we go back and explain to the court how you and Serena met?'

I suddenly see her sitting at a long bar, drinking champagne, dressed for attention. Those duvet days at the dawn of our relationship, flicking on the peripheries. Her Tinder profile there one day, gone the next. *Lavishlondonlashes* Instagram account gaining "likes" by the second with each fresh post. A would-be influencer on the rise. I never met a single friend or work colleague, except for the two girls who gate-crashed that Friday night and raided our work tab. Even then, I only spoke to one of them briefly. Weekends spent in different hotels and exotic destinations, with my final destination being here. I'm looking at the jury and wondering if they've made up their minds.

Will anything I say make a difference?

Despite everything, meeting Serena that first time is still a pleasant memory. The excitement I felt when I saw her at the conference hums inside of me. Her skilful and often cutting sense of humour. The way she could see through to the core of someone's personality.

It all appealed to me.

How I would ache to see her during the week.

I still don't know how it turned into a more charged relationship. It crept up on me when I wasn't looking. My traits that had attracted her, became an annoyance. Serena was more sexually experienced. I never held it against her, enjoying the liberation. It freed me from my reserved chains and allowed me to explore who I was. The photographs were taken without my consent. However, if she'd asked, I would have agreed. I thought it was safe between us in that way.

Two consenting adults.

Two people enjoying each other.

Trust, explicit.

I pause, hoping the jury will make the connection between my supply and Serena's narcissistic needs—two words David has warned me against using in open court.

I push on.

I would find myself apologising for things that I hadn't done, accused of incidents that had never happened. These incidents were figments in her imagination that would come to haunt our days.

Arguments dragged out of nowhere that I couldn't explain.

It drained me.

'Like the incident at *Line Caught*,' David adds. 'When Serena accused you of looking at the waitress in a sexual manner?'

I nod.

'I could list dozens of similar stories. It's only now, looking back, that I see we had highs or lows and never a medium. We'd fallen into a weekend-only romance. I had grown bored of the dynamic. I wanted something more. It was maybe the first time I noticed a pattern from previous relationships.'

'That you were trauma-bonded?'

'I'm still understanding what that means in relation to myself. But yes. What I wanted from Serena was a commitment to us as a couple.'

'And that's when the serious issues began?'

'No, the problems were already there. I thought breaking the weekend-only relationship was the fix. In the past, we'd discussed buying a place together. Looking back on it, Serena never committed. She had a knack of agreeing to things without agreeing. In April, she had to move out of her place. I asked her to live with me. She said it was too "mine". That she would never feel comfortable. It was then she told me a friend of hers was travelling and needed someone to flat-sit for three months. "Let's do something after that?" I remember her saying those exact words. We were having a drink in a bar in the West End.'

'You must have been in love with her to ask her to live with you?'

'I was. She was everything to me. The arguments I had put down to nothing more than teething issues linked into the gaps in the week when we didn't see each other. I thought she was beautiful. I thought we had enough in common. That in time, it would be a good union for us both. I was thinking marriage and family.'

'Then everything changed?'

'Yes. She moved into the flat she died in on the Friday.'

I suddenly fight the urge to cry.

I push on, my voice croaky, my vision blurring. 'I was booked to go to Edinburgh for business on the Monday. I would be gone for the week. I had blocked out the Friday to help her move, with an understanding that we would spend the weekend together.'

'But that didn't happen?'

'She first cancelled the Friday day, saying she had a friend helping her move and that we should meet up in the evening. She then cancelled the Friday evening at about four o'clock, asking me to come on Saturday morning. Saturday morning I got a message asking if we could make it in the afternoon. She again cancelled the Saturday afternoon, saying she was too exhausted after the move and that she was going to do some admin and then have an early night. I'd booked Sunday Lunch a few weeks before. To be honest, I was half expecting her to cancel that.'

'How did it make you feel—all the cancellations?'

'I was disappointed and hurt. It was then that I knew our relationship would never be any different and that I either accepted it as a weekend romance or move on. For me, her responses were calling time on our relationship.'

'And this upset you?'

'Long before the weekend we're discussing, friends, even my father, had hinted that I should move on. There was this part of me that hoped they were wrong. Like I said, I was disappointed and upset that I was left hanging around.'

'Tell the court about that final night?'

It falls through me as it has so many times before. Then I gently shake my head, or that's how it feels. I'm scrolling through her Instagram account on her phone. Shocked that she is the same person I am dating.

She's not the person I know.

But who do I know?

Then I'm at Dan's.

He's handing me my coat.

I watch him in the reflection of the mirror pick out Serena's keys while he thinks I'm using the toilet. I see his old BMW Tourer in Fredrick's footage, and I'm sitting in it, talking to Dan. We've driven to Newquay for a stag weekend. I'm laughing at one of his stories.

Goa.

The elephant taxi.

Then it hits me.

He's fucking her behind my back.

And has been for weeks.

I know he went in after I left.

Tears well in my eyes.

'Tell us about that final night, Kieran?'

There's an urgent nudge in my barrister's voice.

'I didn't kill her. I loved her. I came back, and I climbed over the wall, and I was shouting at her because she'd lied to me about us living together. She never let me in. I left. That was the last time I saw her. She was alive when I left.'

'Thank you, Kieran. Now, could you please start from when Serena first let you in on the Sunday—before you two went for lunch?'

'I can't.'

A tension pushes at the silence in the court.

'Why is that Kieran? Do you need a few minutes?'

'All I can remember is being in Dan's car in Newquay.'

David's voice stays at a low rumble in the corners of my mind. I identify a softer tone, one I'm not used to from him. He's dispensed with his feint surprise and cutting cynicism. He's trying to pull me out of my stupor.

I want to get there, too, and join him on our ride to innocence.

But I can't seem to move.

I'm stuck in Dan's car, and we're somewhere near Newquay Harbour, looking out to sea.

He bought the car ten years ago, and it was six years old when he purchased it. If you count in the pollution taxes and overall fuel inefficiency, any normal person would have long sold it or sent it for scrap.

It's why I'm utterly certain the car in the picture belongs to him. If it wasn't for the lamp-post, I'd be looking at the dog-chewed headrest.

'Do you need more time? Perhaps a drink of water?' David asks.

I shake my head.

David smiles reassuringly.

No longer the Lagos gangster.

A priest.

'Kieran, would you like to tell the court why you went back to Serena's after you initially left?'

Tears well. I can't remember. It's a blank, but it's okay because now he's managing to answer my questions by the way he frames the next. He's using my statement like an actor would a prompt at a read-through. He's attempting to take the sting right out of what is sure to be Patricia's line of attack. I agree with another point, then another, thankful for his prompts.

That Sunday has mostly been a lost sequence of events within the history of my life.

I glance across to the public gallery to see my dad has left, and there are faces I no longer recognise, and some that I do.

DCI Carter, for one.

Teddy-Boy.

The Russian waitress.

The Uber driver.

Serena's two friends.

Behind them all is Serena herself.

She waves at me, childlike, followed by a beaming smile.

She looks radiant.

Sexy and sultry and happy and playful all wrapped into one.

'Why did you come back, darling? What was on your mind, honey?'

'I don't know. It was a good idea at the time? I thought we could fuck and make up like we always do.' I whisper.

'Sorry,' David says. 'I'm not sure the court is following you. It was a good idea at the time?'

Serena winks at me.

Then cuffs her hair into her hands and pins it to the top of her head. She stands and turns. It's then I see her skull is caved in. Next to her is my mother and Henry. They are discussing something, and my mum is showing off the rock on her finger to Serena. Proclaiming how it's bigger with fewer flaws than the one our dad bought her.

Two whole carats.

Then I hear Ryan calling the ambulance and telling me I've killed her.

'Who?' I shout back. 'Serena? My mother? You? Ryan? Who's dead?'

'Serena Brown is dead,' David says.

Ryan doesn't answer me because he knows that all those relationships were long gone and buried before any of them left my life.

I had repeatedly and desperately tried to revive each and every one of them.

A pointless waste of my time.

Exhausting.

'Serena repeatedly cancelling at such short notice must have made you angry?' David asks.

I look at him, or is it Patricia who asked the question?

I honestly don't care any more as I search the courtroom for my dad.

Why has he gone when I need him the most? But that's my dad all over. When it gets to those

crucial points. That time, in the moment, when he
needs to step up and step in, he goes fucking AWOL.

He always did.

He left me to the whims of my mother.

She walked all over him for their entire
relationship, and he fucking let her.

Scared she might leave.

But she did anyway.

He should have grown some balls.

'Do you understand the question, Kieran?'

There's a fear and exasperation in my
barrister's voice I've never heard before.

'You have to understand I wasn't angry. I was
upset, like now. More at myself than with Serena
because I sensed it was coming. I knew in my heart-of-
hearts that she had taken a lease and it wasn't a
house-sit and that our relationship was no more than
me being used each weekend. Honestly, she was a
manipulative fucking bitch, and I gave my power away
to her.'

I hear someone gasp.

It's low and barely audible, but it's definitely a
gasp.

A member of the jury, maybe.

Someone in the public gallery.

David stares at me. Pleading with his eyes for
me to stay calm. Somewhere within, I know he's right,
but Patricia is going to bait me, so what does it
matter? It's true. Serena was manipulative, controlling,
and sadistic. I didn't understand it until Harriet said I

had gone through the stages of "idealisation" to "devaluation" to being "discarded" like a used tissue.

'When Serena wouldn't let you in, why did you go to the rear of the building and climb over the wall?' Patricia says.

I look at David for the answer, but it doesn't come.

I look for my dad, but he's gone.

I look at my palm.

The scar red with new skin.

I took her keys.

'I don't know why I did that. It's out of character.'

Or is it, I think?

Patricia is doing what David has told me a hundred times she'd do. She's going to make me confess my love for Serena. Then she's going to tell me it was the kind of love that smothers. Serena had seen enough to be scared of my temper. She knew better than to let me in for a second time. I climbed the wall, thinking I wouldn't be seen. I either knew or suspected the back door would be easier to open. Serena anticipated my move and came down to dissuade me. Either she let me in under duress, or I forced open the door. Then, in the next nine minutes and twenty-eight seconds, I entered Serena's apartment and brutally killed her. I then stole her mobile phone, expertly cleaned up my DNA, dumping my blood-soaked jacket in the bin, believing the weekly collection would take it on the Monday. I went to bed and woke the next day, calmly catching my flight to Edinburgh as if nothing had happened. My actions fit the profile of a malignant narcissist with homicidal intentions.

Patricia's right on one point.

I climbed the wall because I thought I'd get in.

I'm not sure Serena ever loved me. I was no more than an extension to be used. She'd grown bored, and it was time for her to move on. I'd wasted her time, but even that didn't matter any more because she was pregnant.

And I wasn't the father.

The fuck we'd had earlier was nothing more than a sympathy fuck to keep me calm and under control.

And that's what she told me at the door.

She was pregnant.

The noise of those words collapsing my mind into balls of flashing white light that crowded out any rational thoughts.

I wish I could have remembered it all before now because I have one simple question that's never been answered.

If she was pregnant, why didn't it come up in the autopsy?

The coroner wouldn't have missed it.

I hear shouting at the court door.

Everyone turns.

I see my dad.

He's managed to get a baseball bat that he starts to smash into the wooden panelling.

A woman screams.

He's shouting that I'm not guilty.

That it wasn't me.

I stand and call his name.

The judge is banging his gavel.

A security guard rushes in and grapples my father to the floor.

He's an old man.

He's sick, and he needs my help.

I jump over the dock wall and see the security guard come running for me.

I turn and throw a punch.

It hits him in the face.

He keeps coming, and we're wrestling on the floor, throwing punches. He's suddenly joined by another guard, and I'm shouting for my dad as I'm flipped on my front, a knee rammed between my shoulder blades, my wrists twisted and handcuffed behind my back.

'Dad!' I hear myself say.

'Dad... you ok?!'

'Put your shoes on. Your brief's here to see you.'

I swing my feet off the cell bed and rock my head from side to side, easing the stiffness out of my shoulders. I've spent the night on a thin rubber-covered mattress and pillow no thicker than my wrist.

After the melee in the court, I was taken to the court cells in the basement and then transferred to Paddington Police Station, where I've spent the night. Apparently, it was too late in the day to process me into remand, otherwise, I'd have gone to a real prison until my trial was over.

I'm assuming my bail's been revoked.

One night in a police cell has told me enough that I'm not cut out for prison life.

I'd rather be dead, and I think about suicide and if I have it in me to do it.

I tie my laces and stand.

'What's the time?'

'Ten-thirty two.'

'How's my dad?'

'I see nothing. I hear nothing. I do as I'm told, and I pick up my monthly salary. Do you want to see your brief or not?'

I half expect him to handcuff me, but he doesn't, instead nodding for me to follow him.

He leads the way, casually tucking his thumbs into his stab jacket, looking like a cartoon version of a chicken. The rubber soles of his work boots squeak on the linoleum floor.

We walk past the remaining blue cell doors and head upstairs, turning into a windowless corridor. My police guide stops by a door and nods me in. He walks off, and I'm suddenly all alone.

I pulse with an uneasy feeling.

I tentatively knock on the door and wait.

'Come in.'

It's David's voice, and I open the door to see him sitting at an interview desk. He's dressed in jeans and a jumper and smelling shower fresh. Something I'm desperately in need of myself.

On the table in front of him is a Styrofoam cup and a white sandwich bag. The grease and residue of tomato sauce are seeping through one corner of what I assume is a bacon sandwich.

'I thought you might be hungry,' he says, not looking at me but pointing to the chair in front of him.

'Thanks.'

I sit and pry open the lid to smell fresh-brewed coffee.

'I can't remember if you take sugar, so I added one for good measure.'

'I don't, but it's okay—I need the fuel.'

I was close with the sandwich. It's sausage-and-egg. I'm hungry. I haven't eaten since the lunch break at court yesterday. I take a huge bite and a long sip of lukewarm coffee. I wipe the corner of my mouth and say.

'How's my dad?'

David stares at me like he doesn't understand the question. We're suddenly two foreigners with no history. We're starting all over again, and his natural hostility has returned.

I watch him reach down and pull a folder of paperwork from within his rucksack. He drops it on the table, his left hand flat on top, like he's playing a game of Snap.

'For the record. Anything you say in here can't be used against you. You're covered by client confidentiality.'

'What's going on?'

'You're a funny guy, do you know that?'

'You're worrying me. Is my dad okay?'

'You don't know?'

'Know what?'

'I can't decide if you guys are geniuses or just lottery fucking lucky. Which one is it, Kieran?'

'The last time I saw my seventy-six-year-old father, he was being wrestled to the floor by two fifteen-stone security guards who were forty years his junior. Is he okay?'

'That tends to happen if you break into court like a suicide bomber.'

'How is he?'

'Watch your tone. You still need me. Your father confessed to the killing Serena Brown.'

'WHAT! My dad... did that thing to Serena? That's impossible!'

'By all accounts, he took out twenty-thousand pounds in cash to pay her off. He wanted her to stop seeing you. Looks like she refused. His DNA matches one of the samples found on the towel in her bathroom. He washed his hands after killing her. His car was picked up by the CCTV just before midnight on the fifth. Nobody spotted it, but nobody was looking for it.'

'How did he get in and not be seen?'

'The secret door into the garden was open. He walked straight in. You didn't have to climb the wall and scar yourself for life. You could have just opened the door, like he did, but I'm wondering if you knew that anyway.'

I think about that for a minute.

I'm sure it was locked.

I continue.

'And nobody saw him?'

'You tell me.'

'I don't believe it.'

'For what it's worth, neither do I, but he locked the door after he left. He has her keys to prove it. They are checking the rear door as we speak to see if they can find his fingerprints. Strange, but I have this sneaking suspicion they will. Call me a cynic, and I'm not even old.'

My energy starts to drain. I can feel myself falling backwards into who I am. I push the remaining sandwich and drink away from me.

'Can I see him?'

'He's being held at Islington Police Station. You need to go there and arrange that with them.'

'Can you help him?'

'No, Kieran, I can't. I wouldn't, even if I could. Conflict of interest and all that. I'm not even going to recommend someone to you. Our relationship is officially terminated.'

David opens the folder in front of him.

'I need you to sign these?'

'What are they?'

'Your release forms. You are still technically under arrest, but I expect that to be formally dropped by the Crown Prosecution Service. As part of my service, I will deal with them for you. For now, the court will keep your Passport. I would be prepared for further investigation from the police. However, your father is adamant this was a solo crime, and you had nothing to do with it. I've requested the electronic tag be removed. If they charge you again, you'll need to find another barrister. My file and notes will be available once my invoice is paid. Now sign this.'

'What is it?'

'It exonerates me if you turn out to be the biggest fucking liar and conman I've ever met. And I've met a few.'

'Why did my dad confess now?'

'That's between you and him, but after your performance in court you were going down. You're one lucky guy. Sign the fucking form.'

I take David's pen and do as he asks without even reading the contents.

He breathes a sigh of relief.

'We're done. You're free to go. You might want to look at this. It makes an interesting read.' He pushes a smaller folder towards me. 'I was right about Carter. He's not only lazy but incompetent. The number Serena called was traced to a location in Holborn. Or more precisely, to a large development called *Evolve*. It's a new Street Food Hall Gallery and Shops, that kind of thing. Have you been?'

'No.'

'Part of the development houses new business offices. Like a WeWork. It specialises in short-term lets for start-ups and young entrepreneurs. Seems your mate, Dan King's IT Security company, rented one of the offices. They moved in late June.'

I jolt upright.

My heart thumps.

My stomach cement tight.

I knew Dan had moved offices shortly after I was arrested. I never went and never gave it a second thought, preoccupied with my own stresses.

David continues. 'I'm not a betting person, but if I were, I'd list all the times Serena made those eighty-six calls. I'd then make a formal request for all the security footage from the Street Food Hall and the

Office Buildings above. My bet is you'll see Dan King talking on a mobile phone. Match it enough times to those calls, and I'd say he's in deep shit. The forensic lab also matched his car to the one in Olsen's footage. Let's call it a ninety-three-point-four per cent match. That's enough in a British Court of Law.'

I say nothing.

'You know what I'd do if I was DCI Carter?'

I shake my head.

'I'd take that second DNA sample from Serena's hand towel and see if it matched your so-called best friend. Make sure you pay my bill.'

I nod.

'Have a good life, Kieran.'

I stand in the visitors' line outside Pentonville Prison, waiting for the gates to open. The Victorian building has lost none of its grimness in the decades which have passed since it was first built.

A grimness that seems to be laughing at my fate.

It's taken four stressful days to get to this point. Contacting an inmate at Guantanamo Bay might have been easier. The police applied for an extension to continue interviewing my father, which was granted. As I was still technically charged with Serena's murder, it meant I hit a golden patch for the pencil pushers of the world.

At least David was true to his word.

He ensured that the electronic tag was removed and followed up with the Crown Prosecution Service. His bill duly arrived in my inbox the day after we met for the final time. With everything, it was close to a hundred-and-three thousand pounds, including VAT. The private investigation firm came in at another twenty-two thousand, plus taxes. True to form, David even invoiced me for that last drink we had together and the cab to meet Jake De-White at The Heron Tower. I never did get around to asking if he was adopted or not.

I've calculated that once I sell my flat, pay back my dad, and cover the remaining bills and some other expenses I've accumulated while waiting for my trial to go to court, I'll be debt-free, but without a home, nothing in the bank, and no job.

That's all assuming the charges are all formally dropped.

A buzzer sounds, and the locks on the main gate open. The line moves, and we trundle in, a chain gang of sorts. It takes another fifteen minutes to go through security and have my paperwork checked. I walk in the shadow of what I dreaded for all those months. The smell of institution sticks to my skin. To add to my pain, I'll be walking out of here in an hour and leaving my father behind.

The thought tears at my heart.

I slide into a seat in the visiting room, a small table in front of me. Everything is plastic and Formica and worn and tired. I could be in any one of the interview rooms I'd graced with DCI Carter. There's a buzz and a noisy chatter I didn't expect. A dystopian playpen of sorts. Children cry and run about. There's an array of sweets and biscuits that magically appear, along with packets of cigarettes and other goodies that seem allowed.

I realise I've brought nothing with me.

I pulse with the stupidity.

I've been so desperate to see my dad I wasn't thinking. I don't even know if he has a toothbrush or not.

The main doors finally open, and in walk the remand prisoners. I stand searching for my dad, seeing him amongst the last batch to arrive. I fight back the urge to cry. He's stooped, unshaven, and looking more his age and ill than I can ever remember. The golden tan he's honed with his years in Majorca has turned to a full jaundiced hue.

He spots me and attempts a smile.

I step around the table and give him a hug, holding him like I'm the father and he's my son. He gently pushes me away, and we sit facing each other. I spot a coffee machine in the far corner and ask him if he needs a drink. He shakes his head and reaches out to hold my hand.

'I didn't bring you anything,' I finally say. 'I wasn't thinking. What do you need?'

'I'm okay.'

We stare at each other.

He smiles.

Children shout and scream nearby.

'Be careful what you say in here. You'd be surprised who's listening,' he finally says in a low, hoarse whisper.

I nod and shrug at the same time, wondering who could possibly be listening.

'What's going on?' I ask.

'I killed her.'

He looks at me.

I wait.

He coughs and then speaks.

'I thought you'd be cleared and that I'd get away with it. I'm sorry I put you through all that hell, but I never thought it would get as far as it did. I was sure someone of David's credentials would see you clear with your career intact. I'm hoping you'll forgive your dad. I'm hoping you're going to come and visit me after I'm sentenced?'

I stare at him, wondering who this man in front of me is. This person I've called dad for thirty-three years is really someone else.

Like Serena wasn't the person I thought she was.

Tears well in my eyes and roll down my cheeks. I wipe them away with the back of my hand.

'All I ask is you stay with me on this. Trust your old dad for one last time. Can you do that?'

'What... tell everyone my dad killed my girlfriend?'

'I went to pay her off so she would leave you alone. She was ruining the life you had built and worked hard for. You were too close, too in the mix, to see it. She told me it was none of my business. She told me to fuck off and that I was nothing but an old man. She told me she might make it her personal game to bring you down. So I brought her down. I killed her. She should have taken the money, and none of this would have happened.'

I don't believe him.

Not a word.

'How did you get her keys?'

'I took it when I left.'

'But how did you get in?'

'Through the back garden and then the back door to the block. I then knocked on her door, and she let me in.'

I nod.

'Trust your old dad!' he repeats.

I nod again.

'What's next?'

'I've got magistrate's court on Thursday, where I'll plead guilty. I'm a flight risk as I don't spend enough time in the UK. This is going to be my home for the foreseeable future. I'm seeing another solicitor later. I've sacked the first one. Have the police spoken to you yet?'

'Not formally.'

'They will. They want to believe this is some sort of conspiracy on our part. It won't wash. Don't get bullied by them. Say nothing.'

'What do you need me to do?'

'Nothing. Do nothing. Say nothing. Can you do that?'

I nod.

'What about Mum?'

'What about her?'

'Do you want me to tell her?'

'Why?'

I shrug.

'I wouldn't give her any more for any more. She's abandoned us all for the last time, and you've abandoned yourself enough for a lifetime. It's time to stop. You have a new life that you have to live.'

I don't understand what he means, but I do. Teddy-Boy made me understand that family patterns can be blindly repeated to the next generation. The negative ones can ruin your life if you let them. It takes a seismic shock to get them changed unless you're blessed with an insight that most of us don't have or even care to cultivate.

'Oh… yeah,' my dad adds. 'Bring me some decent books to read. I have the time.'

'Anything in particular?'

'*The Idiot*, by Dostoevsky.'

The bell rings, and it's time to go.

Chairs scrape the floor.

Kids start to cry.

There's a strange inevitability about the whole process that cascades through me from nowhere.

We stand and stare at each other.

Strangers and profound friends entangled in one.

I have no idea what's going on, but we share a single truth that has stayed unvoiced.

We both know who killed Serena Brown.

And it wasn't my dad or me.

Chapter 54

'Hey, dude… finally! It's been too long,' Dan says, greeting me at the entrance to the pub in Highbury.

Before I can say anything, he gives me a bear hug like old times.

I feel listless within his grip.

I'm sure he notices.

We enter the pub, and I spot a couple leaving one of the tall tables by the window. I hijack the space as Dan heads to the bar to get our drinks. I watch him placing our order as I review our life together in chunks. We've canoed, surfed, parachuted, got drunk, slept on each other's sofas, borrowed money, travelled—the list goes on. For years, I thought of him as the brother I'd lost in Ryan. But I'm now watching him through a different set of lenses. I'd give and give, and he'd take and take. It's a mirror of my relationship with Serena. How many times have I turned a blind eye to his controlling nature, quick temper, and the latent bully who lurks beneath his happy-go-lucky image? Even Hatti grumbles about his impatience when she's alone with me, and alcohol has loosened her tongue.

He returns with two pints.

'Cheers,' he says. 'Good to see ya.'

We clink glasses, and I watch him gulp and enjoy those first cold mouthfuls.

'Dude… where do we start?' he says.

'Fourteen years ago!'

He laughs.

It's nervous.

Unsure.

'It's closer to sixteen.'

'A long time,' I say.

He nods.

'How's the old man?'

'He's not great.'

'Has he been charged with Serena's murder?'

'He's pleaded guilty.'

We stare at each other.

Uncomfortable.

I continue. 'We expect a court date early next year—probably after Easter. That's it, from what I can see. He's seventy-seven in July. He's never walking out of prison.'

Dan blows out hard.

'Sorry, dude… I'm sorry for him, you, everyone. Where is he now?'

'Pentonville on remand. Flight risk. Once the charge is formally dropped against me, I'm hoping he'll get bail. Then he should be able to come and stay with me, hopefully until sentencing. It's all extremely complicated, and the police are still investigating the case. Technically, I'm still a suspect, but I'm not. There's a lot of moving parts.'

I take a long sip of my drink, more for the time to think than my thirst or love of beer.

Dan does the same.

For the same reasons.

He knows, I know, he's a murderer.

He'd be stupid not to.

We all have a dark side. A shadow we hide from the public. It haunts us relentlessly unless we address the monster that lurks within us all.

I'm no different.

There's much I have to learn about myself.

But I'm not a killer.

And neither is my dad.

I'm guessing Serena was drawn to Dan's high-energy personality. It ticked her requirements. She wouldn't have cared about his relationship or child or anything else as long as she was getting what she wanted.

Needed.

I see Dan's problem as sharply as he's stood in front of me.

He's wanting the exact same thing from Serena.

Supply.

Her energy.

Her attention.

It's never going to come.

Two people can't suck the lifeblood out of each other and expect each of them to survive.

Someone has to lose.

I'd never thought about it before until now, but all those things they said about me in court are true for Dan. Not me. It's why he never came to court to give his support. He couldn't bear the shame of hearing what a flawed individual he was, albeit via proxy.

A mere mortal and not the grandiose God of his dreams.

She insulted him.

Damaged his ego, and he killed her because of it.

He's insane.

Maybe all narcissists are.

'How did your dad get into Serena's apartment?' Dan asks, gulping the rest of his pint.

'I need another drink before I even start on that one'.

'I'm with you. You hungry?'

'I'll take a burger if you're buying'.

Dan gets up and heads to the bar to order our food and drinks. I stare at the glass he's left behind. There's a centimetre or two of beer left in the bottom. The whole thing is going to be contaminated with his DNA. I glance over to see where he is and realise he's been watching me staring at his glass.

It's like he's reading my mind but struggling to compute it at the same time.

I give him the clarity he wants.

I grab his glass and drop it into a container I have brought in my rucksack.

Dan's face suddenly twists with both anger and disbelief. He turns from the bar as a man steps in front of his path heading to get a drink.

Dan shoves him to one side.

I grab my jacket, but Dan is fast enough to block my path.

'Why are you stealing that glass?'

'Fuck-off.'

'How did your dad get in?'

'You know how he got in!'

His dark side flickering bright behind the veneer of our friendship.

'You don't know what you're talking about.'

'She was dressed up. She was going out to meet someone else. She wasn't interested in you or even me, for that matter, because she had someone else. Your ego couldn't take it!'

People nearby clear to one side, sensing the danger.

I glance beyond him at the exit.

Dan's strong.

I'm quick.

But I want to have my say.

It's why I came.

It's why we're out in public.

'My dad saw you arrive and leave. He picked her keys out of the gutter five minutes after you threw them away.'

'You're full of shit and can't prove a thing.'

'There are photos of your car parked outside
her place. It's on Olson's phone. You cut your hand
when you killed her, didn't you? You were so confident
you wouldn't get caught you wiped your fucking hands
on her towel?'

'Give me the fucking glass.'

'How did you meet Serena?'

'You're delusional.'

'Then why are you blocking my path?'

He smiles.

It lacks the years of our friendship.

'Come on… tell me… how did you meet her?'

'She came to my office. Hunted me down. She
was a fucking shark, relentless.'

'You know. I believe you. Here's the thing,
though. You could have said, *no*.'

'If it wasn't me, it would have been somebody
else. She was no good.'

'But it was you. That's the point.'

'Get over yourself.'

'She told you she was pregnant, didn't she?'

The tense flicker of the memory haunts his
face.

'Did it ever cross your mind that it never came
up in the autopsy? She got a kick from watching
people dance on flames. It's part of her sickness and
her way of telling you she hated you for cheating on
your friend. It's called projection. You should
understand that because you have the same disease
coursing in your veins.'

'She was nuts.'

'No, she wasn't. She was a lost individual who needed drama to feel alive. You killed her for it. She wasn't even pregnant, but you didn't know that. You've lived with the idea that you killed two that night, and it's never bothered you one bit.'

His eyes bulge, and a rage swarms within him in a way that I could never imagine. Then he comes at me in a single gust. I wrap my hands around my head as I fall to the floor.

People around me scatter.

I hear glasses smash.

A nearby table and stool tumble over.

A girl screams as Dan kicks my rucksack away, grabs my head, and starts to smash the back of my skull into the floor.

One.

Two.

The thud reverberates through my head.

My vision starts to glaze over.

Thud.

Thud.

I see Serena in my mind's eye.

Her beauty.

Her flaws.

Her death unwinding in the same way as mine is about to.

Tragic.

Alone.

Dan screaming abuse as two men pull him off me. Flaying his arms and kicking his legs like a rabid dog. I'm looking at Dan, but I'm seeing evil. His true agency exposed for all the ugliness it contains.

I've seen the same in Serena.

The same in my mother.

It's narcissistic rage in full throttle.

Nothing tempered.

A man helps me to my feet, but I'm shoving him away. I'm terrified for my own life in the way that Serena must have been on that night in May.

I hit the outside.

Cold December air fills my lungs.

I sprint down the hill.

I'm not only running from Dan but all the narcissists I've accumulated in my life.

I'm leaving them behind as I cut hard left towards Highbury Fields.

I hear running feet behind me.

I turn to see Dan and his demented, raging face sprinting towards me. He's frothing at the mouth.

Rabid.

I sprint on, driven by an energy to save myself, my dad, and even Serena.

I stand in the middle of the park and glance back to see Dan bent double, catching his breath, looking more like the Dan I know.

The false one.

'Don't do it… dude. Your old man's seventy-six, soon to be seventy-seven. We've got years ahead of ourselves. He's made his choice. Honour it, for the both of us?'

'How could you look me in the eye and know that you killed her? Were you going to come and visit me in prison? Support my appeal?'

He takes a step forward, and I match it with a step backwards.

'You kept the fact you stole her keys a secret. Your dirty little lie. You're not innocent here. The whole world knows how you like to get fucked in the ass. I'll do it better than Serena ever could, and you won't need the photos to remember it.'

'Tell Hatti I'm sorry I ever introduced you two. I hope she sees the truth.'

'She'll never leave me. She's too scared. Weak, like you.'

I turn and sprint toward the station, hearing Dan scream how he's going to bring me down and fuck me in the ass. Fuck my dad. Fuck the rest of my life up.'

He's wrong.

He can't do any of those things because he's freed me from myself.

Finally.

Chapter 55

To my immense joy, I get to spend Christmas with my dad.

Once out of remand, he announced he had terminal cancer, and so many unanswered questions fell into place. The courts haven't set a sentencing date as of yet. I don't think it'll ever come, but the paper-pushers of the world have their own agendas, so for now, we'll see what happens.

Lunch was a joint effort, and even our mince pies hit the gourmet scale, albeit they resembled damp sandcastles when we took them out of the oven. It was another reason to laugh, and I'm cherishing every moment. I had long dreamt that if I was found not guilty, then my friends would flock back, and everything would be as it was. That hasn't happened, and in retrospect, I'm glad they've gone from my life.

The truth was it was one-way traffic with me doing all the work.

A habit I've finally broken.

I glance across at my dad watching the news as I finish cleaning up. It's been an intense month since Dan tried to replicate Serena's death on me. I heard through the grapevine that he got married on the twelfth of December in Stockholm as planned. A guy called Alex ended up being the best man. I've never met this Alex before, and I don't recall him from our university days. I wonder what he's told Hatti about our relationship and how it ended, and if she even knows the new best man?

She hasn't called and won't.

I worry for her safety. It's a tough journey out from under a narcissist, and I'm still shocked at Dan's iron nerve around the whole affair.

Maybe that's part of the narcissistic disease.

My heart cries out for their newborn daughter.

Being raised by a narcissist is the worst kind of abandonment anyone can suffer.

I heard his car was stolen and found burnt out in Epping Forest.

The police still have the hand towel from Serena's bathroom, and I'd stake my life on it that it's covered in Dan's DNA. I was all for going to the police, but my dad begged me not to. He strongly believes Serena's behaviour brought her to her tragic end.

An inevitability.

It's the point in our conversation where we part ways and have to agree to disagree.

Dan won't go down without a fight, and it's where my moral dilemma begins. He'll drag me into the fray, and I might not be so lucky next time. For now, I'm agreeing with my dad. It's a decision I'm not even close to coming to terms with, as Dan has to pay the price for what he did.

As crazy as it all sounds, I did love Serena.

On discovering he had less than a year to live, my dad came to London to speak with me and sort out his affairs. He'd bought tickets to Australia for us to visit Ryan. Unbeknown to me, he had long harboured the idea of paying off Serena behind my back. He saw what it was doing to me, and he could see the future: another failed marriage, abandoned children within a relationship, nothing but toxic interactions that never get resolved, all accumulating into a wasted life dripping in ongoing misery.

He'd flown into London late on the Sunday, having sourced Serena's new address. He'd gone straight to see her from the airport when he watched me climb the wall, and Dan park up.

It was a miracle that we all didn't see each other.

Perhaps, because nobody expected the other to be there, nobody was looking.

He tells me it was the saddest day of his life, sadder than the terminal diagnosis. He was witnessing history cycle, a mirror he never wanted to look into. I guess that was his confession that our mother had spent a lifetime cheating on him, and he had accepted it.

He sat in the car thinking about his own life and that he would come back in the morning and try and catch Serena going to work when he saw Dan leave via the secret door. He tossed the keys into the storm drain opposite where my dad was parked.

A premonition cascaded through my dad.

It was clear and bright.

No doubt in his mind.

Serena was dead.

Dan drove off, and my dad climbed out of his car and fished the keys from the drain. He went in via the secret garden door. It wasn't locked. I never did try it, just assumed it would be. The main back wasn't locked either, but we think Dan didn't close it because of the noise. I have often wondered if the opening of the door by Dan was the noise that Olson heard and thought was me going in.

Not that it matters any more.

My dad walked straight in. He found her apartment and let himself in to find Serena dead on the floor; blood pooled at the rear of her skull. He thought about calling the police, but it slowly dawned on him that it would be me who took the blame despite him seeing Dan leave. He told me that he sat down and stared at her body for nearly three hours, wondering what to do and how he should play it, his own history continuing to pound through him.

He went to the toilet and washed his hands, more out of habit, which is why his DNA was on the towel.

Then, my dad decided to leave.

He still couldn't tell me why he did leave, other than he thought it was the right thing to do. He knew he was dying, and he didn't have the space or time to deal with what he'd witnessed.

He stepped out of the bathroom and shut the door behind him, locking her door and taking the keys, which have been in the glove compartment of his car all this time.

In the passing months, my dad never thought it would go as far as it did. It's why he found the likes of David and pushed for the private investigator, confident that between them and the police, Dan's name would fall into the frame.

It didn't.

Then time.

And his own paranoia and old age worked against him, scared of how it would look for me if he came forward. My performance in the run-up and finally in court meant he had no choice, which isn't true because we all have a choice.

In the two months since that moment, I've been thinking clearly again. It turns out that Teddy-Boy was correct from the off, and had I not lied to him in those early sessions, he may well have become an ally instead of the enemy I hated so much.

I'm "trauma-bonded".

A belief that the highs and lows of an intense personal relationship are the norm, something Harriet picked up on immediately. The dynamic stems from my fear of abandonment, a fear my mother instilled early on in my life to keep myself and Ryan in check.

It's the ugliest form of control, and if anyone should be in the dock, it should be her. I want to believe she didn't do it deliberately, although I'm not that convinced.

Harriet has taught me that a parent's intentions are mostly read by the child as deliberate—intentional.

I think of that a lot.

Intentional.

My task now as an adult is to re-wire that interpretation.

To loosen the grip on my poor mental health in that part of myself.

It's not easy, but at least I can see what needs to be done, and I've started the work.

When I saw Serena at the back door on the night she died, I went into a state of trauma shock. The news that she was pregnant by someone else and knowing that she was about to leave me triggered all those fears of abandonment I had endured as a child. Those memories flooded my body, and in order to protect myself, my brain closed down and blocked out the emotional pain, trying to mitigate the internal damage that was unfolding within.

The upside to all this is I'm naturally sensitive and overly empathic. If harnessed right, it gives me a road to recovery and the potential to have a meaningful personal relationship in my life. I'm almost thirty-four, so I still have time to fix this. The downside is that I'm a natural fit for the narcissists who float in our society. I will have to find a better way to recognise them and then to protect myself as I'll be vulnerable my whole life.

I hear my dad yawn, and I turn to see him stand.

'Goodnight, son. I'll see you in the morning.'

'Goodnight, Dad.'

'Don't do it,' he says, smiling at me over his shoulder as he walks to the bathroom.

I received a letter from Serena's friend, Carole. She was the one who failed to show in court as the final witness. She skipped London that same afternoon and is somewhere in Spain. She never thought I was guilty, and she felt pressured by the police and the prosecution to give evidence against me. It's why she ducked at the last minute.

In the previous June, she had gone to Serena's funeral with Daryl, the other blonde who gate-crashed our drinks. It was Daryl who had sat in the public gallery until my outburst.

Only four other people turned up to see Serena buried. Friends apparently, but with no tangible connections and not a single family member. The ceremony was conducted by a "funeral celebrant"—whatever that is—who gave a speech that made no sense of Serena's life. They even played an Elvis song as the final curtain closed.

Serena's favourite music artist, apparently.

Carole asked me if I was a racing driver in a previous life?

The question made me smile.

Another story from Serena's past that had become woven into the mystery of her life that I'll never know the truth of.

Although, I have my suspicions.

The real purpose of the letter was that Carole had ended up with Serena's urn, and she had left it in her flat in East London, thinking she would return.

But she's not coming back, and the bailiffs will shortly arrive.

If I want Serena's ashes, I have to get there before the ninth of January.

There's still a side of me that is hooked.

It's not love, but it's a glue of sorts, and it's sticky.

My dad tells me to move on, and he's right, and I am, but she deserves a better final ending than the bailiffs.

My dad has three to five months to live, and after he's gone, I might fly to Canada and scatter her ashes. Then I'll see my brother in Australia, stopping off in Japan on the way. A country I've wanted to visit and have never been to.

Serena's Instagram account is still active.

I wonder when it'll be taken down and by whom?

The last post was made on the night she died, and she's wearing the dress that ignited all my fears.

I believe she posted it moments before Dan arrived.

I still wonder who she was off to see.

She looked stunning.

Utterly beautiful.

But it wasn't her.

It was an image she'd manufactured. An outer representation of the false self she had created when she was nothing but a child.

Even her Instagram profile was a false self.

A manufactured person.

She was utterly lost.

If it's true that a narcissist's inner worlds are bleak and desolate places, then for all the trauma she put me through, I'm the lucky one.

I have a true self and it's functioning.

I have hope where she had none.

I sit and crack open a cold beer.

I toast Serena in my mind, as I do Ryan and even my mother, hoping Hatti will find a way out. I save the biggest toast for my dad as I hear his gentle snores vibrate out of my spare room.

Then they stop.

I listen hard, but I'm wasting my time as tears stream down my face.

It's not the silence of sleep.

But the silence of death.

He couldn't have passed in a better place, and he's taught me an important lesson through these last few months.

When I have my own family, I have a choice.

I can drag the ghosts of the past into their lives, or I can stand tall like an ancestor.

I stand, toasting him again.
I'm Big Chief Sitting Bull all the way.

The End

About the Author

SJ Sherwood grew up in a small town in the Midlands. He was always fascinated by the power of storytelling and wanted to be a writer from an early age. He has an MA in Drama from UCL, and has had a successful career selling software in the financial sector, having worked for several FTSE 100 companies.

He is the author of the dystopian trilogy *The Denounced*. *Am I…* is his debut psychological thriller. His first non-fiction title *Apologise… Hell, No! The Power of an Apology in an Entitled World* will shortly be available.

He lives in London with his wife and two young children. He can be found at www.sjsherwood.com